ALSO BY PHILIP SHIRLEY

FICTION
Oh Don't You Cry For Me

NONFICTION
Sweet Spot: 125 Years of Baseball and the Louisville Slugger

POETRY
Endings

THE WHITE LIE

Philip Shirley

[signature: Philip Shirley]

MINDBRIDGE PRESS
Florence, Alabama

Library of Congress Control Number 2014936717

ISBN 978-0-9822151-7-3

Book Cover by James Harwell
Book Interior Design by Felicia Kahn

Printed in United States of America
Published in Florence, Alabama, by MINDBRIDGE PRESS

First Edition

"The five county metropolitan area of Jackson, Mississippi, has a total population of 539,057. The size of Jackson, as well as its location along major Southern highways Interstate 55, Interstate 20, Interstate 220, United States Highway 49, and United States Highway 89, make it a popular destination for drug traffickers looking to bring drugs not only into the city of Jackson but also through the city into the interior of the United States and also to the East and West Coasts of the country via the Mexico border and Florida."

from *How to Become a DEA Agent in Jackson, Mississippi*

Many of us are fortunate enough to receive second chances. Mine came in 1990, by which time I had already learned from a great friend that second chances are treasure. For that reason, this book about second chances is dedicated to Larry "Launcher" Baker.

chapter 1

When real life happens—Peter Brantley thought, gripping the wheel of his Jeep Cherokee at a red light and wearing a Brooks Brothers white shirt with a red-striped tie he had just loosened after work—*it's never what you think it will be.*

A man reeking of tobacco and sweat crouched in the back seat directly behind Peter and breathed hard into the back of Peter's head. He pushed a blunt metal object against Peter's neck. "Move it, you son of a bitch. Now!"

Specks of saliva hit the back of Peter's neck like acid, making him flinch. He could smell the man's stale, rank breath. Peter wanted to speak, to protest, but the words turned to powder in his throat. He usually felt safe with a Beretta .380 tucked under the front seat of the Cherokee. Not now.

Sure, he had often daydreamed of how he would react if he ever needed to defend himself. He always saw himself the victor, surprising the bad guys when he pulled out the Beretta. But as the stranger with the scraggly ponytail had scrambled in a flash into the back seat and now sat firmly behind Peter, Peter felt a rope tighten around his chest. He didn't reach for his own pistol or throw an elbow into the nose of the intruder as he had mentally prepared himself to do time after time. He couldn't force a word from his lips.

Peter looked in the rearview mirror to get a better view. His mind still processed the man's words. *Move it.* Did the man want Peter to get out of the car, right in the middle of the street? He caught the eyes of the man in the rearview mirror.

"What are you looking at, asshole! Drive!"

Peter twisted his head just enough to size up the danger he was up against.

The ponytailed man held a nickel-plated automatic in his left hand and clutched a blue Dallas Cowboys bag in his right, jailhouse tattoo letters L-O-V-E scratched above the first knuckles. And the man's eyes were not the brown-sugar eyes of a stray dog. They were the steel-gray eyes of a wolf. Real trouble.

"I said NOW!"

His adrenaline kicking in, Peter turned his eyes back to the road and pushed down hard on the gas pedal. The Jeep lurched forward, tires barking like a startled dog. He hardly noticed the red traffic light. Looking back in the side mirror at the Greyhound parking lot where the man must have come from, Peter glimpsed two men in black uniforms, their knees pressed into the back of another man face down on the hot parking lot pavement. He was almost certain he saw the two men in uniform jam pistols into the back of the man on the asphalt. The brick wall of the bus station reflected a flashing blue light, so Peter knew not only that the police must be on the scene but that Ponytail here in the backseat must be on the run. In the mirror view, a row of bright pink crape myrtles lined the road, obscuring the rest of the view of the parking lot. When a bus rolled into the lot, there was nothing left to see but the shiny blue and white logo of a dog in mid stride.

Approaching the I-55 ramp, Peter watched the speedometer needle sweep toward seventy and knew he had to keep his eyes on the road. Here the highway entrance forked north to Memphis and south toward New Orleans. He didn't dare turn his head.

"Which way?"

"Just drive." The guy still seemed winded. And tense.

Peter eased off the gas and stayed in the left lane, taking them under a sign reading Grenada/Memphis. A 360-degree loop delivered them onto the interstate heading north. He pulled into the middle lane and brought the car up to eighty as he weaved through the heavy traffic as if he were being chased.

"Slow down, and don't do anything to get us stopped," the ponytailed man said as he leaned over the seat and nudged the pistol into Peter's cheek. "And don't talk. Don't do nothing. If you try anything I'll blow your damn head off. Just drive." In the rearview, Peter saw the man sweating heavily, checking out every car and every exit.

Peter drove north past Woodrow Wilson, Lakeland, Meadowbrook, Northside Drive—finally nearing the busy County Line Road exit, his usual turn for home. With each exit they passed, he felt the air growing thinner in the car. He could hear his own breathing.

Peter took a deep breath and cleared his throat. "Look, just take the car. It has plenty of gas. I can pull over at this exit."

"Shut the hell up and drive! If you stop or if we get stopped by cops, I'll shoot your ass first thing."

Peter continued north past the Ridgeland city limits and began to worry about the police and what would happen if they were spotted. The retail shopping strips and car dealers lining the interstate frontage road in Jackson soon were replaced by thick stands of oak and hickory hardwoods pressing in on the highway and the occasional flat pasture dotted with brown and white cows kept inside only by double strands of barbed wire on thin steel posts. "They might have a road block up here heading out of town."

Ponytail spoke after what seemed like minutes. "Pull off at this exit."

Peter veered right onto the Madison exit and drove past the string of gas stations and fast food restaurants toward downtown. He slowed at the railroad tracks and looked over at Rita's Flowers to see if the kind older woman who worked there might be looking out as he passed. Back in happier days before his marriage stalled and started coasting downhill, she would recognize Peter's Jeep when he parked in front of the shop and would help him pick out flowers for him to take home for a surprise for

Mary Beth. The woman was nowhere in sight.

At the Highway 51 intersection, Ponytail said, "Turn left here."

The main thoroughfare led north out of Jackson toward numerous subdivisions that lined both sides of the road in Madison. The four lanes were crowded in both directions, creating slow traffic as people hurried home from work. Three lights in a row turned red, and Peter was careful to stop at each one. At the third stoplight, a Madison Police cruiser waited in line, headed the opposite direction.

Ponytail saw the policeman, too. He spoke in a slow, even voice. "Just keep your damn eyes straight ahead."

Peter cut his eyes left as he passed, but the policeman never glanced his way. Within minutes they were out of the business district, beyond the heavy residential areas. The cotton fields they now passed formed a blanket of white along the highway to Canton. He drove in silence and thought about how unreal this whole thing felt, like a prank someone might clue him in on at any minute. He knew that the odds were that if an abductor gets a victim away from the scene in a vehicle, the outcome is usually grim. He tried to figure out where he had gone wrong. Earlier he had been bored numb as he got on the elevator to leave the downtown building where he worked, four floors up, overlooking the bright white Corinthian columns of the Greek Revival-style Mississippi Governor's Mansion. He'd taken long, slow strides the block and a half to the parking lot, unaware of his surroundings, trying to shake out the stiffness of one more long plodding day spent by choice alone at his desk. Once in the driver's seat, he hadn't wanted to listen to the news since it would be more of the same miniscule details regarding Bill Clinton's grand jury impeachment hearings that he had heard for months, so instead he'd cranked up the volume on a new CD, Everlast's *Whitey Ford Sings the Blues*, feeling the heavy beat wash over him in a pleasant relief. He knew he had the music really blasting because when he'd driven the Jeep with its vibrating windows past the parking lot attendant, the guy gave Peter a toothy grin. Looking back now, the loud music in the isolation of his car had also kept him lulled from reality. It offered one of the few escapes he'd found in months from thoughts of a strained home life as well as the relentless remorse he felt over his brother's death the year before. When he'd missed the green light at the long traffic signal next to the Greyhound station and sat drumming his fingers on the steering wheel as the speakers pounded inside the Cherokee, he'd felt something wasn't right. Instinctively. Just a feeling, but he'd turned down the music and glanced left toward the bus station. Even with the music off, it still was hard to hear anything outside the car with the windows up and the air conditioner fan set on high to fend off the muggy heat of the late Mississippi summer. But he thought he'd heard tires screeching.

He'd been surprised when the lush, green ligustrum bushes separating the bus station parking lot from Pascagoula Street swept forward over a short, cinder-block wall as if driven by a violent gust of wind and the man with the ponytail had hopped into the backseat as easily as getting into a waiting taxi.

One tiny flick of the door locks switch back in the parking garage, Peter knew, and he would not be in this situation. Not locking his doors was error number one. But allowing the guy to get into the back seat and escape the scene with Peter as hostage was the biggest error of all. Sweat poured down Peter's face. He reached to adjust the air conditioner.

"Hey, Asshole, just drive. Keep your damn hands on the wheel."

Peter spoke in even tones, trying to sound confident. "I'm only making the air cooler."

"Like I said, just drive. Where does this road go?"

Peter could catch enough in the rearview mirror to tell Ponytail looked around at every crossroad and sign.

"It goes to Canton. Just a few miles ahead. After that, I don't know," Peter said. Then, not much more than a whisper, "You don't need me. I haven't done anything to you. I can pull over here. There's no phone out here, so I can't call the police. Why don't you just take the car?"

"'Cause I want you to drive, Asshole. If something happens to me, something happens to you. Let's just call it insurance. Turn right at this next road."

Peter could hear the smile in Ponytail's voice for the first time since the man had jerked open the back door and jumped into the Jeep. Ponytail was in charge of the situation and growing more and more confident. Peter felt his shirt soak through with sweat.

"Turn here," the man repeated as they approached the crossroad.

The road Peter turned onto was narrower, with uneven pavement along the edge and deep potholes he had to steer between to avoid a flat tire. He heard a zipper and looked back quickly over his shoulder to see the man open the gym bag.

"What are you looking at? Keep your damn eyes on the road." Ponytail looked inside the bag. He seemed to be counting something.

Peter glanced in the rearview mirror again but couldn't see the contents of the bag. He thought about the .380 but was afraid he couldn't reach under the seat without being noticed.

Then he heard the stern voice of his father saying what he had heard a thousand times growing up, *Be a man, Peter.*

When Peter was afraid to go off the high diving board at the age of eight, *Be a man, Peter.* And when he had trouble hitting the fastest pitches from the batting cage when he was only ten, *Be a man, Peter.*

Be a man, he thought. *No matter what, don't drive past Canton without doing something.*

There were no cars behind them, but Ponytail kept looking back every minute or two. Peter would have to use Ponytail's lapses in attention to force something to happen.

Peter made himself take slow, easy breaths. He noticed the late afternoon shadows of the tall corn and telephone poles reaching across the narrow, two-lane road. Then he decided.

He picked out a telephone pole about a mile ahead, one that seemed a little closer to the road than the others. He casually dropped his right hand from the steering wheel and tested the buckle on his seat belt without looking down. He looked in the mirror and pushed down on the gas pedal, trying to build speed without being noticed.

Seated in the middle of the back seat, Ponytail turned his head to the left and glanced back just as they neared the pole. When he did, Peter gripped the wheel as hard as he could, swerved right, and slammed on the brakes. He felt the tires shimmy in the sandy soil just beneath the grass surface of the roadside and fought hard to steer the Jeep in a straight course.

Ponytail—along with his gun and gym bag—hurtled over the back seat and hit the top of the dash just as the car crashed into the telephone pole. Despite his seatbelt, Peter's head hit the steering wheel hard, but not before he had heard the sound of grinding metal and a muffled pop he hoped were Ponytail's cheekbones snapping as the car came to an abrupt stop. After his own head hit the steering wheel, he felt for one brief moment time suspended before the crush of pain made his vision blur. Even then, he continued to look through the windshield and try to make sense of the slant of the late afternoon sunlight, wondering for a moment where he was and what inside his head was throbbing. He watched a cloud of dust settle like a thin shroud over the red hood of the car before he lost consciousness.

chapter 2

Mary Beth Brantley leaned forward to reach for her computer mouse and click on Internet Explorer. The office had been almost deserted today, leaving her time to spend on pet projects. Most of her co-workers—all men except for a secretary she shared with the group—had left at two o'clock to play golf with a legislator who sat on the senate appropriations committee. They didn't invite her or the secretary to play, which suited her fine.

She decided to kill the last few minutes of the work day surfing the Internet. She began reading an article on the recent embassy truck bombings in Kenya and Tanzania that killed over two hundred people and maimed thousands more, but she only made it through the first paragraph before the gore was too graphic to read. She clicked the electronic bookmark to the Website bulletin board she checked daily. Keeping up with the local politics of Cedar Key, Florida, she could be a part of the community, even if she couldn't yet live there. She read the comments on the site frequented by Cedar Key's locals as well as vacation homeowners and retirees, many from cold-sounding places like Sodus Point, New York, and Watersmeet, Michigan.

Holding her favorite hand-thrown pottery coffee mug in both hands, she sat back in her chair and scanned the message board on the Website as she sipped the strong coffee. She kicked off her black pumps and pulled one leg under her.

The Cedar Key Beacon served as the official island news. Mary Beth read it dutifully each week when it arrived by mail. She tried to understand the island as she developed her dream plan of starting a small business there.

Her current salary as assistant director for the auto dealers' association did not help much with her early retirement ideas. If she could just start a business at Cedar Key, she and Peter could enjoy leisurely weekends exploring the tiny nearby barrier islands easily reached by canoe.

She wanted to get Peter away from the memories of the ordeal of not being able to help his brother Christopher through his drug addiction. And she wanted Peter out of a business that had lost much of its appeal. Peter had started out loving his work in advertising, but during the last decade client loyalty had disappeared. Old friendships faded and with them the fun was gone. As Peter described it, the new young turks in advertising were MBAs who replaced long-term ad agency partners with specialist firms whose only goal was to boost short-term profits instead of growing strong companies. Peter feared this would come to a bad end, so what was once an upbeat Peter had become a man who found little pleasure in his work. Yet what scared her most was the fact that she knew she had already taken the first steps down the path to a broken marriage. She wanted off that path. Maybe starting over in another place would help.

The big issue on Cedar Key today was how to deal with growing numbers of tourists. Some thought more police were needed while others wondered if the new condominiums would overburden the sewer systems. She knew that somewhere in the midst of this debate was a business opportunity if only she kept looking.

Mary Beth clicked over to real estate listings and browsed through the homes and lots for sale on Cedar Key even though she knew the island was financially out of reach. She constantly toyed with finances and calculated how much money they needed in order to move and live at Cedar Key. If Peter could get a good price for his agency shares and if they sold their house, she thought the move could work even if they did not find great jobs. They'd just have to be careful and plan well. She made a few notes before turning her thoughts to dinner and how Peter was doing. She

wished he could forgive himself for his role in Christopher's problems, but
she knew Peter felt the whole thing was his fault.

She'd talked to Peter's partner, Johnston Baynes, about how worried she
was, though she could never tell Peter how that first meeting had gone.
John had said Peter had a lot of people worried at work. She and John had
become close, too close, she knew, since they had started talking about the
private details of Peter and Mary Beth's married life. John's financial
advice was always sound when she asked him about investments and
strategies as she hammered out the day-to-day in her and Peter's finances.
And John gave her insights about how Peter was perceived at work, how
Peter was handling the pressure and regret over Christopher's death. But
it was more than just that. She was flattered that John took an interest in
her in a personal way, flattered that he seemed to care about her welfare,
even the day-to-day struggles of her life. Then just two days ago they had
met by chance when she ran an errand downtown at the end of the day,
and they had become so involved in conversation that John Baynes had
walked her to her car. When she struggled with the squeaky driver's door,
he had touched her hand and said "If you were *my* wife." He never finished
the thought. He had not had to. She knew that he meant he was just
enough older to be from a generation of men who took care of things,
who opened car doors and kept cars and doors and yards and finances
running smoothly. She also knew he had meant it in another, more
personal way, before he had pulled himself back.

Mary Beth was about to shut down the machine when an email arrived.
She leaned back in her chair, focused on the few brief lines, and then read
them over again. Soon her hands trembled and her eyes felt ready to
overflow. She continued to sit there as the daylight slanted lower and
lower through the office blinds.

Peter's face felt raw as he forced his eyes open and touched his fingertips to the throbbing wound on his forehead. He could only see out of his right eye until he used his sleeve to wipe the thick sticky blood covering his left. He saw Ponytail lying still, his head down on the floorboard. Ponytail's arms jutted at odd angles and blood covered his face. The man's feet, pointing in opposite directions, pressed against the back of the front seat.

Peter opened the driver's door and was hit by the blast of summer heat. He tried to keep his balance as he walked around to the passenger side, leaning on the car as he walked and holding his right hand over the cut on his forehead in an attempt to keep the trickle of blood out of his eye. He opened the passenger door. Ponytail rolled halfway out of the car, his breath coming in shallow gulps as gurgling sounds rose from his throat. Peter grabbed the gun from the floor and threw the nickel-plated pistol over his shoulder into the cornfield. He looked down the road but saw no cars. He snatched up the front of Ponytail's blue denim shirt and pulled him from the car as if unloading a bag of potting soil. Ponytail lay on his back on the sweltering, dusty roadside. A small red bubble appeared from his left nostril then burst. Peter stood above him, wondering what to do.

Inside the Jeep, Peter noticed several small taped bundles about the size of a brick. One bundle was ripped open, leaving white powder scattered on the seat and floor. He'd been to enough parties in college to know the powder was a drug. The packages looked like the cocaine he'd once discovered in his brother's car. Whatever the powder was, there was a lot of it. He'd never seen that much except on the six o'clock news after one of the many drug busts that seemed so common in Jackson.

Ponytail groaned and tried to roll over, but his arms didn't work. Peter noticed the letters H-A-T-E above the knuckles of Ponytail's left hand, the crude letters like the jailhouse tattoos he'd seen on the back of the hands of a man he had once run out of his brother's apartment when he caught the man selling drugs to Chris. The memory caused anger to surge through Peter's veins like adrenaline and, before he had thought better, he kicked Ponytail in the stomach. He heard the sickening sound of air expel from the man's lungs with the sigh of winter wind.

Peter thought about calling for help on his cell phone as he walked to the front of the car, but he hesitated. He wasn't even sure his phone would work out here, and he found no serious damage to the Jeep, only a dented bumper and a small crease in the hood. He bent down to check Ponytail and ripped loose the man's wallet and chain from a blue-jean belt loop. He looked down the road again before he walked around to the driver's side and sat sideways in the driver's seat. He began flipping through the wallet.

Ten one-hundreds, plus a few twenties. No credit cards, no surprise. A Louisiana driver's license indicated Ponytail was Robert Alvin Jenkins of 1005 Opelika Avenue, Apt. 4-B, Baton Rouge, Louisiana. There were a few phone numbers on scraps of paper and a folded sheet ripped from a spiral bound notebook with the words, "5:30 p.m., Friday, Greyhound from Dallas."

Peter gripped the steering wheel and leaned forward with his hands resting on the back of his head. He felt dazed, but Robert Jenkins must feel worse, judging from his moans on the scorching roadside. Peter knew he should at least leave Jenkins where he would be found quickly. He looked down the road before getting back out of the car and moving as fast as he dared. He grabbed Jenkins' leg and dragged him to the edge of the pavement. The man's groans grew louder, his arms trailing behind him like wet towels.

Back at the Jeep, Peter grabbed the Cowboys bag and, gathering the scattered bags of white powder, crammed them back into it. He tossed the broken package near where Jenkins lay in the grass before he reached into his own front pocket, took out Jenkins's wallet, and dropped it into the Cowboys bag, too.

Stumbling back out of the Jeep, he wandered into the six-foot tall corn, weaving back and forth among the rows and kicking up clouds of dust as he searched for the gun. His arms itched from the rough cornstalks, and he decided he'd have to leave the gun, but as he turned to walk back, he spotted the shiny pistol propped against a cornstalk. He picked it up, pulled his shirttail out to get to his clean white cotton t-shirt, and wiped the gun clean of prints before tossing it back into the rows.

Back in the driver's seat, Peter turned the key and felt relief when the car started. *They don't make them like this anymore*, he thought, happy he'd kept the old Cherokee for so long. He backed into the road in a half circle, stared down at his phone, and thought again about calling 911. But instead of reporting to the police what happened, he drove off shaking his head. He looked in the rearview and saw Jenkins lying on the side of the road like a run-over dog.

"Asshole yourself," Peter said as he pulled onto Highway 51 toward his home in Jackson.

chapter 3

Mary Beth sat at her keyboard and typed. "I'm flattered by your kind words. And believe me, kindness is something I can use. But I'm sorry I let things go this far. That just isn't me. Please understand."

She moved the mouse until the arrow pointed at SEND. She hesitated, then moved the tiny arrow on her screen to DELETE and clicked. Her email disappeared from the screen, and a small window displayed, asking if she was certain she wanted to delete the email. She clicked YES. She was glad no one else was around. She knew her eyes were red and swollen.

"So what now?" she said aloud, brushing the back of her hand upward along her moist cheek.

She slipped her feet into the black leather pumps under her desk, opened the top drawer, and removed a small mirror. She applied plum-colored lipstick by running the tip between both lips at once and brushed back her shoulder-length light brown hair with her hand. She pressed a tissue against her eyes and blotted carefully below each one. Satisfied that she looked fine in case she ran into anyone she knew, she locked the glass front door of the red-brick building on what had become known as Association Row. The buildings lining the street were conveniently located for the two-dozen lobbyists who occupied the offices just a block from the Mississippi State Capitol building.

On her way home, she stopped by the Winn Dixie grocery store. Like most locals, she still referred to the small neighborhood store as Jitney Fourteen, the store immortalized in the writing of Eudora Welty who still lived just around the corner. She went through the motions of shopping for dinner by picking up two thick T-bones, two large baking potatoes, and a bag of green salad mix with dressing and croutons included.

But when she drove to Briarwood for wine, a bottle of 1995 Chateau de Sales Bordeaux caught her eye, and she wondered why they still had a '95 on the shelves. She knew the wine would go well with the steak and bought the three extra bottles on the shelf to store. The twenty-five dollar a bottle price was more than the ten to twelve dollars she usually spent on wine for a weekday, but saving a few dollars wasn't her real concern tonight.

Mary Beth knew she was late getting home and was relieved when Peter's Jeep was not in the garage. She rubbed the potatoes with oil and then salted the skins before popping them into the oven. She set the table, opened the wine to breathe, and was regretting the limp salad mixture with its packaged dressing when she heard Peter walk through the door. She was afraid to look at him, afraid he could see that she had been crying earlier. She heard him lock the door before he came into the kitchen to find her.

"Something bad has happened, Bet. I think I may have killed someone."

Mary Beth saw the front of his shirt soaked in blood. Blood smears covered his face, and fresh blood oozed from a cut above one eye. He hadn't called her Bet in months.

Peter turned and walked into the living room, and she followed him, asking questions. "What do you mean? Did you have a wreck? Are you all right?"

He carried a blue bag she'd never seen. He placed the bag on the coffee table before he sat down.

Her instinct was to run to him, but his shirt front was crimson from the collar down to his belt, and there had not been many hugs since Christopher died. Whenever she'd tried, Peter turned or brushed her away.

"I'm fine, Bet. At least, I don't think anything is broken. But something bad has happened. And I need your help sorting it out."

Mary Beth rushed to the kitchen and returned with a wet hand towel.

She bent over Peter and wiped blood off his face, taking a closer look at the cut. "You need a doctor."

"I'm okay. But right now we need to talk."

Mary Beth remained quiet as Peter told her the whole story, starting with sitting at the traffic light near the Greyhound station and ending with the details of leaving the man he believed to be a drug dealer on the side of the road.

Mary Beth tried to wrap her mind around this. "Why'd you just leave him there?"

"I don't know. I just wanted to get away. I was angry. And scared."

"Did anyone see you?"

"No, I don't think so. But I passed a car about a mile or two down the road, heading in the right direction, so I'm sure someone found him."

"Well, we've got to be *really* sure. You have to call the police. You can do it from a pay phone, but you've got to report it, Peter." She rose and leaned over him as she spoke. "Let me get a better look at that cut."

She made Peter go back into the kitchen and sit in a chair where the light was brighter. She put her hands on both sides of his face and turned his head upward. She pulled at the skin on the edge of the deep cut. Thick blood ran down the side of his face when she opened the cut to inspect it. She pressed hard on the wound with the damp towel.

"You need a doctor."

Peter looked deeply into her eyes, as if pleading with her to understand. "I don't want a doctor. I don't want to answer their questions about it."

"Peter, that doesn't make any sense. They don't care how it happened."

"I just don't want a record of getting hurt. I have a reason."

"A reason? What reason?" she asked, though her tone was more an accusation than a question. "What reason could you possibly have not to get a cut sewn up?"

He looked away. "Please, Bet, just bandage it. If you put one of those butterfly clips on it, that'll close it up fine."

Mary Beth stood back and looked at Peter for a few seconds, wondering if the impact of the wreck still had him confused. She didn't like the way he was talking, but he seemed adamant, so she decided to listen first. As she opened a kitchen drawer to find bandages and hydrogen peroxide to clean the wound, Peter told her the idea he had while driving home.

"I know this sounds crazy, but I don't want to turn over these drugs to the police. Not yet anyway," he said, sounding hesitant. "Bet, I don't know exactly what I want to do, but those bags of coke or whatever belong to the kind of men I've come to hate. And it's worth lots of money to them. Losing money is the only way to hurt them. The police seem unable to do anything. And I want to hurt them where it hurts the most."

"What are you saying?" she asked, louder than she meant. She made herself change her tone. "I don't understand."

"This stuff must be worth hundreds of thousands of dollars, maybe even millions." He opened the bag for her to see the bundles of white powder. "I want to take their drugs. *And* their money."

"How did you come up with such a crazy idea?"

"I was driving back, wondering what to do, what to say. I can't explain exactly, but I'm just so mad I want to do something. Get even, I guess."

"Peter, listen to yourself. We're not drug dealers. And how are you going to get even? I think you're hurt worse than you know." Mary Beth forced herself to take deep breath. "After what happened to Christopher, how could you even think about doing anything with drugs?"

Peter surprised Mary Beth as he suddenly pulled her to her feet and held her tight. She couldn't recall him holding her so close in months. She had missed his touch. Yet, a wave of shame passed over her.

Peter spoke softly with his face pressed against her hair. "Nothing bad is going to happen. I won't let it."

After a couple of minutes Mary Beth pulled herself from his arms and sat down. He sat across from her at the kitchen table.

"I can't let this chance pass," he said.

"Why not just turn the drugs all over to the police and let them catch the dealers who did this? That's their job." She went to the sink and rinsed the towel in hot water and wrung it out. She leaned over and held the warm cloth against his eyebrow before looking to see if the bleeding had stopped.

Peter spoke slowly to Mary Beth, and she could tell he was gauging her reaction. "I know I sound crazy, but what if I pretend to sell the drugs back to the people who own them, but don't really turn them over? The police can't do that. They haven't even caught the people who sold Christopher the drugs that killed him."

Mary Beth could tell from the look on Peter's face that it was painful for Peter just to say his brother's name. "That does sound crazy. And why would you?"

"I have a better chance of getting the dealers in a trap than the police. I have the one thing drug dealers want than more than anything else. Their own product. If I hold the drugs for ransom, get the money, and then destroy the bag, it would just be taking drug money from maybe the same guys who sold to Christopher. You hate these guys as much as I do. We wouldn't hurt anyone except the ones who deserve to be hurt."

"You'd probably end up dead."

Peter sat back in his chair and closed his eyes.

Mary Beth watched him. Her eyes were steady, but her hand trembled slightly. "I don't want anything to do with such an idiotic idea."

He remained silent. She wondered if he had a mild concussion because this just didn't seem like the Peter she knew. She swallowed hard and took another deep breath. "I won't let you do it. We don't know how to deal with this kind of thing."

"I understand, but just imagine one thing for me. If I could do it and not get hurt or caught, how would you feel?"

"I'm not interested in playing this game with you."

"Would it really be such a bad thing to take money away from drug dealers?"

Mary Beth looked into Peter's eyes that had become a dark tunnel in the past few months, and she struggled to see something beyond. She thought of the many conversations through the years she'd had with Peter about the drugs he'd used in college and how he often said they hadn't hurt him or anyone else. Since Christopher's problems had begun, Peter had never said such words again.

Though she had smoked pot a couple of times like everyone she knew in college, she had never been around any hard drugs. She was glad they had gradually stopped even seeing anyone smoking pot at a party over the last ten years. "Just because you bought a bag of pot or two with your friends at Birmingham-Southern doesn't mean you know how to deal with these guys."

"Well, let's just think about it tonight. Please, Mary Beth, just think about it."

"I don't think we're doing the right thing."

"We don't have to do anything. No one saw him get into my car or the police would already be here. No one knows what's happened except one guy, and he doesn't know who I am." Peter took Mary Beth's left hand between both of his hands before he spoke softly, "You know how helpless I felt in trying to save Chris. This could be my chance to do something for him. Maybe I'm wrong or even childish, but I want to hurt these people. Not physically, but they need to pay someway or other."

Mary Beth didn't answer right away. Peter was scaring her, but this was the first time in months she had seen him excited about anything. They hardly talked any more. And she couldn't remember the last time he had kissed her other than a quick goodbye kiss. She knew he was holding her hand only as a way to manipulate her, but she didn't care.

She chose to hold her answer. She made Peter strip to his underwear so she could be sure he didn't have other injuries.

After he got dressed again, she insisted on driving him to a pay phone to call the police.

The first two places they tried had too many people around, but despite Peter wanting just to go home, Mary Beth kept driving until she found a pay phone that was deserted. When they returned home from making the anonymous call to 911, Peter held her as they sat on the couch. Neither spoke. Finally, they decided to try to get some sleep.

In bed, they were still and quiet, but wide awake. After being together for twenty years, Mary Beth understood Peter better than anyone. She already knew what was going to happen. As she watched Peter stare up at the ceiling, she knew he had made up his mind that the drugs were his chance to do something for Chris, or for himself. For months their life together had been falling apart. If his insane idea of a fake drug deal was what it took to bring them back together, to feel Peter's touch again the way she had tonight, then maybe she'd go along. Maybe.

chapter 4

Roy Gant felt the Mississippi August afternoon heat, but he didn't sweat. He was a slight man with black hair combed straight back, showing streaks of silver at the temple. He had on dark glasses, ironed jeans over Dan Post black cowboy boots, and a long-sleeved, studded red shirt buttoned to the collar. He looked like a top Oklahoma ranch hand on Saturday night.

Standing outside the Texaco Station on High Street across from the Mississippi State Fairgrounds, he seemed like a man without a trouble or care. He used his thumb to peel back foil and pop the last of the roll of Tums into his mouth. He had finished the pack in two hours. For the tenth time, he imagined the conversation he was about to have with his boss, William McNabb. At exactly four, he dialed the number. McNabb picked up after one ring.

"Don't say anything," McNabb said. "Just go to the usual place."

Gant thought it odd that a man with McNabb's money and numerous businesses, as well as an office used only by the two of them in the back of McNabb's liquor store, often wanted to meet in his car and talk while they rode through the countryside. Gant never asked and assumed it was simply a habit that went back to the days when McNabb was a small-time drug dealer doing most of his business out of his trunk.

Gant climbed into his red El Dorado Cadillac and pulled onto High Street toward I-55. He reached into his right boot and pulled out the Browning Baby .25 automatic and laid the gun on the seat. If there were a problem, the .45 caliber Smith & Wesson under the seat would be his choice of weapons, but the .25 was rubbing his ankle raw.

He drove onto the interstate. At Lakeland Drive he veered right toward

the Ross Barnett Reservoir and countless retail stores with gleaming neon
signs. Orange and white barrels blocked off one lane for miles where the
State was widening the road. He wondered if the highway department
would ever finish adding new lanes to the highway and thought how glad
he was that he lived across town in South Jackson. South Jackson had once
been a fashionable part of town where pockets of old money maintained
spacious white homes with large front porches. Now no one sat outside
anymore, and the area had gradually become more of a blue-collar
community.

He looked at the large new homes crammed together on too-small lots
as he drove and wondered why anyone would want to live there. He hated
the rows of apartment buildings full of eager graduates from Ole Miss,
anxious to make their mark in politics and state government.

He pulled into the parking lot of the United Artists Theatre known as
Park Place, drove to the back of the lot, and backed into an empty space
between two cars. An empty popcorn bag rolled across the parking lot,
propelled by a light breeze. He tuned the radio to country music and
adjusted the air conditioner to blow cooler. After five minutes he saw
McNabb pull into the lot, drive past him, and stop at the end of the row of
cars. Gant walked over to McNabb's white Lincoln Town Car and got in
the front passenger side.

As McNabb drove out of the lot, Gant thought about how the man's
expensive dark-blue suit, manicured fingernails, and razor-cut hair did
little to elevate his looks beyond average.

"William, even the blacks are moving out of here. Don't nobody think
Jackson's a fit place to live no more."

"Well, we're not here to talk politics are we? What in god's name
happened at the bus station?" McNabb asked, his eyes never leaving the
road.

"I got to the Greyhound station in Houston early and was first to board.
Took a seat in the very back where I could watch everything on the bus."

"You didn't see anything unusual at all? Had to be something."

"No, the mule drove up in a cab with the two gym bags and carried them onto the bus. Never knew he's being watched. He never left the bags alone. Neither one of us talked with anyone the whole trip."

"Who was he? You used him before?" McNabb asked as he looked left, then shifted lanes and passed a pickup truck loaded with mattresses and furniture.

"No, he was just like the rest. Just some old man tired of farming baked soil in Mexico. I'm sure he sneaked across the border, looking for any kind of work for money to send to his family. Two or three days sitting on a bus and he'd have lots of money to send home. They can't say no to it."

"What happened?"

"Everything seemed just like usual. The mule seemed calm. I called Harry Ramsey to make sure he'd be there to back up Jenkins on the pickup."

McNabb reached into the pocket of his blue Oxford pinpoint shirt and removed an open pack of Camel filtered cigarettes. He shook the pack until one cigarette stayed halfway out, placed the cigarette to his lips, and pulled it out. He shook the pack again and offered a cigarette to Gant, who took one and placed it between his lips.

"See if there's a lighter in there," he said to Gant, nodding toward the glove box.

Instead, Gant forced his hand into his tight jeans pocket and removed his worn Zippo, flicked the lighter once, and reached over to hold the flame for McNabb. He lit his own cigarette before he pushed the button to let his window down a couple of inches so he could blow a stream of smoke through the window opening.

McNabb inhaled deeply and then spoke without exhaling, forcing his words out through a cloud of smoke. "Who knew the plan?"

"I never told nobody. Not even Jenkins or Harry knew I'd be on the bus. In Jackson, everything seemed fine," Gant explained, "until the mule walked off the bus."

"Exactly what happened?"

"I waited on the bus. There wasn't no cops around that I could see. But as soon as Jenkins and Harry took the bags, two cops ran from around the building, and an unmarked car pulled out to block the road at the corner. Things got crazy in a hurry."

"Well, how did Jenkins get away?" McNabb asked, his tone implying that Gant wasn't getting to the point. He sucked hard on his cigarette and blew smoke toward the windshield.

"Jenkins grabbed one bag and ran. Harry was slower and two cops tackled him. Jenkins ran through that big hedge and jumped into a car at the light. About that time another bus pulled into the south entrance of the lot. Blocked the police so they weren't able to chase Jenkins."

McNabb ran his hand through his hair and closed his eyes. He slowly shook his head but said nothing. The cigarette tip danced up and down as he held the filter between his lips.

"From where they were, I'm not even sure they knew if Jenkins got in that car," Gant said. "One of those older Jeep Cherokees with the square bodies."

"What'd you do when it started?"

Gant was tiring of this interrogation but had learned to hide his anger with McNabb. "Couldn't do nothing. Just walked into the crowd."

McNabb had said little other than to ask his short questions, but his glare at Gant said enough. He shook his head from side to side. "You got a big damn leak, Roy. Find my drugs and make sure *nothing* can be traced to us." He pulled the car over into the middle lane and braked as a pickup truck ahead stopped at the red light. His eyes were squeezed nearly shut as he turned and spoke slowly. "You sure the Mexican doesn't know anything?"

"Not a damn thing. I found him through our usual contacts, and they paid him a thousand bucks to carry the bags. He don't know anybody's name. Couldn't recognize me. May talk, but he can't track it back to us."

McNabb spoke slowly and deliberately, "I'm worried about Harry Ramsey. He knows too much. We both know he'll never talk if there's any other way out for him. But I don't know what else they might have on him. And what about Jenkins? Will he talk?"

The traffic moved through the intersection as the light changed.

Gant didn't like where this was going, but he knew he had to answer this right. He had to say the truth. "Jenkins and I served time together at Parchman. I can trust him to cover my back during a job, but I'm not sure I can promise he won't say nothing if he gets in a jam about going back. He hated that place."

McNabb nodded once and seemed to be deciding something as he reached over to crush out his cigarette in the ashtray. He brought the car to a complete stop and held his foot on the brake as they reached a four-way stop. No other cars were at the intersection. He turned toward Gant, who fought hard not to look away from McNabb's cold stare. McNabb turned his head back to stare out the windshield for thirty seconds before he spoke, still looking straight ahead as if addressing no one in particular. "Do whatever it takes to make sure no one talks. I mean no one. If Jenkins is really that scared about going back inside, that could be a problem. You better take care of it."

McNabb continued to stare out the window, running his hand through his hair again. After a brief pause, he looked back at Gant and continued, his voice even softer. "Somebody has my drugs. Find them. Do whatever it takes, just get them back. I've lost half a shipment. I don't plan to lose the other half."

Gant said, "I'll put out the word on the street. Stuff turns up, people will know."

"Yeah, a million in coke is too much for some idiot off the street to get rid of. Find him. And fix that leak."

Gant nodded but said nothing more as he climbed out of McNabb's car and back into his own. Although Gant was well paid and had just over one and a half million dollars in cash spread across several savings accounts, he still resented the tone McNabb often used with him. He'd always been loyal. He believed they should be more like partners because he knew McNabb needed him and his contacts for the real dirty work that took place at the street level. He knew McNabb could never go back to working directly with men whose skills were mostly limited to breaking locks and heads without the burden of regrets for either.

Gant sat in his car and held tightly to the steering wheel. He would do what he had to, but he didn't like what McNabb had said about making sure no one would talk. He knew what the words meant for him. And what they meant for two men who passed for the closest thing he could call friends.

chapter 5

Peter threw back the covers and lowered his legs over the side of the bed when he heard the slap of the newspaper hitting the driveway. He'd been awake for hours already. His head throbbed, and his ribs felt tender when he ran his fingers down his side. He noticed a diagonal bruise across his chest from the seat belt. Pulling on gray gym shorts and a t-shirt with Property of MSU Athletic Department in bold letters across the front, he walked out to get *The Clarion-Ledger*. He stood barefoot in the driveway, holding the newspaper as he scanned the headlines. He only took a second to find what he wanted.

On the front page above the fold, the headline read, "Drug Bust Nets Millions in Cocaine." The story said that the Jackson Police Department, acting on a tip, had arrested a Mexican citizen suspected of transporting cocaine by bus to Jackson. Also arrested was Jackson resident Harold Ramsey who was immediately detained after allegedly receiving the drugs in the bus station parking lot. A JPD spokesman was quoted. "With street prices what they are for cocaine, the street value of the drugs we seized could be nearly two million dollars."

A third suspect, believed to be the owner of a car found near the bus station, had escaped on foot with luggage police believed also contained cocaine. A man thought to be that suspect was later found on a roadside near Canton, Mississippi, with severe head and internal injuries, as well as a broken leg and two broken arms. A large amount of cocaine had been found beside him, allowing the police to link him to the bus station bust that same day. The suspect appeared to have been in a car accident. Apparently, someone had driven from the scene after running into a telephone pole. No additional drugs were found.

The man had been identified as convicted felon Robert Alvin Jenkins. He was transported by ambulance to University Medical Center where he remained in critical condition.

Peter walked into the kitchen. He measured out enough ground coffee for eight cups. His breath caught in his throat from a sharp pain as he reached up to pour in the water. He sat and reread the article as the coffee brewed, holding a hand over his ribs. He poured two cups, added cream, and took both cups and the newspaper back to the bedroom. Mary Beth, her wet body wrapped in a towel, walked out of the bathroom and sat down on the side of the bed next to him, not bothering to dress.

"The cocaine in our bag could be worth over a million dollars if this is half the shipment," Peter said, trying to ignore the pain and saying nothing to Mary Beth about the injuries.

Mary Beth took the newspaper from him and started reading. After only a few seconds, she looked up and stabbed her finger at the article as she began talking, her voice angry and pleading. "This is what I was talking about. These aren't just some local teenagers selling pot on the street corner. Ramsey is one of the guys they arrested a year or two ago at another drug bust."

"You know who he is?"

"I remember seeing his name in the paper. Got off for lack of evidence or something."

"I don't remember any of that," Peter said.

"He was tied into that business guy, William McNabb, who owns the liquor stores. They say a lot of McNabb's money came from drugs. These aren't people to mess around with."

"You seem to know a lot about these guys."

Mary Beth was silent for a moment, as if caught off guard. She looked down, then held out the newspaper and looked back up at Peter. "I read the paper, and I listen to the news," she said finally. "After that bust awhile back, the media were all talking about McNabb and his connection with drugs. I've heard people talking about him."

Peter looked hard at Mary Beth. For a moment he had the odd feeling that she knew more than she was saying, that she was hiding something from him, but the thought seemed silly, and he decided it was just the stress of the situation, the paranoia, making him imagine things. "Well, anyway, I think you're right that these are some of the same guys."

"I remember reading about the bust," Mary Beth said. "Ramsey was the guy managing the liquor stores for McNabb. Everyone says those stores are just a front. And I hear McNabb has lots of connections."

Peter felt the side of his face throbbing and wondered if the bruise from his black eye was spreading down his cheek. He was about to ask Mary Beth if his eye was swelling noticeably, but she kept talking with barely a pause.

"What are we going to do with those drugs? We have to do something now. I'm scared to have them here. Can't the police figure out what happened? And what if that guy wakes up and tells them about you?"

"He can't afford to tell the police about me. Kidnapping and carjacking just get him in deeper. But I have an idea."

Mary Beth walked over to her dresser and pulled out a set of matching white panties and bra. She turned toward him wearing just the panties, still holding the bra in her hand. She said nothing, but the look on her face told him she didn't want to hear more. "Peter, this is just crazy."

"Will you at least listen? If you'll listen, and if you still think it's crazy, then I'll put the drugs somewhere and call the police and tell them what happened—just not tell them who I am."

"Okay, I'll listen. But you know how much I hate drugs. I don't want anything to do with them." She fastened the bra clasp in front of her before she slid the bra around her body and put her arms through the straps.

Peter watched her as he considered where he was going with his idea.

"Let's watch the court proceedings and newspaper to see if we can figure out who was behind the drugs. Then if we want, we can contact them secretly and pretend to sell the drugs back to them. Taking their money and their drugs is the best way to hurt dealers."

Peter knew he didn't have enough details yet to convince Mary Beth he could pull off his plan. But she had once told him she believed that Christopher's drug problems and ultimately his death were what had led to the chasm between them. Although she'd never said so outright, he knew that she, too, was still angry for what had happened to Chris.

The events that led to Chris's death had arranged themselves like a perfect storm. Too much change with not enough time for Chris to adjust. First of all, Chris was much younger than Peter, so when their father retired and their parents started doing the traveling they'd always planned, Chris's drug problems got out of control. He wound up in rehab when he was arrested on campus for public intoxication and the police found more than just chewing gum in his pockets. Then after their parents were killed in a car accident in the Smoky Mountains, Chris really lost control and soon went back in for a second rehab. After a third stay in rehab, Peter had convinced Christopher to move to Jackson to be near him and Mary Beth. The move didn't help. Only a few months later, Christopher died on his couch in the middle of the night after a weekend of drugs and drinking. Peter found Christopher two days later when he stopped by to see why the phone wasn't being answered.

Peter blamed himself for Christopher's problems, knowing his younger brother had first tried cocaine at a party at his house years before. Peter had supplied the drug.

"Look, let's just get that crap out of here first," Mary Beth said. "If you get the drugs out of the house now, I'll listen."

While Mary Beth finished dressing, Peter took the blue Cowboys bag outside to the storage room. He put on a pair of new disposable surgical gloves from a box he kept with the paint supplies.

He emptied his large, red toolbox, carefully wiping it inside and out with a clean shop towel, and placed the packages of drugs inside. He wiped down each package for fingerprints as he placed it into the toolbox. He made a tiny slit in the last package, used his knife to dig out a small pile of the drug, and placed it into a plastic sandwich bag from the kitchen pantry. He slid the tip of his pocketknife into the sandwich bag to remove a small pyramid of the white powder. He held the white powder up to inspect it before looking around to make sure Mary Beth wasn't watching. Then he moved the knife tip under his nostril and sniffed the powder into his nose. He rubbed his hand across his nostrils to make sure none of the powder showed.

He placed the sandwich bag into his pocket, grabbed two plastic trash bags and a shovel, and put everything in the back of the Jeep, covering it with a canvas tarp.

After telling Mary Beth he would be gone for a couple of hours to hide the drugs out in the country, he drove north on Interstate 55, following nearly the same route he'd taken the day before.

Instead of exiting at Madison as Jenkins had ordered him, he kept north on the interstate past Canton, taking the Highway 16 exit. He often hunted ducks and deer on a fourteen-hundred-acre tree farm there owned by one of his partners at B&P. In the middle of the twelve-year-old pines was a fifteen-acre swamp formed years before by beavers when they dammed up a small stream. He had walked virtually every acre and knew it was a place few people would visit. If necessary, the drugs could be abandoned there forever.

When the highway came to a fork after several miles, he veered left until pavement gave way to red clay. On both sides of the road, fields of planted pines rose nearly fifteen feet tall. Clouds of red dirt swirled behind his car.

From Wendell Road he turned left onto what was little more than a path and drove three hundred yards before stopping. There was no evidence to suggest anyone had been there since the previous hunting season. Weeds had grown two feet high and appeared undisturbed. Tiny yellow flowers topped most of the stalks.

He grabbed his shovel and red toolbox, stuffed the plastic trash bags into his pocket, and walked down a trail most people would never notice. He had spent three hours the year before cutting the lower limbs from a row of pines to clear a path to his favorite hunting spot on the ridge. The path ended where a small stand of hardwoods had been left to grow in the middle of the planted pines. A bed of pine needles created a thick carpet. He made little noise as he walked.

The hunting place had yielded two does and a six point to Peter over the past four years of bow hunting, though he'd not hunted the previous fall after Christopher had died a few weeks before the season. Last time he'd been here was the previous June when he'd found the skeleton of a massive fourteen-point buck he assumed had died of old age. Most hunters would never dream of looking for a spot like this, so close to a well-traveled road and in the middle of pines that many hunters thought were of no benefit to deer. From the numerous tracks in the sandy earth and the countless deer droppings, he could tell the area supported a sizable and healthy deer herd.

Peter neared the spot where he usually placed his climbing tree stand when bow hunting. He searched around the thickest brush nearby for a suitable spot to dig. The dirt was soft, so it only took five minutes to bury the toolbox, safely dry with the doubled plastic bags around it. He spread leaves and pine needles over the spot and stomped them down until he was satisfied the freshly turned earth was covered.

He put Jenkins' wallet in his pocket and looked around to make sure he could find the spot again, counting off twelve paces northeast from his tree. He removed the surgical gloves as he neared the truck and shoved them under a rotten log.

He drove farther down the old road so no one would notice where he had stopped. He put the Jeep into park and left the engine running at the spot he and his buddies normally parked when duck hunting on the opening day of the season. He remembered how great the hunting had been three years before, but no ducks had shown up for the past two years. He thought about all the time he'd spent building a duck blind near the open water in the center of the swamp. Gazing over the murky water and tall cypress trees, he searched for the beavers he had often heard slapping their tails on the water just after daylight, as if celebrating the new day.

After cramming the money and phone numbers from Jenkins' wallet into his pocket, he buried the wallet under one quick spade of dirt. He turned the Jeep around by a beaver dam at the end of the dirt road, leaving tire tracks mashed into the tall weeds.

chapter 6

Lt. Taylor Nelson merged into the traffic inching toward Jackson. He had just left the parking lot across from the United Artists Theatre after following Roy Gant to what, as he'd expected, turned out to be a meeting with William McNabb. With Nelson was Stanley Jordan Hunt III, known to all his friends as Sleepy because both his eyes drooped at the corners. A veteran police officer, Hunt had been transferred to Nelson's drug task force the previous week.

Nelson unwrapped a hand-rolled cigar and placed the tip in his mouth without lighting it. He steered back and forth in the heavy traffic and passed several cars whenever a momentary opening appeared in front of him.

The two men watched as McNabb drove past and turned north on Highway 25, Gant beside him.

"We don't need to follow," Nelson said, answering what he knew was Hunt's unspoken question. "When they meet here, they just drive around to talk. Usually happens about the time some deal goes down. We've quit tailing them from this spot. The risk of being seen when they drive on back roads with few cars isn't worth it. I just wanted you to see both men."

"How long you been on this assignment, Lieutenant?" Hunt asked.

Taylor knew Hunt meant the Metro Jackson Task Force. "About a year. My only job lately's been to get inside McNabb's organization."

"That's been tough?" Hunt asked as he scribbled notes on a small pad from his shirt pocket.

"Damn near impossible. Gant does most of the work. Keeps the group small and informed only on a need-to-know basis. We hoped the bust at the Greyhound station might split McNabb's organization down the middle and give us someone who'll tie him to the drug deal, but I'm not sure yet. Gant's pretty smart. Keeps McNabb in the background."

"What do we know about Gant?"

"Started as a small-time hood, stealing radios and purses from cars as a teenager. Graduated to boosting cars. His resume includes everything from drugs to fronting for sports bookies."

Hunt scribbled more notes. "Joe Graham told me you suspect Gant was involved last year in those two murdered drug dealers, the ones that got all shot up in West Jackson."

"Yeah. Looks like those guys pissed off McNabb by using an outside supplier. Shot through both kneecaps and twice behind their ears, then dumped on public street corners. A clear message about who runs the drugs in this town. We've got a suspect based out of New Orleans. Young guy Gant knows."

"I've seen Gant's rap sheet." Hunt rolled down the window to throw out the gum he had been chewing. "Lots of arrests, but his only jail time outside a few weeks in county was a sentence of eight years, I think. Is that right?"

"Yeah. Served about half his sentence. Felony possession. Part of his time was suspended. Shaved another year off when the Feds made the state empty the prisons for overcrowding. Been out a couple of years."

Nelson reached over to turn the air conditioner fan on high. "Since then, Gant's managed to avoid any arrests, but we're pretty certain he carries a gun. It's a trump card to hold for the right time when we need to catch him in a parole violation."

"I'm amazed at how many of these cons let the police use that tactic against them." Hunt shifted in the seat to glance over at a new Dodge truck on display atop a large pile of granite riprap at Wilson Dodge. "Somebody told me you were assigned to the Task Force from the Mississippi Bureau of Narcotics?"

"Yep. Sort of a political move to show cooperation among state and local agencies. Elections were coming up, and Metro Jackson has a heavy concentration of voters. The Bureau was told to make sure the people saw them as taking action. I got tapped."

"Well, at least you got someone inside McNabb's main liquor store. Nobody else has gotten close, I hear. And it paid off right away."

"Yeah, could be a real break for us," Nelson spoke without looking at Hunt as he turned his head to check the lane beside him to pass a slower car. "McNabb uses a small office there. Stops by several times a week. Joe never even heard the actual plans for this shipment, but he heard just enough to piece it together. Street talk was that something big was coming in that weekend."

"Have you gotten anything else from Joe being there?"

"Nah, nothing so far to nail McNabb. Though in the past two weeks we've seen Gant coming to the store to meet with McNabb a lot more. They meet in a tiny office walled off in the storage area. Funny thing is, it's a great wine store, one of the best in Mississippi. I'd shop there all the time if I could."

Both men laughed.

Nelson continued. "I got into big-body Cabernets and good ports, when I can afford them, to go with cigars, and my ex-wife liked Merlot. Since she left me a couple of years ago and moved to Panama City Beach, my liquor tab has been cut by about two-thirds. Couldn't take the late nights and unpredictable hours."

Hunt laughed. "Mine's not happy about the hours either, but she don't say much. I don't know much about wine, but I like it sometime."

"Sometime on a weekend maybe you can come by. I'll open an '85 or '87 Warre's Vintage Port to try with a cigar. That'll change your mind about wine. I just hope that this store will still make it after we put McNabb behind bars."

"Liquor stores give McNabb a good place to wash his money," Hunt said.

"We think so. But it seems to turn a nice profit as a side benefit."

Neither man spoke for several miles. Nelson was thinking ahead to what he would do when he got home. He hoped there would be an email from a woman he had recently met.

"You live in town, Lieutenant?"

"Over on the east end of Belhaven, where it borders the interstate. I like the area. Kind of a mix of college students, young lawyers, and leftover hippies struggling as photographers and coffee shop owners. Some retired couples that have lived there for thirty years." Nelson looked out the window, thinking of the person who would definitely not be at his house waiting this time. "Lots of people have moved back in from all those damn treeless, red brick home subdivisions springing up outside of town in every direction."

"My wife likes living in the country. We're way out Highway 18. Pretty rural. She thinks the boys need to be away from city schools."

"My ex is the reason I moved to Belhaven. She loved the different styles of old houses. Big stucco houses with polished hardwood floors. Two-story Georgian homes alongside one-bedroom duplexes built for the young married medical students from the University of Mississippi Medical Center." Nelson eased the car to the curb behind Hunt's Taurus. "Nothing else is going to happen today. Let's call it quits and start fresh in the morning."

———

Nelson parked in the carport of his small, two-story house and walked around back to use the patio door. He cursed himself for not getting the lock fixed on the front door and made a promise that he would repair it that week. He'd made himself that same promise every week for nearly three months.

While the house was well-kept and clean, one glance revealed clues that this was a guy's home. Big cigar ashtrays, a barbell in the corner, and a dart board on the wall. But he was pleased that more than one woman had been impressed by the designer furniture, leather couch, a thick red and black oriental rug, and original oil paintings of landscapes, somehow not expecting good taste in a law enforcement officer. He grabbed a bottled beer and sat on his couch.

Finding female companionship had never been a problem for him. As a baseball player at LSU, he had found that women liked athletes, and he used that background to impress women whenever he needed. But usually his full head of hair, broad shoulders, and trim waistline were enough to get him attention. Most other thirty-five-year-olds he knew were already beginning to add a few inches around the middle, so he stood out a bit at closing time at the bars he visited when feeling like another night alone would be one too many. Tonight was like the last few weeks though, and he had no interest in the bar scene. There was only one woman on his mind. A woman very different from any he had met in a long time. Beautiful without flaunting it. Confident, yet reserved. And unfortunately, involved with someone else.

He pushed the power button on his Compaq laptop that was open in front of him on the coffee table. With one eye on the TV he clicked on AOL and entered his password. Hearing the familiar voice telling he had mail, he sat up and leaned over the keyboard. He scrolled down the three emails and found all were selling something. None was of interest. Not even bothering to delete the messages, he logged out.

After a moment of digging around for the remote under the cushion, he turned on ESPN. He pulled the cigar from his pocket, snipped the tip with a cutter from the coffee table, and held a torch lighter under the end as he rotated the cigar and puffed. He leaned back and blew a series of blue smoke rings toward the ceiling, smiling to think how nice it was to smoke a cigar inside the house without anyone frowning at him.

He flipped the channel around for a few minutes and put his feet up on the sofa. His cigar went out as it rested on the large ceramic ashtray in front on him. He settled on watching *Jaws* for the fifth time, but his eyes grew heavy at the first commercial when local Jackson appliance king Cowboy Maloney pitched his latest greatest price on a new refrigerator with a range to match and nothing down. The last thing he heard was he better hurry and come by before Sunday at five or he'd miss the prices that would never, ever be this low again.

chapter 7

On Sunday morning, Peter hunched over the coffee table and read every page of the newspaper, searching for new details on the drug bust. Finding nothing, he began reading the instructions on the heavy-duty carpet cleaner he'd picked up at Reliable Rentals the day before. He drained the last of a cup of coffee and walked out to the driveway. The sun, already heating up the morning air, created shafts of yellow light across the front yard where rays found an opening in the thick oaks and pines.

He poured yellow liquid Joy into a mop bucket and turned on the hose in the backyard. He filled the bucket, ripped an old white towel in half, and dipped it into the soapy water. He turned on a radio and found the oldies rock show "Tunes Till Two." David Adcock's familiar melodic voice said, "I have a little bit of Dickie Betts' fine guitar work coming up with the Allman Brothers' "Blue Sky," along with some Skynyrd and CDB to finish off an all-Southern set, right after this message from my good friends at Patty Peck Honda."

Starting with the door on the driver's side, Peter began carefully scrubbing the Jeep's vinyl interior to get rid of the bloodstains. The water in the bucket turned red when he squeezed the sponge. He looked up at the front of the car and wondered how the car had such minor damage while his passenger had been broken up so badly. Two hours later, Peter plugged in the carpet cleaner and began applying foam to the seats and carpet. He spent another hour on the first cleaning before deciding to foam each surface one more time and let the fabric soak while he took a break for a large glass of ice water. He worked the foam down into every fold and crevice he could. Peter knew it would be impossible to hide every trace of dirt and drugs, but he also had faith that the police in Jackson would not be thorough if they had reason to inspect his car.

Inside the house, he found Mary Beth sitting at the computer. She seemed startled when she saw him and quickly closed the email she was reading and opened another window.

"Sorry, didn't mean to sneak up on you."

"Oh, it's nothing. I just didn't hear you."

Peter noticed *The Cedar Key* discussion board on the screen, explaining in no uncertain terms exactly what residents thought the little town needed to do. The State of Florida's ban on net fishing was the big topic of controversy. The ban had practically destroyed the part of the town's economy based on mullet fishing. The mullet fishermen complained they could barely make a living with small cast nets to get the fish necessary to make the island's famous smoked mullet.

"Bet." He'd begun to call her Bet after her two-year-old nephew started calling her Aunt Mary Bet, finding the "th" sound somehow impossible. The name was beginning to stick, and he knew she liked it. "I have an idea for the swap. You want to hear it?"

She stood and walked past him into the kitchen and opened the refrigerator. "You want a Coke or something?"

"Yeah, a Coke is fine." Peter realized he was still thirsty after the glass of water.

She pulled two cans of soda from the bottom shelf and opened a Diet Dr. Pepper for herself. "Okay, what are you thinking?"

Peter sat at the kitchen table, directly across from Mary Beth. He picked up a cloth napkin left beside his normal place at the table and wiped sweat from his forehead. "Well, we need to plan the same way I'd plan a marketing campaign. Decide what our obstacles to success may be, what our strengths and weaknesses are, and our information gaps. What advantages do we have over our competition? What are our alternatives?"

He was sorry as soon as he spoke. Listening to himself aloud, he felt the

blood rush to his face. His words sounded naïve. Or worse. He looked at
Mary Beth to see if she thought the way he was talking was silly. If she did,
it didn't show.

"I've been thinking, too," Mary Beth said. "I think getting involved with
drug dealers is crazy. And besides, even if we wanted to go through with
something so stupid, we have some other questions that need answers
first."

"Like what?"

"Like who the drugs belong to, much less how to contact them? And
how do we prove we've got the drugs without meeting face to face? And
here's the thing that scares me the most, how can we be sure they aren't
working with the police? Can't you see this won't work?"

"Peter started to speak, but Mary Beth interrupted."

"And how do we make the exchange, or fake it, without getting killed?"
She slammed her hand on the table. The more she talked, the angrier she
seemed and the louder she talked.

"I don't have an answer to all of those questions," Peter said, being
careful to keep his voice conversational in tone. He was excited that she
had even imagined what would be involved in going through with the
plan. "But I think I know how to find out if this McNabb guy is the right
guy. That's the starting point. If contact with him doesn't go well, then we
don't have any further to go anyway."

Mary Beth grew quiet. Peter could tell from the way she crossed her
arms she was angry that he was still trying to win her over. He'd seen the
look before. During the past few months, he'd seen it far too often as
more and more of their conversations became arguments. Too many
ended without resolution.

"I need to finish cleaning the car first," Peter said. "Then there'll be no
way anyone can connect us. I promise that not getting caught will always
be my first priority."

Mary Beth walked back to her desk without replying and sat down without looking at Peter.

Peter knew he had to convince Mary Beth that he would be cautious if he wanted her to take the next step. He also admired her smarts and knew she could help make his plan work. As he reached for a wet sponge, he suddenly began thinking about what he would do with hundreds of thousands of dollars in cash before reminding himself the goal wasn't money.

He finished the inside of the car after another hour and was sure there was no obvious trace of Jenkins. From all the cop shows on TV now, he knew there might be blood hidden in some tiny crevice, but he had to do something. As a last step he sprayed the interior with Clorox and water and wiped it down. He remembered that on some movie he'd seen Clorox made it hard to trace the DNA in blood.

Next he started on the exterior of the car. He took lighter fluid and the other half of the towel and began to scrub the bumper to remove the black creosote marks where it had hit the telephone pole. Satisfied the marks were gone, he washed the entire outside of the car, paying particular attention to the tires. He felt a little foolish doing so, but he lay on his back and squirted the hose all over the underside of the car until he felt certain he'd washed down every speck of dirt from the wreck. He didn't plan to give anyone an easy way to link him to the incident at the bus station or to the wreck that had put Jenkins in the hospital. Still uneasy, he left the Jeep in the backyard out of sight from the street.

When he came back inside and sat down in the den to drink a big glass of iced tea and cool off, Peter saw on a high shelf his collection of cone-top beer cans from the 1930s and 40s. Funky old labels and rich colors. He used to love to sneak time on the Internet to bid on these, and he was still missing a few key pieces. He felt like taking them all and putting them in a box and then putting the box inside a dark closet. The Peter who had that kind of passion had left when Christopher died. And now it looked as if that Peter wasn't coming back.

———

The hospital-green cloth cap and heavy black glasses made Roy Gant feel transformed as he sat in the University Medical Center employee parking lot. A middle-aged male nurse had appeared in his place. Even his friends wouldn't have recognized him in the disguise without his usual creased blue jeans, gold horseshoe belt buckle, and western shirt with mother-of-pearl buttons. He wore light-green hospital scrubs, taken the night before from a storage closet in the hospital. They'd been right where his nephew had said they would be, and his plan for not being seen had worked perfectly. His nephew, a male nurse in the emergency room, was the only family member he was close to. Gant sat in his Cadillac, waiting for the afternoon shift change.

That old lady looks like my mama. Drives like her, too, Gant thought as he watched a little gray-haired lady creep through the parking lot in a two-toned lime green and white thirty-year-old Buick that looked twice as big as newer cars. Yeah, she could be his mama, with her skinny arm propped on the window, filling the car with her rings of blue smoke.

Gant felt his eyes grow full and a lump swell in his throat. He swallowed hard. He could see his mother standing in the front door of her run-down, two-bedroom trailer on the edge of a cotton field outside Eden, Mississippi. She stood there leaning against the doorframe on one foot while he loaded his few possessions into the trunk of a Ford Fairlane with rusted-out fenders and seats repaired with duct tape until they were almost completely silver. Her faded flowered dress was so thin from hand washing he could see her skin through the material.

At seventeen, he had been one of the only white people living around the little Delta town just north of Yazoo City that was dusty all summer and muddy all winter.

There was no good work for the black families or the white families if you didn't own one of the ten-thousand-acre farms that stretched for miles in every direction. He had no reason to expect much with his 10th-grade education, no money, and no daddy. But his mother said she had hope for him, the youngest of her four children and for some reason the only one she said had a chance.

That day had been the last time he had seen her, but he could still remember her yelling as he drove off, her words barely loud enough to hear over the rumble of the dual Cherry Bomb glasspack mufflers. She was standing there with an unfiltered Camel waving up and down on her mouth like a signal flag. The last thing she said to him was, "Your day will come, son." She died two years later from a heart attack while hanging laundry out behind the trailer. By the time he heard, when he ran into a first cousin in a bar in Biloxi, she'd already been buried. He had never been back to Eden.

As groups of hospital workers began to file out in twos and threes, Gant walked to the hospital side entrance. Inside, the smell—an odd combination of decay and disinfectant—immediately reminded him why he avoided hospitals.

At the second door, he used the key his nephew had given him, entered a storage room marked Hospital Personnel Only, and selected a wheelchair. On a shelf, he found two small towels and wrapped one around each of the handles before pulling a pair of surgical gloves from a box and slipping them into his pocket.

Pushing the chair, Gant walked past Jenkins's room and glanced in. The door stood partially open, enough to see. A folding chair beside the door indicated that the police guard was still on duty somewhere nearby.

Gant walked toward the elevators and looked down the hallway. He saw the young uniformed officer leaning against the nurses' station, his back to Gant, talking to two nurses behind the counter. The nurses laughed as the policeman gestured, obviously telling some story about cops and crooks. A cup of coffee on the counter and the laughter of the nurses told Gant what he needed to know. He pushed the wheelchair to the end of the hall and left it. He walked back to Jenkins's room and, with a last look both ways down the hall, entered the room and closed the door with his elbow as he slipped on the gloves.

For several seconds he stood there, simply looking at Jenkins. The man's face was swollen and covered with a combination of deep blue and red bruises. He was almost unrecognizable. His eyes were shut, and bottles of clear fluid dripped into both arms. Gant looked around the room and saw nothing to indicate any family or friends had visited. No flowers, magazines, or personal items were on the chair or window sill.

A hospital pillow and thin blanket remained neatly stacked on the chair beside the bed where no one had sat. Bending over Jenkins, he whispered, "I'm sorry, Robert." He pushed the pillow over the man's face and held it there with both hands as he pressed down with the weight of his body. After a few seconds, Jenkins's chest began heaving and his arms struggled against the leather straps that held them in place.

———

On Monday, Mary Beth was up early, before Peter. She went straight to the front driveway to find the newspaper. She sat on the front porch steps, enjoying the warm morning air as she flipped through the paper. Nothing was on the front page, but at the bottom of the State/Metro section she read, "Suspect in major drug case dies." She sat back against the front door and scanned the article, her breathing shallow and rapid.

The article indicated that Harold Ramsey, manager of a Best Price Liquor store, and Santiago Cuevas, a Mexican citizen, both remained in custody following the recent drug raid. She took the paper inside to Peter and handed it to him in bed without saying a word.

The story offered little additional information except that a hospital source said Robert Alvin Jenkins had died without regaining consciousness.

Peter sat up and leaned his head back against the wooden headboard.

"I can't go to the police now." He spoke in a monotone. "How could I explain it all? They might think I tried to kill him for the drugs."

"I know." Mary Beth said, her tone flat. "There's no way to roll back the clock." Her eyes met Peter's, and she waited for him to explain their way out of the situation. "You said they don't know anything. Just leave the drugs in the woods, and no one will ever know. Peter, you did nothing wrong in defending yourself, and you shouldn't suffer just because a criminal picked your car to steal while running from a drug bust." Despite her feelings of a void between them, she still loved Peter. "Do you really think your scheme is what Christopher would want us to do?"

Peter's eyes grew larger, his emotions barely contained when Mary Beth brought Chris into the conversation. "Christopher would want us to get our fucking lives back," Peter said, louder than normal but not quite yelling, as he tossed the newspaper to the floor.

Mary Beth turned and walked out of the room.

chapter 8

On Saturday morning, after a week during which Peter and Mary Beth had argued about the drugs every time they talked, they were on the interstate highway driving home from Bessemer, Alabama, having dropped off Peter's car for repairs. They had figured that two hundred and fifty miles was far enough away from Jackson. The police would never look there. They'd spent the prior evening with friends in nearby Birmingham, drinking beer and telling old stories about other friends who weren't there to defend themselves.

"Are we in over our heads?" Mary Beth asked.

Her tone was matter-of-fact. He could see she was trying to keep her voice even to avoid another angry conversation. The answer to her question wasn't in the rehearsed speech he'd been waiting to make when she brought up the subject. And now that she opened the door for him to make a strong argument and settle the matter once and for all, he wanted exactly the right answer. He wanted to sound cautious yet confident. His mind went blank. He didn't respond in time.

"Well that's just great," she said after enough time passed, unable now to keep her voice down. "I've spent days deciding that this drug crap, as bad as it is, could be the way to give us something to do that will pull us together. I finally resolve to go along with something idiotic, just to show you how much I want to support you and now you're not sure!"

"I never said I wasn't sure. I think we can. What do you mean pull us back together?"

She turned in the seat and looked directly at Peter, her voice softer, more confident. "Oh, come on, you know exactly what I mean. You've been in your own world since Christopher died last year. You've shut me out. You don't even touch me anymore. Not the way you used to."

"I just need some time to get over Chris. I want to do something for him." He switched lanes at the last second as his car overtook another vehicle slowing down as they started up a steep incline.

"Damn it, Peter. Listen to you. This isn't about Christopher. This is about you. You need to feel it's okay to go on living. Well, it *is* okay. Life goes on. I loved Christopher, too. But we can't bring him back, and we can't get him to tell us everything is all right. Listen to yourself. You're absolutely right that Christopher would want us to have a fucking life again, as you so eloquently put it the other night. But I know you, and I know you're going to do something with those drugs. And I've decided something, too. If you're going to do something crazy then damn it I am, too. So make up your mind, and get on with whatever the hell you're going to do."

Peter was stunned. It was the first time he'd heard Mary Beth say that word in a long time. Yet, there it was. She hated the word, but she had made the impression he knew she wanted. After a pause, Peter simply said, "Then it's decided."

They sat without speaking for the next half hour, until Mary Beth's words cut through the heavy cloud of silence. "I have an idea that might help. We need to know more about McNabb and who works for him in case the drugs do belong to him. I have lots of experience with newspaper microfilm to look up the campaign promises of politicians. And you can find all kinds of stuff on a Yahoo search. If he's been in the news, I can find out."

"Okay, that's good. I think you should do that."

They spent the next three hours saying virtually nothing as Mary Beth fed one CD after another into the player.

After arriving home in the early afternoon, Mary Beth logged into her computer while Peter lay on the bed and slept. After a two-hour nap, he sat up on the side of the bed and rubbed his eyes.

"You hungry?" Mary Beth asked as she walked into the bedroom.

"No, you go ahead and make yourself something. I'm going for a drive to look at a place I thought about for the exchange."

Fifteen minutes later, after getting off I-55 at High Street and passing the State Fairgrounds, Peter was southbound on Jefferson Street. He passed in front of the bus station, unable to resist reliving the scene of Jenkins jumping into the backseat, before continuing south past the WLBT television station. He came to the dead end at Silas Brown Road and veered onto the old Woodrow Wilson Bridge over the Pearl River. He began smiling for the first time in days. He turned the car around in the parking lot of the old Spur station just across the river and drove home.

Peter thought about how appropriate it would be to try to do a drug deal—even a fake one—right along what was once called the Gold Coast. At one time, the area was the central locale for illegal whiskey, drugs, and prostitution. Today, he saw only a couple of run-down gas stations and a store that wasn't anything more than a shack with a stove and refrigerator, with TAMALES painted across the front wall above a sliding window. Next door was an auto repair shop guarded by an assortment of rusted-out wrecked cars and one ancient German Shepherd with matted fur, tied to a metal pole with a tattered rope.

———————

With Peter gone, Mary Beth logged in remotely to her office email. There was only one new email, but the message wasn't about work. She stared at the sender address for a few seconds before she deleted the email without opening it. She typed an address and composed an email:

Please do not contact me anymore. I know you'll understand. I simply cannot do this.

MB

The second she finished, she hit SEND. She pushed her chair back and bent over, holding her face in her hands, determined not to let this throw her.

She heard the computer make a single tone indicating an incoming email. She looked up and saw the email was a reply to the one she had just sent:

No, I don't understand. At least meet me at lunch tomorrow and tell me why to my face.

chapter 9

A major deadline faced Peter at work on Monday morning. Without the Cherokee, they had to drive Mary Beth's car. After dropping Mary Beth at her office, Peter parked her car in his usual spot and walked to his building.

He had promised that a marketing analysis would be written and faxed to a client by noon, but at 11:00 he was still on page one. He couldn't concentrate. Rather than wait until the last moment, he decided to call and lower his client's expectations. He needed to buy some time.

Picking up the phone, he dialed the direct number for the ad manager at Southern Food Distributors, the parent company for Mrs. Peters' Cakes. After getting agreement that he could take another two or three hours to complete the project, he hung up. He would have to work through lunch, but now he could meet his deadline.

He took off his reading glasses and leaned back in the chair. He turned to look out the window at the corner of Capitol and Congress streets, as he often did when thinking. Four times in the last few years he had been watching that corner just as a car ran the red light and banged into another. Once, he'd seen a truck broadside a car, causing it to jump the curb and hit a telephone pole.

Peter noticed a man sitting in a parked car. Peter stopped breathing. The man looked like the same one he had seen looking at him from across the street earlier. While Peter watched from the window, the man pulled out of the parking space and drove off. Peter couldn't tell conclusively if the man was the same person, but he told himself to begin watching more carefully. He was still staring out the window when the agency's runner, Jeff, knocked on the door.

"Mr. Brantley, here's the package you were waiting for." Jeff laid a small wooden box on the corner of the antique desk Peter had retrieved from his father's study after his parents died.

"Thanks, Jeff."

He walked over to look at the small box, a sample for a direct mail project. The concept called for a small container to hold a goose call. On the lid was a mock-up of artwork showing a line of geese crossing the road in front of the Goose Pond Tower, heading for a scenic lake that surrounded three sides of the office building. The message read, "Sorry, but our rush hour can sometimes create a brief traffic jam." The piece would be hand-delivered to fifty key downtown prospects for a real estate client that had recently opened a high-rise office building on Colony Parkway on the edge of town.

As he reached for the box, Peter suddenly stopped and smiled. He stared at the box, realizing how he could make contact with McNabb to find out if he was the one who originally owned the drugs.

Peter couldn't wait to tell Mary Beth and see if she thought his idea might work. He felt as if a burden had been lifted. After taping a note that read "On Deadline. Can it wait?" to the outside of his door, he touched the Do Not Disturb button on his phone.

———

Mary Beth's secretary said she'd run out to pick up lunch for the office, so Mary Beth scanned the take-out menu from Keifer's Deli. Nothing appealed to her. "Just order me the salad with sliced chicken breast. Iced tea," she said looking up at the young woman standing in her doorway. "Thanks. And please pull my door shut. I've got to make some calls."

She turned back to her computer and typed an Instant Message, I don't know why we're having this conversation.

I think you do, came the Instant Message reply.

What does that mean?

I'm not trying to make things worse. But not talking doesn't help. You can't just send an email and say goodbye.

Mary Beth thought for a moment and then started typing again. Sometimes talking only makes things worse. Talking things out is overrated.

Moments later a response came that made it harder for Mary Beth to keep up the conversation.

Has something happened in the last few days? Things just seem to have changed all of a sudden. One day you're laughing and your eyes sparkle, the next it seems like someone has died. I'm concerned. Is that a crime?

Before she could respond a second message appeared. I just get this message that you're so busy you can't even talk. Then you don't want to meet for lunch. And now you say don't even contact you. I don't get it.

Mary Beth tried to type something that made sense, but each time she started her hands trembled. She clenched her jaw, trying not to feel weak. I'm sorry, I shouldn't even be having this conversation, she typed and then pressed Enter to send the message. She hoped her secretary would be gone for a long time. She poked around in her purse until she found her lipstick, applying it to both lips at once in one quick motion.

———

Peter handed his assistant a draft of the analysis for Mrs. Peters' Cakes. He'd finished in an afternoon what often took at least a day and a half.

He dropped off the report to be bound for delivery, walked back to his office, and closed the door. He picked up the box from his desk and felt the smooth unvarnished wood. *Mary Beth might like this idea,* he thought. He put down the box and spent the afternoon catching up on the work he had neglected for several days. He answered nearly two dozen emails on various topics before sorting through a stack of unopened mail. The last hour was nothing more than filing a stack of internal memos and various documents pertaining to client projects in progress.

He looked at his watch. It was nearly 5:30. Knowing Mary Beth would be waiting, he started for the car. He realized how much of a hassle it was to have only one car and thought about how much he took for granted. He closed the car door, turned the switch, and the radio came on with a blast of Elton John from an oldies station. In his car with the music blaring, the rest of the world disappeared.

Peter saw Mary Beth standing inside the small lobby, staring out the narrow floor-to-ceiling window beside the front door. He turned down the volume on the radio, not wanting to hear a comment about how loud he kept the music. Mary Beth was outside and locking the office building door before he was completely stopped. She opened the door and slung her purse between them as she sat down.

"How was your day?" Mary Beth asked.

Peter noticed she didn't look at him, but he assumed she was just tired, same as he was. He wasted no time in launching into his new idea. "I know how to make contact. We can package one bag of the powder and deliver it to McNabb. That'll prove I have the drugs and that I'm not the police. The police couldn't do that. It would be entrapment."

Peter had used direct marketing to sell everything from condos to lawnmowers. He laid out his plan. "His response will tell me if he's the right guy. I can control exactly how he has to respond. I'll just send him a package that can't be traced back to me even if he's working with the cops."

Mary Beth listened. "That might work. But we don't know for sure that McNabb's the right person, or that he'll go along. Or that he has the money and will pay."

"But don't you think we should at least try?"

"Peter, I agree this might be the safest way to approach McNabb, but it's still not too late to drop this whole thing."

"Maybe you're right, Bet. And maybe the whole thing is crazy. I change my mind twenty times a day, but let me do this one thing. All I ask of you is to find out where McNabb lives."

chapter 10

John Baynes held a fork loaded with black-eyed peas from a plate mounded with rice and gravy, sliced tomatoes, and fried chicken. "What's going on, Peter? You seem a million miles away." Baynes, president and CEO of Baynes and Powell, had long been Peter's closest friend at the agency, so when he had asked Peter to lunch, Peter was glad to oblige. But Peter had also known the conversation was bound to come around to this. "I've thought for some months now that your concentration and focus on work are getting worse."

Peter didn't answer immediately. He hated lying to John, and after the owners' meeting a few weeks back, he knew all the other partners were unhappy with his performance for the last year. Because of his brother's death, for a few months they had held back their criticism and were forgiving of problems with his work, but it was now clear that they thought he should be back contributing more to the agency.

As he and Peter sat across from each other at Laura's Place on the below-ground level of the Petroleum Building, John did not jump to fill the silence in the conversation. He seemed to wait for an answer.

Peter considered how to respond to a friend who knew him better than anyone except his wife. On a daily basis, John was too busy to pay attention to what Peter did, so Peter knew the situation at the office was worse than he'd suspected if John felt the need to take him to lunch to talk. Peter had great respect for John and wanted to answer in the least deceitful way. But in this situation, he could think of no good way to tell the truth, as much as he wanted to.

Ten years ago, they'd met at an American Association of Advertising

Agencies conference in Louisville where they hit it off big. In the bar atop the north tower of the Galt House Hotel, after one long night of sampling top-rated bourbons from the Largest Collection of Kentucky Bourbons in the World, they had felt like old friends. They loved the bar with its seafaring theme of fishnets, crab pot marker buoys, and a topless mermaid on the front of a ship facade who kept a vigilant watch over the customers.

They had kept up the friendship even before Peter's move to Mississippi. On several occasions, the two had taken their wives and met for golf weekends in Birmingham and Memphis, or taken an extra day at ad conferences to play whatever famous course was nearby. Over time, the four of them began to vacation together and spent many nights and weekends at each other's home.

"And where'd you get that black eye last week?" John asked. "I tried not to ask after you said you banged it on a table, but everyone in the office has been making bets on what really happened."

"Nothing's wrong, I've just been busy and a little tired lately. Why do you ask?"

"Bullshit. I know you. Something's bothering you, Peter. The whole damn agency knows your head is somewhere else."

"I'm fine. Really, there's nothing wrong. And there's no great story about the eye. I hit it on the corner of the table in my workshop when I bent down to get something. As I said."

"Well, you need to be careful about how you react to people. A couple of people on your account team have asked me what's wrong. They said you don't seem interested in their work right now and you let creative concept boards go through without your usual interest in picking at little details. Your team may not like you sticking your nose in, but it scares the hell out of them when you don't. And it scares me, too."

Peter took a bite of chicken after tearing a strip from the breast and smiled, "I guess I need to be more of a worrier so they won't think I don't care." He laughed but was afraid it sounded forced.

"Look, I've covered for you about all I can, Peter. You have to get back in the game. And you better do it now," John said.

Peter knew John didn't make idle threats. He was simply being honest with a friend while doing his job as CEO at the same time. Peter tried to lighten the mood. He smiled. "John, if I didn't know you loved me, I'd take that as a threat."

John didn't follow suit and said nothing, his face unyielding, without a smile.

Peter decided to change the subject. "How's Janie?"

"She's fine. She's been following the kids around to swim meets all summer," John answered.

"You guys need to come over for dinner soon. It's our turn to cook. I think we've been over to your house the last two times. And Bet and I were, shall we say, *overserved* last time at your house."

Both men laughed more than the joke deserved, welcoming something to break the tension.

"Yeah, that sounds good to me. Maybe this weekend," Baynes said.

They walked out into the bright sunlight, each reaching for sunglasses as they turned the corner to the Lamar Life Building where their offices were located. Like men often do when they're together, they drifted off to separate thoughts. Neither of them said anything as they walked down the street, and neither cared that no one spoke.

"What's your afternoon like?" Peter asked as they neared the building.

"I'm trying to get a meeting with the new president of Perdido Hotel to talk about that research project. What about you?"

"I'm trying to decide how to follow up on that direct mail project," Peter lied. Actually he was wondering if cell phone calls could be tracked to a specific location.

As they reached the front door of their office building, Peter noticed a man in a dark suit standing across the street in front of the governor's mansion. The man seemed to be watching them. Peter turned casually and tried to act as if he weren't looking. They reached the elevators just in time to catch one before the doors closed.

Exiting the elevator, Peter walked through the lobby to the corner conference room with a view of the governor's mansion. He looked down the street, but the man in the dark suit was gone.

———

Peter waited until after dinner on Friday night to bring up the next part of his plan.

"I want to bring Danny in on this," Peter said.

Mary Beth turned toward him on the sofa. "What do you think he can do?"

Her question sounded more like an accusation. "I know I can trust him. He'd do anything for me."

"I know Danny was where you got those bags of pot you sold to your fraternity brothers at Birmingham-Southern, but does that mean he knows what to do with these guys? They're real criminals, not a bunch of college kids."

Peter put his wine glass on the coffee table, then reached over and placed his hand lightly on Mary Beth's arm. He looked into her eyes. "I never told you everything about Danny, but maybe you should know now. He hung out with a pretty wild bunch in high school and later it was the same at the community college."

"I sort of knew that."

"There's more you don't know. He had several run-ins with the law and only managed to stay out of jail by luck. He was deeper into the drug scene than you knew. I saw him with guys that clearly didn't give a damn about police or laws."

"What do you mean you saw these guys? And what has that got to do with helping us?"

"Do you remember Danny's best friend, Nick? They called him Juice?"

"Yeah, I've heard the stories. But I never really got to know him." She sipped her wine and looked over the rim of the glass at Peter.

"Juice was the first person I ever knew who carried a gun for something other than hunting. One time Juice and Danny shot out the windows of a liquor store when the guys wouldn't sell them beer on Sunday. Another time they robbed a drug dealer's apartment. And Juice has spent time in juvenile custody and he did a few months for breaking and entering for something up in Huntsville. Maybe another night or two in the Birmingham jail for drunk and disorderly conduct."

"OH, lovely. They certainly sound like they come highly recommended with those stellar resumes."

Peter ignored the sarcasm. "Look, you know Danny's been straight for a long time. And Juice, too. They were kids then. I just think Danny—and maybe Juice if we need help from someone who isn't afraid to take a little risk—are people we can trust to help. And they know what drug dealers are capable of doing."

———

The next morning, Peter and Mary Beth drove to Bessemer to pick up the Jeep. With a new bumper, no dents, and a paint job, it looked like new. Mary Beth had picked out a deep burgundy color.

By mid-afternoon, they were on their way to Danny's house to talk. Mary Beth had agreed that Peter should at least get Danny's help, but she was still skeptical about Juice.

Soon after they passed through downtown Birmingham, Peter turned off the interstate to the Center Point neighborhood and weaved through the local streets to Danny's house. The house sat at the end of a dead end street formed when the new interstate loop cut the neighborhood in half twenty years before, blocking all the through streets.

Danny's house sat in the middle of three nearly identical homes, each
one a single story house with white-siding and a carport held up at the
corner by a round metal pipe. Two small bicycles, a baseball bat, and a
large blue and yellow plastic dump truck lay scattered in the freshly cut
front yard, but no children were visible. Peter parked on the street, and he
and Mary Beth made their way up a walkway of round concrete stepping
stones that curved in a gentle s-shape from the mailbox at the street to the
small front porch.

"Peter. Mary Beth. Come on in," Danny said as he held open the screen
door with an outstretched arm. He hugged them both before he shouted
toward the back of the house. "Cindy, they're here."

The four of them took seats in the living room, clean but modestly
furnished, unlike Peter and Mary Beth's home filled with thick rugs and
modern furniture.

"Where are the kids?" Mary Beth asked.

"Oh, the two youngest had a skating party. And Danny Junior's off
somewhere on his bike with a bunch of boys."

Peter asked, "How's the computer business?"

"It's going pretty well," Danny said. "The more they sell the more they
need us troubleshooters around. Job security I guess."

After a few minutes of casual conversation to get caught up on what
they'd all been doing, Peter said, "Danny, you got time to take a ride with
me while Mary Beth stays with Cindy? We don't need to bore the women
with work talk. I've got a project we need some help on at the office."

"Sure, let's go."

Cindy grabbed Mary Beth by the hand and motioned toward the kitchen
with her head. "Come on, Mary Beth. Let's get a cup of coffee."

"You sure this is all right?" Peter asked.

"Hell, yeah. Don't we always manage to drive around and drink a six-
pack in the car when you're in town? Cindy don't mind me having a few
beers, but since her daddy was an alcoholic she don't like me to drink

around the kids. I'd already reminded her that we might need to go out for a little while to talk business."

"You know, I miss driving our big motorcycles together. But I guess the days of going for a ride out to the river and drinking a few beers on the sandbar are gone forever."

"Hell man, when the kids started coming along, I sold mine and never thought about it again," Danny replied.

"I've still got an old Triumph Lightning from the early seventies in the garage, but Mary Beth and I rarely take it out anymore. It's mint, though. Got that great 654cc engine that'll run forever. I just can't seem to decide to sell it." Peter fiddled with the rearview mirror and took a deep breath. "Danny, I need to tell you something. I'm into something big, and it's not good. I may need your help. And I might need another person, too. Is Juice still around?"

"Damn, man. That sounds kind of heavy. Ad business too boring? You robbing banks or something now?" Danny said, laughing.

Before Peter answered, he pulled into the Jr. Food Mart parking lot. "Is Miller Lite OK?" he asked, as he all but jumped out of the car.

"Yeah, anything. Hurry up. I want to hear what kind of shit you've gotten into. Is this another one of your crazy business deals? And you won't believe what Juice is doing." Danny was barely able to get the words out before he started laughing again.

Peter was forced to wait in line as a kid in baggy shorts at least ten inches too big in the waist counted out nickels, dimes, and pennies to pay for two dollars' worth of gas.

When Peter returned, he handed the beer to Danny who opened two cans and started talking. "Juice is selling houses. He doesn't like anybody calling him Juice anymore. Of course, I still do, but not if anyone is around. He didn't tell anybody he was doing it. Just studied and got his license. I think he must be good at it. He bought a great house in Southside last summer and is fixing it up. I still see him on weekends once in a while."

"Is he still doing drugs?"

"Not really. He hasn't done hard drugs for about four or five years, but he might smoke a little pot sometimes. What've you got yourself into?"

Peter told the story from the beginning, starting at the bus station, as he had with Mary Beth.

When Peter finished, Danny whistled a long, low whistle. "That asshole never knew what hit him, did he. You did the right thing. You don't need to feel bad at all about that slimy little frog of a man. What did you do with the dope?"

Peter realized he had made the story sound as if he knew right off what he had to do when he was carjacked, as if Jenkins never had a chance. He had left out how his shirt had been completely drenched in sweat, and then blood.

"Well, that's why I think I may need your help. I have a plan to sell the drugs back. No one gets hurt. If we need Juice, do you think he'll help? I'd pay him fifty thousand dollars for one day if my plan works."

"If you're in, I'm in. For fifty grand, Juice would lick sweat off a donkey's ass. I know he's in if you want him."

"Can he keep it quiet?"

"Don't worry about him talking. He could have got off from doing six months' time back when we got caught ripping off that drug dealer in Huntsville if he'd just gave them my name. But he wouldn't do it. The cops were watching that apartment and saw us do the whole thing. They just didn't know who I was. When they came to get him, he never said a word about me. All they could get him for was the B and E because the drugs were gone by then. That's why he did the six months."

"I hope you understand, Danny, that we're not doing this for the money. We won't keep it. I mean, at least we're not going to keep our part. We'll give you some of course, but this is about something bigger than money."

Peter then spent twenty minutes telling Danny what items they needed, items Peter didn't want to buy in Jackson. He handed Danny six hundred dollars and told him not to mention anything to Cindy and not to bring in Juice unless they needed him, and only at the last minute if they did. "There's just one last thing."

"Yeah boss, what's that?"

"The whole thing's going to be a rip-off. I don't plan on letting those drugs back on the street."

"What? You better tell me a little more about that part," Danny said. He tilted his head back and chugged his beer. He opened another one right away and looked over at Peter, his eyes wide in disbelief.

chapter 11

After studying every radio and CB in the store, Danny settled on three of the newest FRS band radios that could fit in a shirt pocket and had a port for a microphone and earpiece. They were advertised to have a range of two miles, enough for what he had in mind if the terrain was flat. He knew just enough about radios to know that the Family Radio Service frequency had been set aside by the FCC for private use, mostly hunters or hikers who needed a small, simple radio. There would be no interference from business or government frequencies.

The purchase would take most of the six hundred dollars from Peter after he added hands-free lapel mikes and earpieces for two of the radios. He carried everything to the sporting goods counter at the back of the Rogers Army-Navy Store and paid the clerk in cash. He pocketed ninety-six dollars and change.

Danny's next stop was the Party Store, where he picked up four masks, all fashioned to cover just the eyes, somewhat in the style of Zorro. They were small enough to hide in a pocket but provided enough cover over the face to hide someone's identity.

Walking back to his car, Danny removed the NAPA hat he'd worn pulled down as low as it would go and the dark wrap-around sunglasses he'd been wearing. He casually tossed them both into a trash can on the sidewalk, just in case he showed up on a store surveillance camera. While he thought that Peter was paranoid making him take such precautions to hide items no one would ever know about, he went along. He certainly didn't want to do hard time just because he let some security camera take a picture of him.

Danny stuffed the radios and masks into a green duffle bag and left it in his trunk, where he'd earlier placed his rifle in a metal carrying case. He slammed the trunk lid and drove toward the old quarry up Highway 75 in Blount County. The quarry had been a good place for target shooting for several years, and no one ever bothered him there.

He drove down the quarry road feeling uneasy, though he'd been there at least half a dozen times in the past couple of years. What if some cop stopped him or caught him shooting and found the masks? You're just getting paranoid like Peter, he told himself as he stopped the car in front of a fifty-foot wall of sheer limestone rock that served as a great backstop for target practice. The area was littered with broken bottles and cans that had been peppered with bullets.

Opening the trunk, Danny removed three targets and six push pins. He found an old refrigerator box someone had drawn circles on as targets and pinned his own orange and white paper targets to the side. He stepped off twenty-five paces and marked a line in the red dirt with the toe of his shoe, noticing two dried condoms and six crushed Miller beer cans nearby. He went back to his car and drove it up to the mark he'd made so he could use the hood as a rest for his rifle. He opened the trunk and flipped the four latches on the gun case, removed the Winchester Model 70 topped with a Tasco 3x9 scope, and brought it up to his shoulder. Through the scope, he aimed at a crow sitting on a fence post some two hundred yards away, lightly fingering the trigger as if he were firing. He reached up and cranked the magnification power up to nine. He could see the yellow in the crow's eye.

There were many higher priced scopes that gathered a little more light late in the afternoon, and he had been tempted to buy a Leopold or a Nikon. But he couldn't quite force himself to give up a scope that worked fine to buy a new one for three or four hundred dollars just to be able to hunt for five minutes longer in the evening. Besides, he'd always had good luck with a Tasco. He killed more deer than most of his friends.

Danny hadn't shot the rifle since last hunting season. He tried to remember exactly when he had fired his last shot and decided it was between Christmas and New Year's when he had taken a trophy one-hundred-ninety-six-pound eight-point buck with a twenty-inch antler spread while hunting near Montevallo on Anderson Tully timberland.

He smiled when he remembered how the magnificent animal slumped —even before the sound reached it—without taking a step. A quick kill meant everything. The bullet had neatly clipped major arteries at the top of the heart as the Silvertip had mushroomed to dump its staggering load of energy just behind the animal's front shoulder. The bullet killed the deer instantly from shock. He knew the animal was dead before it hit the ground.

As he looked through the scope, he remembered a few years before when a neck shot hadn't resulted in a quick kill, and a young buck had made a sound like a woman's scream as he approached the wounded animal. Tears poured down his cheeks as he held the animal's head in his lap. He felt the animal struggling to stand, its legs kicking the air as he sliced deeply into the deer's soft throat with a six-inch knife. As the blood gushed onto his pants, soaking them through, he held the animal tightly until the yearling buck no longer kicked and its eyes became cloudy and vacant.

Danny vowed never to take another shot not meant to kill within seconds, and he learned to shoot better than anyone he knew once he understood why a carefully placed shot was so important. He was smart enough to see the irony in his deep respect for the whitetail deer's beauty and grace, mixed with his passion for hunting. Like several hunters he had hunted with, the actual kill was neither the most important nor the most satisfying part of the hunt, but he had long since quit trying to explain to his non-hunting friends why he was still somehow driven to complete the act of harvesting the animal. He didn't understand the need himself, yet there was no denying the desire he felt to continue hunting. He knew he could never explain the thrill of sitting alone in the darkness in a remote area, feeling the chill as the wind picked up just before sunrise, knowing there may be no one for miles, seeing the thin line of yellow light painting the edge of the dark horizon, hearing the birds as they awakened. At these moments he blended with nature, feeling natural and right.

A quilt spread across the hood, with a small sandbag, made a great gun rest. After chambering a shell and slamming the bolt shut, he leaned over the front of the car and placed the rifle on the sandbag. He loved the sound and feel of the well-engineered bolt-action rifle when he chambered a shell, and he couldn't understand why some of his friends opted for an autoloader. One shot should be enough for a good hunter with a scoped rifle, and autos simply didn't shoot as accurately. Anyone watching a real shooting competition could see that the bolt action was the rifle of choice among shooting purists. He considered himself one.

Danny placed the cross hairs on the target and took a deep breath. He let out half of the breath, held it, and tried his best to squeeze the trigger gently without blinking at the report. A perfectly round hole the diameter of a pencil appeared a half inch right of the bullseye. The next shot was also right and slightly below the first shot. A third shot was an inch farther right but near the height of the first shot. He put the rifle down and walked to the target. He found the center point of the three holes and calculated that he needed to move the cross hairs up a quarter of an inch and three-quarters of an inch to the left.

Three more shots to the second target were in or touching the bulls eye. He felt confident and congratulated himself on being a good shot, though he could never figure out why. He usually only fired eight or ten shots to make sure the scope was sighted in correctly. He'd practice two or three more times during the season, mostly to make sure he hadn't knocked the scope off line while climbing into tree stands or hauling the gun in his car trunk down bumpy roads.

With the one-hundred-fifty-grain bullet in the .30-06 caliber, Danny knew that setting his scope correctly at twenty-five yards would make the gun shoot only a couple of inches high at one hundred yards and dead on again at one-hundred-fifty yards. At two hundred yards, he would be only four or five inches low. This method of sighting a rifle meant he could ignore the need to adjust shots on distances out to two hundred yards and still make the killing shot on a deer, where the kill zone just behind the front shoulder was about the size of a sheet of notebook paper. Shoot at the top third of the paper and you would make a heart or lung shot. For a moment he wondered about the kill zone on a person but quickly told himself not even to think about that.

Danny hoped there would be no shooting when the time came to help Peter. At least not at people. He didn't think he could shoot at a person again unless someone was shooting at him. He guessed most people had some deep dark secret. His was the time he and a friend had broken into a car trunk they believed held a box with thousands of LSD tablets. When they broke the trunk lock, the breaking metal made enough noise to wake someone in the house, who began shooting from a window. Without thinking, he had returned fire as they ran for their car, putting six shots from a .45 automatic into the side of the house. He'd shot high to make sure he hit no one, just trying to scare the shooter back from the window. He had vowed never to use a gun again except for hunting. Now he was breaking that vow to himself, but only because someone he loved as much as anyone in the world asked him to.

chapter 12

"I need to concentrate so I can get the membership report finished before the board meeting next week," Mary Beth said to her secretary as she closed her office door. She glanced through the window and saw a wiry-haired mutt picking through the trash cans in the alley. She started to rap on the window but then smiled and turned back to the work of the day.

Mary Beth sat at her desk and scanned through the priorities list she'd written the day before in a spiral-bound notebook. Then she quickly calculated in her head that the membership report would only take two hours since she was fast and kept her computer records up to date. The report was the only thing pressing. That would leave her plenty of time for what she really wanted to do, which was to learn all about William McNabb.

Usually when a board meeting approached and she was caught up on urgent matters on her own list, she would ask if others needed help. But today she needed time to think. The idea of ransoming drugs for cash was no longer just a crazy plan. The deal might really happen. One moment she was arguing with Peter to stop while the next she tried to think of how to make the plan work.

She smiled at herself for arguing both sides before she spun around in her chair, leaned back with her hands behind her head, and without focusing on anything in particular gazed out the window at the small landscaped flower bed beside the rear parking lot. She'd played by the rules for her entire life. She never cheated on tests in school or even on her taxes. Rules were rules, and the world worked better if everyone followed them.

But Peter's words kept coming back to her. What would it hurt if all they did was take money from a drug dealer? Drugs had turned their lives upside down. Maybe getting even would bring them back together. At least they were talking more now than they had in months.

If she could concentrate, she could finish the report and still have time for research on McNabb. An hour and a half later, she sat back and realized she had finished without stopping once. She emailed the report to her secretary to proof and print.

Mary Beth straightened her desk and reached for her purse before pausing and turning back to her computer screen. She had one unopened email. She opened the email and saw the words, "Please call me on my private line, John." She deleted the message and sat back in her chair, the ache of a small fear in her throat. She knew John was worried, but she didn't know what to say to him. She decided to get out of the office. She had to think before she called back, but she also knew she could do her research on McNabb while she decided what to say.

Walking through the office lobby, she turned to the secretary, "I need to check on some language in a couple of pre-filed bills in the House. I'll be at the library the rest of the day." No one even looked up as she walked out the door.

In ten minutes she was in her usual spot where she'd spent many hours doing research, a corner room of the Eudora Welty Library, spooling through microfilm copies of the old stories in *The Clarion-Ledger* about drug busts in the area. She checked drug-related stories going back ten years. She found one story about a drug bust in South Jackson at a Best Price Liquor store. Although nothing was ever tied to McNabb, one of his managers named Roy Gant had been sentenced to prison. Doing the math in her head, she realized the guy could be out by now. She knew she could find out soon enough with her connections.

Mary Beth made photocopies of the story, including a close-up photograph of Roy Gant. She was becoming convinced that McNabb was the head of a drug ring. The paper hadn't said so in so many words, but there were obvious criminal ties to him and his businesses. All indications were that McNabb was a major drug dealer in Jackson and that Gant was one of the main people who worked for him.

Rising from the table, she thought about all the interesting talks she'd had over the past three months sitting at this very spot. The lively conversations were like those she had once had with Peter.

She put a hand to her neck, thinking of how she had felt when fingers brushed softly across the side of her throat one day as she was in the middle of a sentence. The touch had been unexpected, but the emotion hadn't scared her. The feel had seemed somehow right. No man but Peter had touched her like that in many years. She decided not to be mad at herself for letting him touch her. The situation was so innocent on her part. Or was it? She told herself she hadn't invited the attention. But as she walked from the cool, quiet library into the blast of heat and traffic noises of State Street, she couldn't quite forget how much she had liked the smooth touch of his hand. She wanted more. She could fight it, but she could not deny it.

———

When Mary Beth arrived home from work and walked into the kitchen, she saw Peter grilling hamburgers on the back deck. After calling to him, she changed from the heels and work clothes into just a tee shirt and jeans. No shoes, no bra. Just the comfort level she needed.

The nights were still warm, so Peter suggested they sit at their wrought-iron patio table on the deck. He'd already covered the round table with a red and white tablecloth, and a candle burned beside an acrylic salt shaker and pepper grinder built into one. A light breeze made the temperature pleasant. Two squirrels scampered around the yard, preparing for the coming winter by burying acorns that had begun falling from the large white oak near the back of the yard.

They finished eating and sat sipping the last half of a cheap bottle of Fetzer cabernet. Mary Beth knew the attention Peter had given to making this a pleasurable dinner was no accident. She made no comment, enjoying her meal and waiting for Peter to say what was on his mind.

Peter poured a little more wine into the two glasses and set the bottle aside. "It's time to contact McNabb."

After a few moments to reassure herself that she was really ready, she replied. "I'm not going to let you do it without me." She hadn't intended to sound like she was so eager to get involved and immediately began backing up a bit. "I mean, I'm at least ready to take baby steps. The whole thing is scary and stupid, but if this is something you have to do, I want to be as much involved as you are."

Peter was quiet and took Mary Beth's hand. She noticed he'd started doing that more lately, the way he used to when they first met. She liked it, but it made her wonder if Peter was finally sensing the deep chasm that had opened between them. She wondered if he was trying to find his way back to the place they had once enjoyed together, the place where neither could imagine life without the other. "We can do this. I know we can. I just want ..."

Mary Beth shook her head in small movements and held up her hand to stop him in mid-sentence. She sat up in her chair and leaned forward, pulling a loose lock of hair back behind her ear. "Let me tell you some things I've been thinking."

Peter sat up in his chair, and she noticed his posture was a mirror image of hers. "Sure. Tell me."

"First, we don't do anything that can be traced back to us. I know you've been careful with fingerprints and the car and all, but we need to think about everything else that could lead McNabb or the police back to us. Maybe we sell the car."

Peter nodded. "Okay, that might be good."

"I mean, if he gets caught, we have to make sure they can't find us, too.

We'll only make phones calls from pay phones—a different one each time. And no more calls to Danny from home." She paused and looked over at a squirrel that had hopped onto the deck railing just a few feet away to fuss and chatter. "We have to learn about McNabb and anyone else we know who might work for him. If we need anything, we buy it with cash and throw everything away after we finish. If we wear clothes people can recognize, we throw them away."

She sipped her wine and then put both hands around the stem as she leaned over the table toward Peter. She wanted her tone to be perfect, a mix of understanding and warning. "And last, you have to promise me to back out and just walk away if things get too dangerous or if we can't find a way to do the deal without the drugs getting back on the street. We have to agree about this."

"Great," Peter said, still nodding. He stood and stepped around the table to Mary Beth's chair. "I'm okay with everything you've said."

He pulled her to her feet and hugged her. Neither said anything. He held her tightly as tears built up in his eyes and ran down one cheek. She could tell he was hiding his face in her hair, but with his face turned he didn't see that she was crying, too. She felt the warm breeze as he held her and rocked them slightly from side to side.

Mary Beth turned her face toward Peter's, put the backs of her wrists behind his head, and pulled his lips hard to hers. She pushed her tongue forcefully into his mouth and leaned her body into his. She felt his body respond. Peter grabbed the bottom of her t-shirt, lifted it over her head, and put his lips to her breast. He pulled her tightly to him with one arm behind her and a hand cupping her other breast. She stood for a moment with both hands behind his head and pulled him into her almost painfully, her head back and her eyes closed as she felt the sensation, like electricity through her body. She pushed him away, sat down on a lounge chair, and reached up to unbuckle his belt as he stood beside her.

———

"Something's just not right about the whole deal," Taylor Nelson said to himself as he sat in his Lumina behind the strip shopping center where McNabb had one of his three Best Price Liquor stores. The afternoon sun was just going behind the old red oaks lining the other end of the short street, leaving long shadows down the pavement in front of Nelson. The radio was tuned to public radio on low, and a reporter told about how the embassy bombings a few weeks ago were linked to some rich Saudi named Usama bin Laden and his Islamic terrorist group that no one had ever heard of before. With the window down, he could smell the faint smoky odor of withering fall leaves. The ninety-degree afternoon still felt like the middle of summer to him in a car where the wind did little to cool the air.

Someone must have those drugs, he thought, as he sat staking out the Best Price, a duty he liked to share with his men once in a while. There was no reason for Jenkins to have two cars at the bus station, and he wouldn't have had a backup coming down Pascagoula Street where there was no good place to pull over after coming through the underpass. Unless this was a planned out-of-state heist, that vehicle had to have been someone just happening by. Pure luck for Jenkins, although the picture of him in the hospital with a dozen tubes in him, casts on both arms, and a broken leg didn't look exactly lucky. And Jenkins' head had looked more like a basketball with a face than a human head. Nelson chuckled, thinking about when he had seen Jenkins on Sunday afternoon just hours before he'd been murdered. Nelson had been lucky to keep the facts of Jenkins' murder out of the newspapers, at least for now. He regretted he hadn't had an opportunity to question him.

Had Jenkins really escaped with someone just happening by? And whoever it was had somehow had a wreck and survived. Nothing else made as much sense when he thought about Jenkins leaving his car behind in the bus station parking lot.

Was there someone out there with a lot of drugs who didn't have a clue what to do with them? The cocaine wasn't on the street. He'd have heard by now if drugs that pure had hit the street. The drugs seized at the bus station had proven to be virtually uncut, still too high in the drug dealer food chain to be near street sales yet. And now, on top of it all, the boys from homicide were poking around. He hoped the news that Jenkins was murdered could be kept quiet and his investigation didn't get pushed aside.

Nelson got out to stretch his legs. He turned off the radio, locked the car, and slid his Glock 23 into the back of his belt, under the loose fitting yellow golf shirt. He walked toward the McRae's Department Store as if he were just another customer. Just as he stepped out from between two parked cars, he saw Gant coming down the parking lot in his Cadillac from the other end. Nelson turned his head away and waved at a woman in a flowered sundress as if they were old friends. She smiled a slight, timid, almost fearful smile and looked away. He hurried into the side door of the department store just as the Cadillac passed behind him. He turned as soon as the car passed, opened the glass door a crack, and watched Gant's car turn right and go behind the row of stores. He walked back to his own car certain that Gant hadn't noticed him.

An hour later, Gant came out the back door of the liquor store and drove away. Nelson decided to wait and see if McNabb would leave soon. When McNabb rushed out of the store five minutes later and drove toward downtown, Nelson followed, lagging two blocks back. McNabb drove straight through the streets of downtown to South Jackson, stopping at Hillside Bar & Grill. Nelson pulled around the side of the building to see if anyone else of interest showed up. After an hour he eased out and drove home. McNabb was known to stay at Hillside Bar drinking Johnny Walker Black and soda for hours. Nelson decided that if any deals were to be made tonight, they would have to be made without him there to catch the bad guys.

At home, Nelson headed for the back door, still uncertain that someone had made off with a shipment of cocaine. But it sure felt that way. Inside, he reached for an unopened cigar he had left beside the ashtray the night before and held a wooden match under it until his puffing left a thick cloud around his head. He pushed the power button on his computer to let the machine warm up. Grabbing a Sam Adams from the refrigerator, he sat down in front of the screen, clicking on AOL when the computer was ready. He was surprised when he saw he had no new emails.

———

Peter stepped into his pants and zipped them up. "If we hurry we can still get to the mall before the stores close. We need a few more things. You want to go?"

"Sure," Mary Beth said, reaching for her blouse. Ten minutes later they were inside Northpark Mall. They shopped carefully, selecting shipping tape, a large flashlight in a box that seemed just about the right size to hold one of the bundles of drugs, a package of typing paper that was the most common brand they could find, brown shipping paper, and half a dozen black Sharpie pens. Next they purchased two sets of red gym shorts and bright yellow t-shirts for Peter. The last purchase was for a small, inexpensive backpack like most kids used for schoolbooks. At each stop they paid in cash, avoided extra help from any sales clerks, and left without speaking to anyone. They also purchased a gym bag the same size as the one the drugs originally had been carried in, along with materials to create packages that looked just like the real bundles of drugs. They were careful not to touch any items more than necessary, holding them by their edges.

chapter 13

Peter was up earlier than usual, even for a Monday. The orange streaks of daylight were just spreading across the horizon, silhouetting the pines outside their bedroom window. He dressed in jogging shorts and a t-shirt, white socks and Nikes.

After a quick cup of coffee, he loaded his mountain bike, along with a blue helmet, into the back of the Cherokee and drove the three miles down Ridgewood Road to the Eastside Elementary School at the edge of Eastover, a neighborhood of nice homes and money. Real money. Not just a good living like he could claim, but money that meant Christmas in Colorado and vacations in the Bahamas every year. Peter wanted a last look at McNabb's house before he took the next step and delivered his message.

He took his bike from the Jeep and hopped on, heading into the heart of Eastover like just another forty-something guy fighting an expanding waistline and trying his best to keep a little of his youthful energy intact. He passed four or five walkers, then a couple of obviously serious women runners who looked as though they were right off the pages of a *LOOK* magazine from 1946. He had visions of them as black and white photographs from a Nazi concentration camp, with their drawn faces and hollow cheeks, no fat on their bodies after the hours of running each day. Neither runner was pretty, though with a few pounds to round out their sharp features both could be.

Passing the upper lake that sat near the center of Eastover, he saw three swans gliding across the middle of the small lake. *The rest of us don't live like this*, he thought. He watched the swans and began to notice the size and

grace of the homes around the lake, each with a perfect lawn and splashes
of color from bed after bed of annual flowers. He turned left onto Lakeview
and began watching for McNabb. As he neared the end of the block, he
saw on his right the red brick column standing like a sentry alongside
McNabb's curved driveway, its fellow soldier at attention on the opposite
side.

Peter pulled to the edge of the street and got off his bike directly across
from the front of McNabb's house. He felt good from the exertion and
made a mental note to start riding or running again. Squatting and
fiddling with the chain as if something were wrong, he checked the details
of the front of the house. He didn't really know what he was looking for,
so he decided to memorize everything he could. Circular drive in front of
wide steps leading to a broad front porch with white columns. White sheer
curtains blocking the view from floor-to-ceiling windows on both sides of
the front door. To the left of the front door a mailbox. Not a slot in the
front door but a real mailbox, quite large. A tall white wooden fence
extended from both sides of the house, blocking any view of the back yard.

After thirty seconds he mounted the bike and rode on. He peddled
another two blocks and turned around for another pass. Without stopping,
he slowed and looked again to memorize the front of the house. He biked
back to his car. He was loaded and driving home within forty-five minutes
of first arriving at the elementary school. The plan to contact McNabb
would work, but the drop wouldn't be as easy as he had hoped.

He didn't notice anything unusual about the white Ford Taurus that
passed him as he loaded his bike.

For more than a week, Peter followed this same routine, hauling his bike
to the school and riding past McNabb's house twice between 6:30 a.m. and
7:00 a.m. The newspaper was usually there if he came by about 6:30, but
was gone if he came by at 7:00. He saw McNabb one morning at about 6:50
walking down the driveway to get his newspaper, so Peter figured the man
had a morning routine he kept.

After only a few mornings, he knew what walkers to expect. They also seemed to have a precise schedule.

———

Back home, Peter sat at the kitchen table with Mary Beth long enough for each to finish a large mug of coffee. They studied the plan to make the first contact with McNabb, discussing problems that might occur and how they would deal with them.

"What if police stop you for some reason?" Mary Beth asked.

Peter took a deep breath, growing tired of repeated questions. He searched her facial expression for a clue about what thoughts were really inside her head. He tried to be as patient as possible to erase her doubts, so he made sure his voice didn't show irritation. "If they do, it'll just be for a routine traffic ticket. And even then they won't search me. I'm too normal looking."

He studied her face. Her questions seemed to be less about the real problems they would face and more about hypothetical situations that would probably never occur.

"What if McNabb comes to the door just as you ride up the driveway?" she asked.

He reminded himself to be patient and take each question seriously. "I'll be in and out of his yard in less than twenty seconds. I'll get there before time for him to pick up his paper. If he does, I'll just turn around and ride off. Even if he sees me he won't have time to chase me by the time he realizes he should, and I'll be disguised just in case."

After another five minutes, he had satisfied her that the risk of the first move was virtually zero.

———

Before work on Tuesday morning, Peter loaded the bicycle into the Cherokee as he had the day before. He knew that anyone who saw him, including the Hart Security patrols paid privately by the Eastover neighborhood to watch their streets, would see just another guy on a bike. But today would be different. He knew he was taking a step that would change his world forever. He was ready.

Leaving the rear cargo door open, Peter walked inside to the bedroom where they had laid out the drugs he would deliver. He took a handkerchief, wrapped it around the box containing the package, and placed it in a backpack.

Mary Beth, wearing plastic gloves, had carefully wrapped the package of drugs inside the flashlight box. She had covered the box in brown shipping paper and taped it completely shut. The package looked like a typical UPS delivery. Inside with the drugs was a single sheet of typing paper on which she had written in all cap letters:

I HAVE WHAT YOU WANT. I WANT A FINDERS FEE OF $500,000. THIS SAMPLE PROVES I TELL THE TRUTH. IF I SEE DANGER, I GO AWAY FOREVER AND SO DO YOUR DRUGS. ONE TIME OFFER. IF INTERESTED, PLACE THIS AD IN THE CLARION-LEDGER & I WILL CONTACT DISCREETLY ON MY SCHEDULE: SWM, 45, SEEKS SWF, 35-50. REDHEADS ONLY.

Outside on the brown wrapping paper she wrote:

HAND DELIVER TO WILLIAM MCNABB
PERSONAL AND CONFIDENTIAL

Before he had even pulled the bike from the back of the Cherokee, Peter already felt moisture gathering along his spine and around the hairline of his brow. He wore red shorts over his black shorts, and a bright yellow shirt over a light blue t-shirt. He placed his bike helmet in his pack with the box and put on a brown cap from Hunt's Restaurant, his favorite place to eat raw oysters when he happened to be in Dothan, Alabama.

He watched the first red streaks of dawn appear through the trees and heard birds waking up and calling to each other. There was enough light to see, but the shadows still provided a little comfort. Lights were on in several homes, but he saw little activity outside. He noticed that most people hadn't picked up their morning newspapers.

He approached McNabb's house and was about to steer into the driveway when he saw car lights coming toward him from around the lake. He knew the lights would shine on him in seconds. He swerved his bike across the road and continued past the driveway just as the car passed him. The car was a light-colored Taurus. At least one person around here goes to work early, he thought. He was sure he had seen the car in the neighborhood a few days before.

Peter made the block, passing an older man he had seen several times walking a white standard poodle on a long leash. The poodle began yapping but made no move to chase him. He passed to the left of the man and turned right toward Lakeview.

He noticed a light on at McNabb's house in what looked like the kitchen and saw another lamp in a window at the side of the house. He looked at his watch. Ten after six. The paper lay in the middle of the driveway. He sped up, and then stopped peddling just before the driveway, coasting quietly toward McNabb's house. He made only one turn of the pedal as the bike slowed near the top of the slightly sloped driveway. He was glad he had liberally squirted lubricating oil on the chain the day before.

He stopped in front of the entryway and slid the backpack to the ground. With a quick look up and down the street, he saw no one and nothing unusual. Using a handkerchief, he gingerly removed the package. Instead of placing it inside the mailbox as planned, he laid the package against the front door. He knew McNabb was likely to walk out soon, and he wanted to make sure McNabb saw it first thing. Peter hurried, expecting the front light to come on and someone to throw open the door any second. His heart pounded. As he hopped on his bike and pedaled down the drive, he heard a small dog begin barking frantically inside the house. Peter glanced back just as he reached the street and saw the front light come on. He could see the silhouette of a tiny dog standing on its hind legs, its paws against the large front window.

Peter turned the corner and reached the end of the next block, pumping as hard as he could without appearing to be in a panic. He took another left and coasted down half a block to the turn where a tall hedge grew near the road. The thick hedge blocked the view from anyone who might be following him. Only someone directly across the street could see him.

Crashing through the hedge to a narrow opening between the shrubs and a tall white stucco fence, he quickly took off the red shorts, yellow shirt and hat, and stuffed them into the backpack. He strapped on his bike helmet, slid his arms through the pack straps, and pushed back the bushes to see if anyone was in view on the street. No one was coming. He mounted the bike and started peddling hard back toward his car.

As he turned the corner toward the hill below the elementary school, he saw the same light-colored Taurus turn in his direction off Ridgewood. *I guess I'm not the only one who remembers something halfway to work and has to go back home,* he thought. The car passed, traveling in the opposite direction.

Within minutes he had loaded the bike and was safely on his way back home. The morning traffic had picked up, but he didn't mind the slow pace. He hadn't felt this good in a long time.

Mary Beth was sitting in the kitchen when Peter burst through the door.

"I did it!" he shouted, his adrenaline still pumping. "And the only person

I saw was an old guy I've seen before, walking his poodle. But McNabb has a dog, too, and it started raising hell just as I rode off. I don't think anybody could have seen me from the house, though. Everything worked just like we planned it."

"Slow down," Mary Beth said. Peter could see her eyes were red and swollen and knew at once she had been crying before he burst in. "This scares me. I thought I was ready, but now that it's happening I'm not sure." She paused, as if to gain her composure. "In some ways, what we're doing makes sense, but then I realize how much we have to lose."

Peter remained quiet, allowing Mary Beth to choose her words carefully. "We had a good life, Peter. What happened?"

Peter sat down and pulled his chair out to face hers. He leaned forward with his elbows on his knees and his hands clasped with his fingers intertwined. His tone was intense, but he changed his voice to conversational level. "Let's just see what happens. If his reply is in the paper, we'll decide then if we go ahead." But in his mind there was no reason to stop now. He felt certain there was no way they could be traced by McNabb or the police.

Roy Gant had already showered and shaved. He was buttoning his shirt when his cell phone rang. He flipped the phone open. "Yeah."

He heard McNabb's voice. "Go to the usual place, now."

"I can dress in two minutes, but it'll take me another fifteen minutes to drive," Gant said, calculating the time from his apartment in South Jackson. McNabb lived only five minutes away from the spot. The phone call had Gant worried. McNabb had never called him before 7:00 a.m. Something was wrong. He could tell from McNabb's voice, but he knew better than to ask over the phone.

"Just come now."

Driving into the parking lot of the Park Place movie theatre on Lakeland,

Gant felt out of place. There were no other cars. He was surprised that McNabb wasn't there yet. He parked and waited, hoping no police would drive by and see him parked like an idiot in the middle of the lot. He had barely turned off the ignition switch when McNabb drove up from the opposite direction and waved for him to follow. He started the car and followed McNabb three miles down Lakeland to the parking lot of the Winn Dixie grocery store, which was already half full of cars. McNabb stopped and pointed to a parking spot. Gant parked and got in with McNabb. He was beginning to think that McNabb was losing his edge, and these meetings in the car did nothing to make Gant feel more confident. It might be time for him to move on, but he wasn't ready just yet. Either way, he needed to be ready at short notice.

McNabb started talking before Gant could say a word. "Someone sent me a box with a kilo of cocaine this morning, with a note saying they had what I want and wanted to sell it back. They left the stuff at my house, for god's sake, so there's no doubt they know who I am. Roy, what in the hell is going on? Who knew about this last deal?"

Gant had no idea what was going on and didn't know what to say. He felt his face flush. He could feel the accusation in McNabb's tone. "How? What did ...?"

"Do you know anyone outside Jenkins, Ramsey, and you who could know this was my deal?"

He looked McNabb square in the eye, his gaze steady and his voice completely under control. He knew that whatever had happened was not from his carelessness. He would not be blamed for this. "No, William, no one. No way."

It worked to make McNabb soften his harsh tone a little. "Well, someone left dope on my front porch with a note inside. They want half a million bucks. I guess they read in the paper that the drugs are worth double that on the street. I'm sure as hell not paying for something I already paid for."

Gant couldn't believe someone would just leave a kilo of cocaine worth thousands of dollars on a front porch. "Do you think it could be the police? Is it a set-up?"

"That's what I thought at first, but I don't think so. I don't think cops would leave that much cocaine and I think it would be entrapment anyway. Just doesn't seem like police," McNabb said. "Could be whoever was in the car that Jenkins grabbed figured out a tie between Jenkins and me from the damned newspaper article." McNabb turned in the seat and paused for a second, allowing his words to carry more weight. "There's another way they could know."

"What do you mean?" Gant asked.

"You know damn well we have a freaking leak somewhere. And I'm thinking if it wasn't Jenkins it might be Ramsey. Hell, Roy, maybe they're both in on it."

"What do we do now?"

"I'm going to have a talk with my lawyer and see if this could be a set-up. If not, I want you to place an ad in *The Clarion-Ledger*. We need to see what's going on and get a look at these idiots up close. You better think long and hard about Ramsey, too. I can feel the cops breathing down our necks, and I don't like it. And get this on the street," McNabb said as he reached under the seat for a rolled-up brown grocery bag.

———————

After a couple of meetings to get the new coke on the street, Gant stopped by the Best Price Liquor store office. He'd just poured a cup of coffee from the pot that sat on a small table outside the manager's office when his cellular phone rang. He slid the phone from his pocket and flipped it open. "Gant."

"Go with it. Do you have the note with you?" McNabb said.

Both men had a strong sense of caution and knew to say as little as possible on a cell phone. They had worked together long enough to have learned to use phrases that could mean something innocent if they had to defend them in court.

Gant looked around before answering. The manager was standing nearby, along with the part-time guy he knew only as Joe. He walked quickly toward the office in the back as he answered. "Yeah, I've got it."

"Try for day after tomorrow. Let me know tonight when to expect it. Come by the office this evening."

"Okay, I got it. You talk to the lawyer?"

"Yes, I asked him a hypothetical question about the situation."

"What'd he say?" Gant sipped the steaming coffee as he listened.

"Said the locals wouldn't risk it. National boys might as part of some elaborate operation, but never locals. Call me if there's a problem. Otherwise, meet me at the office this evening." The connection went dead as McNabb hung up without a goodbye.

Gant smiled. For the first time in several days, he thought things were going better. When he put all the pieces together, he figured they were dealing with some rookie who would be scared and didn't know exactly what to do. The guy might be smart enough to figure out who McNabb was, and he even did a good job of letting McNabb know he was serious, but Gant knew the guy wasn't a professional or else he would simply sell the coke himself and keep all the money. Gant knew he and McNabb could beat a rookie at this game. These were his streets, and this was his backyard the shithead had ventured into. No one beat him here.

McNabb had written exactly what the note said to put in the classified personal ad, and he had added a message of his own. Gant removed the message from his buttoned shirt pocket and placed the paper in an envelope he took from a box on the desk. He looked at his watch and realized he had to hurry to make sure the message was delivered to the paper by the deadline. He tilted the cup back and took a last swallow of coffee as he stood up to leave.

Two minutes after McNabb called, Gant walked out the back of the store and drove to The Sports Nut, a bar where he knew several of his friends —none of whom would have what anyone would consider a regular job— would be hanging out and making small-time bets on whatever foreign sporting event was on satellite TV in the middle of the afternoon. It would be easy to find someone there to deliver the envelope.

An hour later a call confirmed the message would run in the Personal Announcement section of *The Clarion-Ledger* on Thursday.

chapter 14

"Nelson."

"It's Joe. I may have something, Lieutenant."

Nelson could sense the excitement in the typically reserved and soft-spoken Joe Graham's voice. "Don't say anything on the cell phone," he cautioned, knowing that others were often listening to random cell phone calls that could be snatched out of the air if one had the right equipment. "Come on by. I've got a couple of cold Sam Adams beers."

Nelson downed the last swallow of his beer, dropped the empty bottle into the trash, and pulled another one from the refrigerator. He sat back is his easy chair and relit his cigar, ignoring the movie on the television.

In less than five minutes, Graham walked to the sliding glass doors on Nelson's patio. He knocked as he slid the door aside and walked in, not waiting for Nelson to get up.

Thick cigar smoke hovered about Nelson like a rain cloud. A thin blue line of smoke rose from the tip of his cigar resting on a long yellow and black Cohiba cigar ashtray. He picked up the TV remote and pushed POWER. The screen went black just as Steve McQueen reloaded a 12 gauge, but Nelson knew McQueen would safely shoot his way down the stairway with Jacqueline Bisset close behind.

Graham got a beer from the refrigerator and took a seat in the overstuffed leather recliner. He twisted off the top and took a long swallow but leaned forward instead of sitting back in the soft, deep chair as he would usually do.

"Start at the beginning," Nelson said as he reached to pick up his cigar. "I hope it's good. We need a break."

"Today was my early day. Gant was at the Best Price off and on all day. I worked in the stock room a lot. You know how fast they empty the cheap liquor shelves in this part of town every two weeks on payday, so I was hustling to get the shelves restocked with half pints of cheap vodka."

"So what'd you hear?"

"First, Gant got a call on his cell phone and he left immediately. All I heard him say was that he had it. He asked about meeting with a lawyer, too. I could tell something was up, so I volunteered to straighten the stockroom where I could hang close to the office," Graham took a deep draw from the longneck bottle. "Around six, McNabb and Gant both showed up and went to the office."

"Could you hear?" Nelson asked.

"As I was getting a case of vodka from a shelf near the office, the door opened a couple of inches. I could hear someone was pissed. At first I couldn't make out the words. Then McNabb started yelling." Graham took a deep breath as if starting on a long speech. "That's when I heard McNabb tell Gant *find my shipment*."

Nelson sat forward in his chair, blowing a stream of smoke into the air above their heads. He placed the cigar back on the ashtray. "What exactly did McNabb say?"

"I wrote it down as soon as I could get in the bathroom with a pen," Graham said. He pulled a sheet of notebook paper from his shirt pocket and unfolded it. At the top were the date, time, and place the note was written, along with Graham's signature as Nelson had instructed, in case their notes were ever needed in court. "Here's the best I could remember of what McNabb said. '*We don't have any more time. You just be ready when they call about my damn shipment.*' That's when the door opened and I quick-stepped out of there. I was almost to the front of the storeroom before Gant appeared through the office door."

"Shipment? That was the word he used?"

"Yeah, that's exactly the word he said. Seemed clear that someone has

McNabb's drugs and he's expecting a call. Don't you figure that has to be the other bag of dope?"

Nelson nodded his agreement. "OK, we've got to get on Gant's ass. I'll set up surveillance in the morning." He picked up the cigar and took a puff, blowing the smoke out in a series of tiny rings as he thought. "Did they mention any names or places, anything like that?"

"No. Nothing that would give us somewhere to watch. But I'll tell you this, when Gant stepped through that door, he looked mad as hell. I have to tell you, just a glimpse of him looking at me with those dark eyes of his and I knew right then he wasn't someone I want behind me in an alley at night."

Nelson nodded and smiled. "Joe, you need to stay as close as you can. If they find this shipment, or if it finds them, we need to be there. We've been waiting a year for this opportunity. Let's hope we can follow the drugs to McNabb."

"Can we tail McNabb?"

"Can't stake out his house very easily in that neighborhood, but I'll have it watched somehow. But with this information, we can get a court order for phone taps. I'll have taps approved for McNabb and Gant by tomorrow morning. Right now, you're our best bet."

Both men grinned. Nelson took a long swallow of his beer, sat back, and held up his cigar. "Maybe we'll get to smoke one of these in celebration soon. I've got a real Cuban in the humidor I've been saving. I think it's about time to enjoy it."

———————

Mary Beth's hair was wet, a large pink towel wrapped around her head like a turban. She stood in the bathroom with a second pink towel around her torso, making faces at the mirror to see if she had developed any facial wrinkles during the night. She forced herself to go through the motions of a routine day, but her heart already pounded as she wondered if the message would be in the newspaper. The moment Peter burst through the bathroom door and she saw the newspaper in his hand, she knew.

"Mary Beth, here it is. We did it."

She grabbed the paper and read where he pointed in the Personals:

SWM, 45, SEEKS SWF, 35-50. REDHEADS ONLY. MUST TALK FIRST AND GET TO BE FRIENDS. MAYBE MORE LATER.

"It's him for sure, but he didn't write the message exactly like we said," Mary Beth said. "I don't have any intention of us getting to know him well enough for him to figure out who we are."

"It makes sense that before he hands over that much money he wants to know something that will reassure him. I'd want assurance, too."

She pulled the towel off her hair and held her head back, shaking her hair down her back in wet curls as she walked past Peter into the bedroom. She sat on the bed and began making long strokes through her damp hair with a pink comb. She stopped combing and glanced toward Peter. He had turned to the side as she walked past, but he still stood in the doorway with his weight on one foot and arms crossed as he leaned against the doorframe.

"Are we ready to go ahead?" she asked, her voice sincere and soft. She walked over and stood a few inches from Peter. "I mean, are you completely sure we should go on? Right now we can still walk away and no one will know who we are. If we go ahead, it gets harder to hide ourselves. We're running out of chances to quit."

She felt an undeniable sexual tension in the danger they were about to face together. She wanted Peter to pull the towel off her breasts and push her back onto the bed. Her bare shoulders had been enough to stir Peter during their first years of marriage, but she hadn't seen that strong sexual urge from him in a long time. Too long. Now she could stand in front of him and wear nothing but a towel or her sexiest panties and he hardly noticed. She wanted not only the intimacy but the heat they had lost. To her, arousal these days brought the thought of someone else's touch on her face and neck. She hoped Peter didn't see her face flush and her nipples grow hard under the towel as she turned away.

Peter's voice brought her back to the present. "I'm not turning back now. I know what I'm doing."

Mary Beth could not stop herself from saying it. "Do you really, Peter? Do you really know what you and everyone else are doing?"

Mary Beth tensed as Peter's hand gripped her shoulder and stopped her from walking away. He tugged at the wet towel, and she felt it slide down and drop to the floor. When he pressed into her from behind and reached around to cup her breasts and take her nipples, she knew that he *had* seen after all. She closed her eyes and let her head fall backward onto his shoulder as his lips brushed the side of her neck. Through his pants she could feel him pressing into her, and she knew he found the risks they were taking every bit as sexual as she did. She bit her lower lip when the fingers from his right hand played lightly across her belly before he slid them with force down between her legs. She had been married to this man long enough to know she had no idea what she was in for except that it would be full of surprises.

After a morning at the office spent going through stacks of computer printouts of electronic timesheets and detailed listings of media bills, Peter left for lunch a few minutes early.

"I might be late getting back," he said to the receptionist as he got to the door. "I have a few errands to run."

Peter spent almost an hour buying a few last items he and Mary Beth had decided they needed: matching red baseball caps, identical bright yellow t-shirts, and two pairs of Mississippi Blues sunglasses that were sold at half the gas station counters in Jackson. He went by the Mardi Gras Costume Store and picked out a fake ponytail similar to the color of his hair that could be pinned to the baseball cap.

Back at B&P Advertising, Peter stepped off the elevator at 2 p.m. As soon as he turned the corner to the hallway leading to his office, he saw John Baynes. Peter immediately realized he had forgotten an important 1:30 conference call with a major client.

He felt a constriction in his chest. Despite the excitement of the drugs situation, he still hated letting down his friends and partners at work. He felt the blood rush to his face.

John followed him into his office and closed the door.

Peter sat heavily into his desk chair and looked up at John, aware of the age that sat on John's features these days and hoping he himself had no part in the newest wrinkles and grayer hair. "Oh, man, I'm sorry. I just ..."

But before he could finish making up an excuse for being late, John stopped him with a raised hand. "Forget it. I covered for you and told Parkinson you had an emergency and would call later today if you could. Unless someone is sick or died, I don't want to hear where you've been. But I hope that whatever the hell is going on with you is over soon. You know I'll help you if I can, but this needs to stop now. You've been on another planet for weeks. This is it, Peter. This is the last time."

John turned and walked out before Peter could think of anything to say. He spun in his chair and stared out the window with his lips pressed tightly together and his fists clenched into hard knots. He watched as a breeze rippled through the flowers in front of the Governor's Mansion.

———

Sitting slumped down in his Cherokee across from the McRae's Department Store parking lot, Peter could just see over the dash. He carefully eased a pair of binoculars up to his eyes and looked at a white Taurus. He felt a shiver run down his spine as he realized the car could be the same one that had passed him the morning he dropped off the package at McNabb's house.

After work Peter had decided to drive past McNabb's house. When McNabb happened to pull out of his drive just as Peter turned onto the far end of Lakeview, Peter followed him to see where he might go.

Two blocks later Peter saw the white Taurus he'd previously noticed in the neighborhood merge between them from a side street. He began to worry that he was following too far back and wouldn't see where McNabb turned. McNabb's car was already well ahead and out of sight around a corner. When Peter reached a long straight stretch of Meadowbrook Road, he saw McNabb a half-mile ahead and was able to close the distance, using the Taurus to shield him from McNabb's rearview mirror. A few blocks later, after each turned into a shopping center behind McNabb, Peter realized he wasn't the only one following. And he also knew McNabb had a store in the strip center.

As McNabb's car disappeared behind the building, the Taurus veered left in the parking lot. Peter backed into a tight space between two vans, cutting the wheels sharply. His tires made a grinding noise on the loose rocks of the aging pavement. Peter wondered if the man in the car was McNabb's security. Or maybe the police?

He had to get a better look. He left his car and walked casually into the department store's side entrance, willing himself not to look around but to act like any other customer. He exited at the front where all the stores in the strip center were connected by a covered walkway. He walked down the sidewalk past the liquor store without stopping. The store was well lit, but there was no sign of McNabb. Peter picked up a pair of socks as he walked back through McRae's and paid cash so he could leave the store looking like a shopper. Back in his car, he sat for a couple of minutes watching the man inside the Taurus. He didn't like the situation. And he didn't think he was just being paranoid this time. Someone was watching McNabb.

———

Leaning over to see inside the refrigerator, Nelson stared at a bottle of ketchup, three beers, an aging package of hot dog wieners, a wilted head of lettuce, and assorted sauces. After nearly half a minute of staring, he settled for a beer and decided pizza delivery sounded good.

Since talking to Graham the previous day, he had been busy. He knew something was up. He had decided to go home from the office right after five, something he almost never did. He often worked until 6:30 or later, but the office was depressing today. He looked at the Pizza Factory magnet on the side of the refrigerator and dialed the number.

"Pizza Factory. How may I help you?" said the familiar, bored voice he recognized as belonging to the girl with all the earrings.

"Yeah, I want a pizza delivered. Is the guy there who makes the Cherry Bombs?"

Nelson had developed a liking for a specialty pizza with lots of hot items on top, though it wasn't on the menu. The special order was a combination of jalapenos, onions, sausage, and red and green peppers, with hot spices sprinkled in before the cheese was added. The Cherry Bomb had been a Manager's Special when the store first opened two years back, and now only one person was left who knew how to make it. The girls who answered the phone knew about the Cherry Bomb since Nelson tried to order it just about every week, but only one guy could make the special pie. Tonight Nelson was in luck. The mystery pizza maker was on duty.

"Yeah he's here. What's your address and phone?"

After hanging up from ordering, he pressed the power button on his computer and logged in to check his email. His heart jumped when he saw he had an email from someone he hadn't expected to hear from. As he sat there without opening the email, he realized it had been years since he felt this excited over a woman. Although part of him knew the relationship was unlikely to work, he couldn't deny the jolt of adrenaline he felt before he even opened the message.

chapter 15

Mary Beth noticed someone else at work had made coffee for a change when she walked past the kitchen on her way to her office. She sat her purse on the break room table and poured a cup. She said good morning to the two men sitting at the table and discussing how surprised everyone seemed to be that Mississippi State had the best football team in the West Division of the SEC. They barely glanced up.

She sat at her desk and sipped coffee while planning how quickly she could finish her deadlines for the day. Her phone message light was on, which surprised her. She pressed the message button and keyed in her password to listen. The message said, "Mary Beth, this is John. Please call me. We need to talk." She pressed the delete key, looking around at the same time to see if anyone had been standing close enough to overhear. She had a good idea of what he wanted, but she would call back when no one was around and she could talk more openly.

Mary Beth kept her door closed for two hours as she considered how to find McNabb's unlisted home number. She often located phone numbers of hard-to-reach people, most frequently legislators or their administrative assistants. She always found a way. It was easy to get people to talk if you just asked them for particular information.

While her office was small—just a desk, a side chair, and a bookshelf that ran all the way down one wall—she felt comfortable there. Tacked to the wall beside her desk, she had half a dozen snapshots of Peter and herself from vacations and holidays over the years.

She opened a drawer and removed a photo from beneath a stack of papers, a photo that would never grace any wall. She stared at a photo of the two of them from a Halloween party several years before. She wore five-inch heels and a mini skirt that showed the tops of black stockings and garters. A leather cat-o-nine-tails was hanging from her belt. Peter, dressed in a police uniform, was handcuffed to her wrist.

Mary Beth realized how sexy she looked with just a tiny bit of her thighs showing above the stocking tops. She had surprised herself and Peter by wearing the costume. She remembered how turned on Peter had been when she first walked into the room to show him the outfit. She'd always heard that guys loved seeing women dressed that way, but she didn't fully understand why looking like a dominatrix was such a turn-on for Peter, or the other men she caught secretly eyeing her during the party.

She held the picture like a book in both hands. The police uniform gave her an idea. She pulled the telephone book from her bottom drawer and looked up the Best Price Liquor address for the South Jackson store and the phone number for the Highway 80 store. Five minutes later she was standing in front of the pay telephone outside the Texaco on High Street.

She inhaled and exhaled several times to make herself out of breath, folded two sticks of Spearmint gum into her mouth, and dialed the Highway 80 store. A man answered after two rings.

"Best Price Liquor. Jimmy speaking." The man's voice sounded tired or bored.

She hesitated, unsure what to say.

"Can I help you?" the now irritated Jimmy said, as if expecting someone to hang up on him.

"Jimmy, this is Dottie at the South Jackson store." Mary Beth chewed the gum as she talked, using her best country-sounding voice. "We just got robbed ... and, you know, I mean, I know I'm, like, supposed to call Mr. McNabb and all, if anything bad ever happened. But I can't find the number."

Jimmy answered, a little more interested but still sounding a bit put out. "Did you call the cops? Anybody get hurt? What happened?"

"The cops are already here. I'm outside at the phone booth while they talk to the customers that was inside. They told me not to touch nothing, so I came out here." She waited for Jimmy, who was quiet. She could tell something bothered him, but she felt it best to remain quiet and not press.

Finally he spoke. "That number should be on the cash register."

"I can't find it. I mean, I don't want to go back in there right now. Can you just gimme the number? Please."

Jimmy let out a loud sigh and muttered "women" quietly under his breath. Mary Beth smiled to herself, knowing she'd get the number. As she held her pen ready, Jimmy read each number to her clearly and slowly, as if reading it to a child.

Without saying thanks or goodbye, she hung up and spit her gum into a large plastic trash barrel beside the phone booth.

———

The vice president of sales and marketing and the ad manager for Greenbrier Equipment showed up unannounced at Peter's office at 8:45 a.m. Peter had finished scanning the front page of the *Wall Street Journal* and was opening his mail when his secretary buzzed his line, "Please tell Mr. Brantley that Mr. Givens and Mr. Stark are here from Greenbrier." She was good. She could always tell when someone arrived without an appointment, and she wanted to give Peter a way out if he needed one. Or at least give him warning to get ready.

Peter hated Givens, the sales and marketing vice president. More than once he'd thought that Givens was proof that only an idiot could have decided that, in Corporate America, sales and marketing should be combined into one position. Peter always dreaded it when he won a new account and found his primary contact had a title like vice president of sales and marketing. He loved and admired good sales guys, but what they did had little to do with the big picture of marketing. He was convinced that the sales guys always rose through the ranks and became head of marketing, but they never knew much about real marketing. From their point of view, and often from that of the CEO as well, sales *brought in* money and marketing *spent* money. Sales guys always got to the top while the marketing guy right beneath them made things work. For Peter that generally meant smaller production budgets and deadlines driven by sales calls instead of strategic marketing thinking.

A meeting with Givens wasn't the type of day Peter had hoped for. He had no heart left for advertising. He spent every free moment planning and plotting. His lunches were spent driving around town imagining ways he could elude police or hoodlums chasing him, or imagining ways to swap money for drugs with minimum risk. He'd skipped lunch so often lately that he noticed his suit pants were beginning to have a little extra room in the waist, and only this morning he'd tightened his belt another hole. He wasn't focused on his job, and those close to him had noticed. Two people had already commented on his weight loss, something he'd be happy about if he were making any effort to lose weight.

Unfortunately, he had no way to dodge the Greenbrier meeting. Besides, he had estimates Givens needed to sign. He grabbed his favorite Mountain Valley coffee cup, tucked in his shirttail better, and walked down the hall.

"Good morning, George. Morning, Mark," Peter said as he approached the two men, wearing his best smile. "Can I get you coffee?"

"Yeah, I'd like some," George Givens answered.

"Sure," Mark said, reaching out and tapping Peter's flat tummy lightly with the back of his fingers. "You losing weight? Wish I could."

Peter faked a smile. "Couple of pounds. I've been riding my bike a lot this summer. Come on, let's grab a cup and we'll meet in my office if you don't mind."

The three of them started down the hall to the kitchen. Peter rummaged through the coffee cup cabinet and managed to find a cup from radio station KKLS and one from University of Southern Mississippi. He poured three coffees and waited while his guests decided what sort of sweeteners and cream to use. They walked into his office and sat down.

Without waiting for Peter to ask, Givens started talking about why they were there. "We had a planning session this weekend, and we're just not sure we're ready for that campaign to break."

Peter was already thinking about the long hours his creative group had put in the week before to finish the concepts in time for Greenbrier to approve the work and still meet deadlines for the trade magazines before the big trade show coming up in less than two months. He knew the deadline had already been extended from the magazine until next Tuesday and they wouldn't be happy to lose the ad this late. He knew the magazine could still charge for the space since the deadline had passed, even if no ad was ready. He wouldn't blame them anyway, and part of him wanted these clients to get stuck with the ad costs just for being such jerks.

His agency spent a lot of money with the magazine and might be able to call in a favor and not be charged, but this was one time he wouldn't offer such a favor to the client. Not this client. Not this time. Not in the mood he was in.

The concept had only been developed after Givens had decided that Greenbrier needed a bigger presence this year for the large trade show in Chicago for outdoor pool and patio furniture. Peter and the others on the account had jumped through hoops to complete the work in time to make the publication deadline. He was already dreading telling his staff that Greenbrier had changed its mind.

Peter allowed the pause in the discussion to become uncomfortable, letting his disapproval be known by his silence. Peter watched the two clients, his eyes steady and his face stoic, waiting to see if Givens had any guilt in making such a decision at the last moment. Peter asked, "What's come up?"

Mark looked down when Peter asked the question.

Givens spoke up. "Well, Peter, we need to do something, of course. But we're just not sure that an ad campaign is the best way to get attention before the trade show. We were thinking maybe that direct mail idea you had would be more effective."

Peter held back what he wanted to say. He had suggested direct mail more than two months earlier, but Givens vetoed it, wanting a splashy ad campaign for the new product line. Peter could tell from the way Mark now remained silent that he was uncomfortable and thought it was a bad idea to change direction this late, but he wasn't ready to take on his boss. Peter thought thirty-year-old Mark was much smarter and had more marketing savvy than fifty-five year old Givens, but he also knew Mark would never publicly challenge his boss.

Two hours later Peter gave up trying to save the campaign. He convinced Givens and Mark to leave it to him to come up with a new plan.

The second the two men were on the elevator, Peter called the entire direct marketing team into a stand-up meeting to see what they could do to convert the ad concepts into direct mail. Peter asked them to develop their best plan by the next morning and told them he would support the plan, regardless of what it was. Cost would not be an issue. "Propose what you think Greenbrier needs to spend to complete the new jobs on time."

The members of the B&P marketing team assigned to Greenbrier all looked at each other and walked out of his office with little to say. He could see in their eyes that all four of them were thinking that he had never allowed them to develop concepts without involving him. He knew word would get around the agency fast and that John might even ask him if he was doing the right thing for Greenbrier, but Peter knew he had given the client good advice. If they chose another marketing direction, that was their decision. The guys at Greenbrier had brought this situation on themselves, and if their indecision cost them a little extra to fix the marketing, he would not lose sleep over it.

He closed his door and stared out the window over the cobblestone street that ran past the eastern side of the Governor's Mansion. The client work was already forgotten now that his team had agreed to take on the assignment. Now his thoughts were only of how to disguise himself. It was time to call Danny and then McNabb. One way or another, his days in advertising were numbered.

———

Danny placed the phone down gently after listening to Peter tell about how he had contacted McNabb. Danny wasn't sure if he was shocked, but he knew the person he'd known growing up had changed. Part of the change was good because Peter sounded more energetic and excited than he'd been since Christopher died. Peter needed his help, but Danny wasn't sure either of them was ready to deal with McNabb and his men. Danny decided he needed to talk to Juice. He dialed Juice, who answered on one ring.

"Nicholas Joyce."

"Juice, it's Danny. That stuff with Peter I mentioned the other day is going down. We need to talk."

"Come on over."

Ten minutes later Danny parked in front of the house. When he stepped onto the sidewalk, a warm breeze blew his hair, suggesting that summer wasn't ready to go just yet. Juice and his girlfriend Susan were on the wide front porch, sitting in rocking chairs. Danny wasn't happy to see Susan, though he always enjoyed the short skirts she wore. More than once he'd caught a glimpse of her red or black panties as she lounged casually around the house. Tonight was no different, and he had to force himself not to stare at her thighs where the skirt had ridden up as she sat rocking with her legs crossed.

He was relieved when Susan jumped up after he walked onto the porch. "I'm going to the gym. You guys can do your business. Whatever that is." She winked at Danny, kissed Juice on the cheek, and skipped down the steps. "Call me later, Sweetie," she yelled from the street as she opened the door to her red Mazda. Her black panties showed for a moment as she hiked up her skirt, dropped into the seat, and swung her legs inside.

They watched her speed around the corner without even slowing at the stop sign, her tires squealing.

"Damn," Juice said under his breath as he looked over at Danny and rolled his eyes, the one word being sufficient to communicate his displeasure at his girlfriend's poor driving. He stood up. "Let's sit inside."

Inside, Juice went to the refrigerator and came back with two Blue Moon beers.

Danny took one and sat on Juice's new couch. Running his hand across the smooth leather surface, he raised his eyebrows. "Man, you must have won the lottery."

"Sort of. Sold a big house to that surgeon I told you about." Juice took a seat in an overstuffed lounge chair and propped his feet on an upholstered stool. "Made nearly twenty grand."

"Damn, you lucky shit."

For the next hour, he told Juice the details as they each finished two beers. Neither of them had heard of McNabb, but they agreed that meant nothing. They knew little about Mississippi's drug scene. But both had been deep enough into the fringes of that scene in Birmingham and Huntsville, even as far south as Panama City, to know being careful wasn't enough. These were people who wouldn't think twice about killing anyone in their way.

When Danny was finished talking, Juice said he didn't have much to add, but he did want to remind Danny of one thing. "I know you remember everything about that deal we did in Huntsville. Did you ever figure out how the dealers who came after us knew it was us?"

"I guess I just quit trying to figure it out."

"I thought about it a lot. And I believe to this day that someone in the police department told them."

Danny turned up the bottle of beer and took a long swallow. "I think that was the worst few months in my life. You taking the fall for it and me not being able to do anything. I still can't believe those bastards watched us steal pot from a dealer's apartment and never did anything about it. Must have been protecting someone undercover. Right after that, my car was demolished by baseball bats and my apartment torn apart. The cops may not have known who I was, but somebody put two and two together."

"Yeah," Juice said. "After you split town, it was at least a year before things settled down, even with me spending half of it in county."

Danny sat back and felt a chill run through him. "Damn, you're right. Had to be the police that told them about us."

"That's my point. If you do this deal," Juice said, "trust no one. Assume everyone knows everything. And believe that these dudes are bad." He reached over and clinked his bottle against Danny's. "Then call me when you get up to your ass in alligators."

chapter 16

As Peter approached the entrance to the Downtown Club parking lot on Friday night, the parking lot was filled with 4x4, full-sized, big-engine Dodge, Chevy, and Ford pickups. Peter had promised Mary Beth this venture into the bar would be the last solo action he took before Danny got there. He needed to know for sure if the bar was Gant's main hangout, as Mary Beth's research had indicated. Peter was constantly surprised at how much information she could find out sitting at her computer or researching files at the library. He wanted to know as much as he could about McNabb and his main man Gant. Peter had already followed McNabb to the Hillside Bar & Grill once, and now he wanted to see inside where Gant hung out. The windows were painted the same green as the cinder block walls, so he had to go inside to see anything.

Peter parked, pulled his Jackson Senators baseball cap down low, and walked to the bar's front entrance. As he opened the door, he felt a cold blast of air and smelled the unique sweet and sour aroma only a bar could generate—a mixture of disinfectant, stale smoke, musky perfume, and spilled beer. He stopped for a moment to allow his eyes to adjust to the dark interior. He held his stomach in and made a conscious effort to appear confident, as if he drank there all the time. The air was red and blue from neon beer signs across the front window that highlighted the thick haze of cigarette smoke.

Gant sat alone at a small round table near the far end of the bar. Peter sat at the other end of the bar on one of two empty stools where he could watch Gant's image in the huge mirror behind the bar. He ordered a draft beer and sat sipping it for forty-five minutes. He tried to read the dates on coins laminated into the bar surface, but there wasn't quite enough light. He was fascinated by a two-gallon jar of bright pink pickled pigs' feet sitting in the middle of the bar. Next to the pigs' feet sat a jar filled with pickled eggs. He had seen such jars in honky tonks all his life, though he couldn't remember anyone eating from them. At Gant's end of the bar sat another huge jar filled with water, a shot glass resting at the bottom. A slot crudely carved into the jar lid allowed patrons to drop in coins in an attempt to ring the shot glass. It wasn't clear to him what prize one might win, but the bottom of the jar was filled with quarters piled two inches deep.

Gant seemed to know everyone in the noisy place. Several men and two women spoke to Gant as they passed by, some pausing momentarily to chat. One man in a black cowboy hat came over from the pool table, stick still in hand, and sat down for a couple of minutes. Gant and the pool shooter leaned toward one another over the scarred bar table and talked in hushed tones. The other player's partner, standing impatiently at the pool table, finally started complaining about holding up the game, and the cowboy pool shooter got up with a shrug and walked back to the red felt-covered table.

Peter studied Gant. From his meticulous appearance and hair combed perfectly and slicked back, Peter sensed the man was precise in his actions and paid attention to detail. Peter sensed a quiet confidence in the man from the way he seemed to look hard into the eyes of everyone who approached his table. He seemed perfectly at ease and comfortable in this setting. Peter laid three dollars on the bar and walked out without looking back. He had his answer. Gant was at home in the Downtown club, but he was not a man to be messed with. Maybe Peter *was* in over his head.

Danny called his boss at home on Saturday morning and said he needed to take off a couple of days the next week to make a long weekend. He had lots of vacation time saved up, and the fishing trip to Destin his buddy had planned came through when someone canceled a charter at the last minute. They had a sweet deal and wanted to go. Of course, his boss said to go ahead, as Danny knew he would. His boss was an avid tournament bass fisherman and spent many weekends driving around to lakes across the State, so Danny knew his fishing story would work well.

His story for Cindy was different. He told her that the computer project Peter needed help with had come through and he was taking a couple of days off to make some extra money. He hated lying to his wife, but he thought it would protect her more if she knew nothing about their real project.

Cindy decided to take the kids shopping with her and kissed him goodbye as she left. He packed his rifle and an old .45 Colt revolver in the trunk, glad to be able to take the guns without Cindy seeing him. Cindy knew he would take the big revolver on a trip and it wouldn't prompt questions, but he could think of no good excuse to take the rifle outside of hunting season. It took him ten minutes to find the old skateboard he had once spent a lot of time riding. He placed the board in the trunk with his guns. He had assured Peter he could no longer ride the board as he once had, and he couldn't think of any reason he needed it, but Peter had said to bring a skateboard and he and Mary Beth would explain why later.

Before leaving, he made one last call to Juice. He asked him if he could be ready to come to Jackson if they needed him. Juice would be ready.

Danny set his cruise control at 78 miles per hour and drove straight down I-20 through Tuscaloosa and Meridian into Jackson to Peter's driveway. The four hour drive had given him plenty of time to think through what he was doing. He realized he didn't want to screw up a life he was happy with. He knew he had taken more than his share of chances—more than Peter knew about—and this one was far riskier than most of the things he had done. He almost pulled the car onto an exit several times to call Peter and back out. But finally he realized he cared too strongly.

———

On Sunday morning, Mary Beth selected a mid-calf, conservative black dress with a wide yellow belt that made the dress look perfect for church. She held the dress in front of her as she looked into the mirror.

She held the dress open and stepped into the smooth cloth, reaching around to zip the back partially until she could get Peter to finish the top later.

She pinned up her hair and chose a large-brimmed yellow hat to match her belt. With sunglasses and gold and silver bracelets, her transformation into an Old South, old-money club member was complete. She looked into the mirror and hardly recognized herself. She felt gracious and pretty, as if she were someone's rich aunt, here to visit the family.

Peter drove her downtown and parked a block from the Crowne Plaza. At the hotel she asked for a room for three days, requesting the second floor.

"Will you be using a credit card for that, ma'am?"

She spoke in her best old-South accent. "Oh, no. I much prefer to use cash." She laid three crisp one hundred dollar bills on the counter.

———

When Peter and Mary Beth arrived home, Danny sat at the kitchen table and studied a city map. His gleaming, oiled rifle and three small radios lay on the table.

"We need to get a bag of cocaine for the bait-and-switch," Peter said, as he sat with Danny and Mary Beth at the kitchen table. "You guys want to go?"

"Hell yeah," Danny said. "I just want to see that much coke at one time."

Peter drove the three of them toward the woods near Canton where the large box was buried. They spent the time reviewing every scenario. What would they do if McNabb pulled a gun? What if he was working with the police? As they played out each scene, they gradually felt they could handle almost any problem.

Danny laughed as Peter stopped the car down a weed-covered dirt road. "Damn man, you wanted to make sure this shit was hidden."

"Hey, I'm not used to doing this kind of thing." Peter stepped to the back of the Jeep to retrieve a shovel. "And we thought we might end up just leaving it buried anyway." He led them through the pines until he found his tree. Then he stepped off twelve paces.

"Are we digging for pirate treasure?" Danny kidded.

Peter unearthed the bags after first struggling with the heavy weight to free them from the hole, as dirt pressed in on the sides.

Danny stopped laughing when Peter opened the box. "Man, I can't believe this." He squatted down to get a better look at the bags. He spoke just above a whisper. "There was a time I would have killed for blow like this."

Peter felt a cold chill as he heard the words. With a half-joking tone, he said, "You still might get that chance."

chapter 17

On Monday morning, Peter sat in his tall-back leather desk chair and answered a frenzy of emails that had piled up over the previous week. He went down the list, deleting one after another, responding with a simple yes or no to some, and writing brief responses where he could. He printed out three or four that required him to edit something or to think more about his answer. Looking at his watch, he realized he'd sat there for over two hours, so he stopped and went for a mid-morning coffee.

Back at his desk, he lifted the stack of mail, magazines, and newspapers from his in-box and placed them in the center of his desk. He picked up each piece in order and didn't put the piece down until it was handled. Three hours later, working through lunch when the phones were quieter and fewer people interrupted, the stack was filed away or tossed into the trash. He had no interest in work. The exchange would be today.

He pushed the speed dial button for John Baynes. "John, I'm caught up right now, and I'm not feeling well. I'm heading home early unless you have something urgent for me." He tried not to sound sick. Nothing was worse than someone trying to sound sick.

"Sure, go ahead. See you tomorrow if you're feeling okay."

Peter stood behind the glass front door of his building lobby for a moment, scanning the street in front for anything unusual. He saw nothing and told himself to quit being so paranoid. No one could know he was the person who had gotten away with a million dollars in drugs. He crossed the street to the sidewalk in front of the Governor's mansion and walked down Capitol Street to the AmSouth Bank building. A flock of English sparrows hopped from tree to tree in the small courtyard of the building.

He hesitated a moment to watch the birds before he cut through the building, passed a row of retail shops, and crossed Amite Street to the Crowne Plaza.

After casually looking around to see if anyone he knew was there, he stepped into the elevator and pushed the button for the second floor. Someone had scratched "eat s" on the polished metal plate above the elevator buttons, likely interrupted before finishing the thought. He shook his head in conversation with himself, walked down the hallway, and used Mary Beth's key to let himself into the room she had taken.

He changed into jeans, topsiders, and one of the bright yellow t-shirts. He pulled on the red cap with the ponytail attached, put on a pair of the dark sunglasses, and walked to the registration desk.

An African-American woman about thirty years old spoke before he reached the counter. "Good afternoon. Checking in, sir?" He noticed her flat accent, as if she were schooled somewhere out of the South, as well as her erect posture and tailored blue suit. She looked Peter directly in the eyes, her chin slightly raised. He realized he had been thinking about her and hadn't answered, but before he could speak up, she spoke again as if he hadn't heard her the first time. "May I help you, sir?"

"I sure hope so. I need a room for a couple of days. Got any vacancies?"

"Of course, sir."

He registered as Robert Johnson, the name of one of his favorite blues men, and listed his hometown as Greenville, a Mississippi Delta city, though he wasn't sure Johnson had lived there. Before walking away, he asked the clerk several questions about nearby restaurants, where he could find a bar, and if there was a mall nearby. He casually turned his head a couple of times while they talked, just to be sure she saw the ponytail.

After visiting the room to make sure it would appear slept in, he returned to Mary Beth's room and changed back into his suit from work, minus the tie that he carefully folded and slid into his side coat pocket.

Peter, Mary Beth, and Danny were each to take separate cars on Monday afternoon to the exchange site. The time was 5:45 p.m. Now that the downtown traffic had thinned out but there was plenty of daylight left, Peter wanted to get moving.

"We have just over a half hour to get everything in place before I call," he said.

"Once I get the skateboard, I'm ready," Mary Beth said. She wore Timberland ankle-high boots, loose boot socks with a red ring around the tops, ragged cutoffs, a tie-dyed t-shirt, and a red bandanna tied around her neck. Her hair was pulled forward to cover the earphones and most of her face. She looked like a kid to anyone who didn't look closely at the tiny wrinkles beginning to show at the corners of her eyes. With a Walkman clipped to the waist of her cutoffs and Danny's skateboard in her hand, she would just be one of the teenagers who used the downtown sidewalks most summer evenings.

"Park two blocks south of the AmSouth Bank building on Pascagoula Street, then make your way to the crosswalk," Peter told her. "Danny, you park north of the hotel and remember to stash the second yellow t-shirt and red cap behind a dumpster in the hotel alley."

Danny nodded that he was ready. "I'll be at the upstairs schoolhouse window long before anyone shows up in the parking lot." He didn't need to say that he would be covering with the rifle they'd hidden there the night before.

The three cars left the house at the same time. Peter drove to the telephone beside the barbershop at Highland Village, two hundred yards from the Amoco station but on the opposite side of the interstate. He walked to the pay phone and dialed McNabb's home number.

"McNabb."

"Bring the money right now. Drive to the pay phones at the Amoco station on Northside Drive. You've got six minutes. If you're late, or if you've got anyone with you, the deal is off. And don't hang up, just put down the phone. I don't want you calling anyone else. Go now and wait for my call."

"Now wait a minute—"

"Just come now," Peter said forcefully, cutting off McNabb. From McNabb's obvious surprise and anger, Peter could tell he wasn't prepared for the call on his unlisted number. "I'm the one who left you a surprise package, so you know I have something else you want. You've got six minutes. No more."

"Don't mess with me."

"The clock is ticking," Peter said, and then he hung up.

———

Gant was opening his front door when he heard one ring and realized he had missed a call. He pressed the button on the answering machine and recognized McNabb's angry voice. "It's me. Call me now on my cell. They've called, and I need you now, damn it."

Gant dialed McNabb. He heard a simple "Yeah."

"It's me," Gant said.

"They had my unlisted home number. I'm two blocks away from another phone they sent me to. Near my house. Just head this way."

Gant knew McNabb was saying as little as he could. They were always careful on cell phones since they knew the signals could be intercepted easily. "William, do you think you should do this?"

"It may be our only shot. But you know I have no intention of paying this son of a bitch if it's bad business, and I haven't gotten the money together yet anyway."

"I'm on my way." Gant grabbed his .45 automatic from the kitchen counter and slid the gun into the back of his belt.

"Just keep your phone close and get your ass up here. I'll call," McNabb said.

As he jumped into his car, Gant wondered if they had underestimated the guy with the drugs. The guy had figured out who McNabb was, and now he had gotten McNabb's unlisted number. That sounded more professional than Gant expected. He suddenly realized that if the guy knew that much, he might know about him, too. Gant slammed his hand down on the steering wheel as the thought sunk in. This guy had made him pay already. If Gant got the chance, he'd make *him* pay. And the price would be dear. He reached for the automatic on the seat beside him and placed it between his legs.

—————

Peter didn't need his binoculars to see McNabb arrive at the Amoco in his Lincoln Town Car. McNabb looked around as he walked to the pay phones, but Peter knew McNabb wouldn't spot him. The traffic was heavy going both directions on Northside, and people were outside at all three gas stations around McNabb.

Peter dialed the number, and McNabb immediately picked up. Peter didn't wait for McNabb to speak. "Drive to the parking lot next to the Crowne Plaza downtown. Go up the ramp until you see me. If you don't see me by the time you get to the fourth floor, just stop and wait. Go to the public parking side, not the hotel parking lot. You got it?"

"Yeah, I got it. But like I said, I want to talk first." McNabb ran his hand through his hair and scanned the cars and buildings nearby.

"Just bring the money. I'll be in a red hat and yellow shirt. Wait where you are exactly two minutes, then leave. We'll know if you leave too soon. You'll have seven minutes after that to get there. Anything goes wrong, this is the last time we'll speak." For the second time, he hung up on McNabb without waiting for a reply.

———

Gant's phone rang just as he turned from I-20 onto I-55 North. Traffic was still heavy, and he had to settle for staying in the far left lane where traffic was at least moving. He listened carefully for whatever message McNabb could give him without saying too much.

"I've set up that meeting with our new partners we've been talking about," McNabb said. "I need you to join us. I think there will be at least two of them meeting with us, but I'm not sure that's all. They're parked in the Central Parking lot next to the Crowne Plaza downtown, on the fourth floor, so I'm going to run by there and drop off that box of papers they asked for. We're meeting in about ten minutes. Can you be there? As you know, I'm not ready to close this deal yet, but we might have a chance if you get there."

Gant answered with equal caution, "Great. I'll meet you there after you drop off your package. Maybe we can have a little surprise celebration for them."

Gant smiled. It would be over soon.

chapter 18

Taylor Nelson was slumped in an overstuffed chair with his feet propped on the corner of his coffee table, but his thoughts were still at work. With his hands behind his head, he stared up at a small oil painting of the Jackson downtown skyline at sunset and tried to connect the pieces of the case. He had a feeling that the evidence was pointing him in the one right direction, but the meaning lay just beyond his grasp. His telephone lay on the chair arm, so he answered on the first ring. "Hello, this is Nelson" was barely out of his mouth before Joe Graham began talking, the excitement in his voice obvious.

"L.T., this is Joe. I was off from the liquor store, so I've been monitoring the clone phones. I've got something that could be important."

"I'm listening."

"Just listened in on a call to McNabb. From Gant. McNabb must have left him a message that something was urgent, and Gant called him back. They're on their way right now to the Central Parking lot next to the Crowne Plaza to meet someone he called their 'new partners.'"

Nelson felt the hair on his arms stand up. This didn't sound like a normal business deal. "Okay, call a backup unit and—no, wait. We need to be careful and not scare them off. Look, do you know if Sleepy's still there? He said he might be working a little late."

"Yeah, he's still on."

"I'll pick you guys up. Grab him and meet me out front in three minutes." Nelson was already running toward the door. He held the phone between his cheek and shoulder. He grabbed his Glock on the kitchen counter and slid the gun into the back of his belt. "Let's find out what's going on." He pushed the off button and tossed the phone on the counter.

He slid the door back and then closed the glass shut behind him as he ran to his car and started downtown. From his home in Belhaven, he thought he could make the mile and a half to the station in two minutes if he ran the traffic lights, which he planned to do.

Graham and Hunt waited outside the department and piled into Nelson's car before the tires even stopped. Both carried Glock pistols with fifteen-round magazines in shoulder holsters under their sport coats, standard issue for the drug task force. Each had two back-up clips as well, in polished black leather pouches in the back of their belts. Joe also carried a .38 caliber five-shot revolver strapped to the outside of his right ankle.

"Joe, will McNabb know you from the liquor store?"

"I don't know, probably, but Gant has seen me for sure."

"Then I'll let you out at the traffic light a block away. Walk through Smith Park, but stay back out of sight." Nelson handed Joe an LSU baseball cap and a windbreaker that had been lying on the seat. "Put these on. Leave your coat in the car, and watch the back of the lot and hotel from across the street."

After letting Graham out, Nelson slowed as he reached the front of the parking garage. "Sleepy, take the elevator to the second floor. Walk up from there until you spot something. I'll drive up and cover each floor by car."

Nelson knew the plan was weak and a long shot, but it was the only plan he had. He turned into the parking lot, pulled a ticket from the machine, and started up the ramp as the wooden arm rose in front of him.

———

From her lookout position on the bank crosswalk, Mary Beth saw a man jump out of a car and run to the parking lot elevator before the car turned onto the parking lot ramp. She couldn't see the driver. She stood up, uncertain about what was going down, but she knew something was wrong. She felt the air freeze inside her lungs as she saw a second car slowly cruise down Amite Street in the turn lane that led into the parking lot. She recognized Gant as the driver. But instead of turning in, Gant shifted left into another lane, sped up, and drove past. She squinted, trying to figure out what had just happened. She had no idea who the first men were. She had assumed they were with McNabb. But when Gant drove past, she realized the first men must have been police.

———

Peter watched McNabb step out of his car on the fourth level of the parking lot and close the door, looking carefully around. McNabb moved to the back of the car, looked around again, unlocked the trunk, and removed a briefcase.

As soon as McNabb stood upright behind the car, Peter yelled "Hey!"

At first McNabb didn't see him in his red hat and yellow shirt since he wasn't in the Central Parking lot but was fifty feet away in the adjacent hotel parking lot. A four-story drop separated them. The parking lots were connected only at the south end where they shared an exit ramp. The exit ramp was where Peter planned to meet for the exchange, knowing he would be long gone down a stairwell before McNabb could have anyone cross the spiral ramp and chase him.

"You looking for me?" Peter said across the open space separating the parking lots.

McNabb turned toward him, looking around. "That depends on you. How do I know who you are?"

"I'm the special delivery man. I left you a note, along with a gift at your house. Does that sound like the right person? Why don't you ..." Suddenly Peter stopped and put his hand to his ear. He then turned and ran toward the hotel elevators as Mary Beth shouted into his radio to run.

Danny heard Mary Beth yelling into the radio, "Get out! It's a trap."

He slid his pistol onto the windowsill. Then he propped his rifle on the sill and took off the safety so he could fire if necessary. His guts were in a knot as he asked himself how he had let the situation come to this. He was no killer, but he would protect Peter and Mary Beth. He knew he could shoot somebody as a last option, but he wasn't sure he could live with himself afterward. He would try to scare them off first.

Through the riflescope, he saw past the man he believed was McNabb and realized another man was getting off the elevator. The new man's sport coat and thick-soled, black shoes said cop. Danny's concern turned to fear as he realized the situation was out of his control. He eased the gun barrel back inside the window and spun around with his back to the wall. He was willing to protect Peter from drug dealers if they tried to harm him, but a fight with police wasn't something he would do. There was no way he would shoot an innocent person. That wasn't the way to help Peter.

He knew running was now the only option for all of them. He picked up the radio. "Peter, there's a cop coming, but he's on the public side. I think the hotel side is clear. Get your ass out of there! I'm gone."

As Peter reached the elevator, he spoke into the radio microphone, "Both of you, go. I'll be fine. I'm at the elevator, and no one is after me. Go now. Just walk away. Don't run, and don't look back."

He switched the elevator button to ON, which he had minutes before switched to OFF to keep the elevator open at his floor. He removed the OUT OF ORDER sign he had taped over the button and stuffed the paper into his pocket. He put the room key into the elevator card reader, and the elevator started down to the second floor. Still inside the elevator, he removed hat and t-shirt and stuffed them into the bag along with the real cocaine and the fake bags. He was now a shorthaired man in a black t-shirt, carrying a typical travel bag. He stuffed the earbud in his pocket just as the elevator door opened.

No one was in the hallway, but as he reached his hotel room door, an older couple came out of a room three doors down. He looked directly at them, knowing they would likely turn away from his stare. Both the man and the woman looked down, though he and the man nodded briefly with just the barest of polite eye contact. He walked past his door until he heard the elevator open again.

When the couple got on the elevator, he doubled back to Mary Beth's room and unlocked the door. His shirt was wet with sweat though he had only run twenty-five feet. *What have we done?*

He put the earbud back into his ear and tried the microphone, willing himself to be calm. "Are you two all right?"

"I'm two blocks away and almost to the car," Mary Beth answered after a few seconds, her voice faint and scratchy. "Are you okay?"

"I'm in the room. No one saw me. I'll be fine," he said. "Big guy, how 'bout you?"

There was no answer from Danny.

"Where are you, man? Can you hear me?" Peter was more than a little concerned. He wanted to be sure that Mary Beth wouldn't try to check on Danny. "Remember, when you get to the car, don't stop, no matter what. Just get to a phone and check in."

"I'm in the car now," she answered.

"Just go. There's nothing more to do here. D? You there?"

Ten seconds later Danny came on the radio. "Don't come this way. There was a cop running down the sidewalk toward me. I just had time to step behind a van parked on the street when I heard his footsteps echoing out of that tunnel behind the hotel. If he hadn't made so much noise running, I'd have never heard him. I'm in the car now. Just follow the plan."

chapter 19

Nelson pulled into a parking space on the fourth floor, catching a glimpse of McNabb entering the elevator. Then he saw Hunt running down the ramp toward his car.

Wheezing from the sprint, Hunt said, "A guy ran across the hotel parking lot in a red hat, yellow shirt, and jeans. Long hair in a ponytail. Had a bag that could be the drugs. We've got to move."

Nelson picked up his police walkie talkie and radioed Graham, who was watching the hotel from across the street. "Joe, watch the back alley for a guy with a red hat and yellow shirt. Let us know if you spot him, but don't do anything. We need you undercover. Sleepy will work his way to the back through the mezzanine level. I'll take the elevator down and start at the front. Meet in the lobby if we don't spot him."

Just as Nelson finished checking the men's room on the first floor, Hunt radioed in. "This is Sleepy, Lieutenant. I found some clothes in the alley back here that may have been our guy. I'm heading out the alley onto Lamar. Cover the West Street side."

"I'm heading there now," Nelson answered.

He sprinted through the front lobby and out the door, crossed to Smith Park, and then doubled back past Graham who simply shrugged as Nelson jogged past where Graham was concealed behind a tall hedge. Nelson continued down West Street and around an old school building. He slowed to a walk when he saw Hunt coming back from the next block over. Joe joined them as they walked back through the alley behind the hotel.

When they neared the rear door of the hotel, Hunt reached behind a dumpster overflowing with cardboard boxes. He brought his hand out with the red hat and yellow t-shirt clutched in his thick, powerful fingers. Flies buzzed around the three of them, and the tart fragrance of food waste rotting in the corners of the dumpster made the air seem thick.

"Just got a glimpse, but this sure looks like what the guy near McNabb was wearing," Hunt said, sounding out of breath.

"Joe, how'd he get past you?" Nelson asked, his tone more puzzled than angry.

Joe shrugged. "I was right across the street looking down the alley the whole time. I never left. Can't see how he got past me. There was a National Linen delivery truck back here that pulled out about then. Maybe he got behind it or something, but I don't see how."

After an hour of talking to guests in the lobby and others who were returning to their cars, the three men drove back to their office to compare notes. They had secured the past two days of videotape from the security camera covering the front entrance and hoped they could use it to identify who had entered the hotel.

Nelson was unhappy. "I can't believe that in 1998 we still can't get cameras on every floor of a public garage or at least the actual hotel lobby so we can find the bad guys. One day, I swear, we're going to have cameras all over."

Hunt laughed. "Yeah, good luck with trying to do that, L.T."

———

Roy Gant sat on the hood of his El Dorado two blocks from the Crowne Plaza where he had watched the trim Lt. Taylor Nelson run out the front door of the hotel and around the building. He had seen another man who also looked like a cop come out of the alley behind the hotel. The man was somehow vaguely familiar. He was fairly certain that the person they were chasing got away. He had seen no one. It seemed that McNabb was in no trouble either. He knew McNabb wouldn't be running from the police, so they had to be after someone else.

After driving past the hotel earlier and seeing cops closing in, Gant had circled a couple of blocks and driven into the Federal Building public parking lot and up to the third floor. From there he could watch the hotel without fear of being seen. He wanted to help McNabb but knew that his presence would only make things worse.

McNabb hadn't answered his call nor left the parking lot in his car. He was somewhere still in the hotel. None of this was making sense, unless the police were chasing the guys who had called McNabb. Either way, this didn't feel right to him. The police were too close, and he had no intention of going back to prison. With the police this close, his backup plan was more important than ever. He'd need to have some cash ready. He would begin today to prepare to get out of town. He'd seen the breaking point coming for the past year as McNabb grew overconfident and careless, and he knew it was time to move if they couldn't settle the problem quickly. No matter what, he wasn't going back inside again to make someone else rich. McNabb was making the business personal and taking too many risks.

———

Mary Beth looked at the clock and was surprised to see it was past one in the morning. She had spent hours talking with Danny, filling in many of her gaps about Danny's life and beginning to understand better why the two cousins were such close friends.

She placed her glass of George Dickel Tennessee Whiskey and Coca-Cola on the table in front of her. "Can I get you another drink?"

"No, thanks, I'm done. I need to be able to drive in the morning." Danny placed his glass of only a few ice cubes and a last swallow of bourbon on the coffee table in front of him. "As soon as we know Peter is out of the hotel and safe, I'm running over to Birmingham. I can come back when you need me."

She realized why Peter liked Danny so much. He listened, and he seemed genuinely interested in anything she had to say. And he was there when needed, even for something as dangerous as what they'd done that afternoon. She had no such friends. "You and Peter had some fun times growing up it sounds like." She tucked her feet up under her in the big chair opposite Danny on the couch.

"Yeah, we got to be close when we were about twelve or thirteen, I guess. Spent a lot of Saturdays at our grandmother's house in Alabaster."

"Peter told me. I remember one story about when you showed Peter how to put a penny on the train track and then find it flattened out. I once found a little smooth, thin copper disk in with his watches and stuff. He said that's what it was."

Danny picked up his glass, tilted his head back and drained the last swallow. "He kept it all this time?"

"Yeah, it's still on top of his dresser. He says it's a good luck charm."

"I remember this one time we bought a can of Prince Albert tobacco and Bugle rolling papers from an older boy that lived at the end of the dirt road behind grandmother's house. We practiced for hours learning how to roll our own cigarettes. Neither of us would inhale, but we spent a lot of time behind granddaddy's run-down auto repair shop, acting like we were smoking."

"He drove me past the shop once and showed it to me. It was still there with a bunch of old cars around." Mary Beth leaned over to reach for the bottle of Dickel and poured a small amount into their glasses. "Here, have one more little one with me."

Danny picked up the glass and swirled the toasted golden liquid around. He looked down, still a bit shy and not completely comfortable being alone with Mary Beth. Taking a sip, he could feel the pleasant burn in his throat. "We'd sit with our backs to the shop, legs stretched out in front of us and the sun in our faces, puffing on lumpy cigarettes and dreaming of the day we would have fast cars of our own with four-barrel carburetors, dual exhaust, and chrome wheels."

She laughed and nodded but said little as she poured more whiskey into their glasses, no longer bothering with ice or Coca-Cola.

Danny took a sip and held the glass in his lap. "Peter was the one cousin who'd spend time at our little dog-eared house when we were growing up." He took another sip and looked away as if remembering something. "Other cousins always had friends with bigger houses, swimming pools, go-carts. And Christopher, he was ten years younger. Peter didn't care that I didn't have such things. And I've never forgotten it."

Mary Beth sat silently for several seconds, a contented smile spreading across her face. When she spoke, her voice was barely above a whisper, as if saying the words out loud would make them untrue. "You love Peter, don't you? I mean, I know he's family and of course you love him. But you really do love him as a friend, don't you?"

Danny nodded yes, even before she finished.

Mary Beth didn't expect Danny to say anything out loud. "I don't mean to embarrass you with some kind of sappy moment, but I'm just now really understanding what you two mean to each other."

"Don't tell him I told you all this, but even in college when Peter had his rich friends at Birmingham-Southern and my junior college buddies were mostly from moms and dads who worked at the steel mills, Peter still found ways to spend time with me." Danny kept his eyes down and spoke slowly. "My friendship with Peter's more than blood, and it's more than friends. There's not really a word for it. There's not many like him."

Mary Beth felt a lump in her throat at the words. Danny was describing the Peter she had fallen in love with, the man with a big, compassionate heart. The man she wanted back. She forced herself not to say too much as she realized she felt a little jealousy, wondering how men—who always wanted to hide their emotions, at least in front of other men—seemed to be the ones who developed the closest bonds. She could think of few women with whom she had felt that close bond in her lifetime. She was uncertain if there was even one she could count on like these two men could count on each other.

She stood up, walked over to Danny, and kissed him on top of the head. "Goodnight, Danny."

chapter 20

After tossing and turning for most of the night, Taylor Nelson arrived at his office just before 7:30 and began piecing together the events of the previous afternoon. He laid his notes and files on the small conference table, along with the items of clothing found the previous day in the alley behind the hotel.

He picked up the yellow t-shirt and red hat from the top of his desk and held them, thinking about the person who had left them. He suddenly slapped his forehead with an open palm and muttered a string of obscenities to himself. He grabbed the hat and t-shirt and yelled to Hunt, who was pouring a cup of coffee, to come with him.

Nelson drove to the Crowne Plaza and parked in front of the main entrance. He slammed the car into park, threw open his door, and practically ran to the registration desk.

Turning to an attractive young African-American woman whose nametag read Melinda, he flashed his badge. "Hello, Melinda. I'm Lt. Nelson with the State Attorney General's office. Do you remember anyone wearing something like this registering here for a room yesterday?" He held up the t-shirt and hat.

Without hesitation, Melinda spoke up. "Yes. I registered him after lunch yesterday."

"What's his name? And what did he look like. And I want to see the room."

"I'm afraid I don't have the authority to provide that information," she said, a little uncertain but working hard to maintain her even voice.

"Then call your manager," Nelson said softly, but firmly. "You may have a criminal fugitive in the hotel."

She turned to walk back to the office, but the manager was already coming through the office door, having heard Nelson's voice.

"What's wrong? Have you found the man from yesterday?" The manager stood with his hands in front of him and his fingers interlocked.

"He might still be inside the hotel."

The manager spoke in low, controlled tones. "Well, do you have some kind of warrant or something? We can't just go around opening up guests' rooms, you know. Or scaring them."

Nelson leaned over to the man and whispered. "Do you want me to bring in half the department and put uniformed officers with guns on every floor and in the lobby and all over the parking lot? We can certainly do it that way if you like. Would that make your guests feel safer?"

The manager had the young front desk manager lead Nelson and Hunt to the room. As they walked down the dark red carpeted hallway, Nelson took the opportunity to quiz her.

"What else can you remember about this guest?"

Nelson noticed the woman straighten up with pride as she answered. "He was a white man in his late thirties or early forties, with long hair and a ponytail. He wore dark glasses and a cap, so I couldn't tell anything else. He registered as Robert Johnson." She hesitated. "The ponytail didn't look real to me."

"Melinda, will you please walk to the end of the hall and stay back," Nelson said as they neared the door to the room. He and Hunt stood on either side of the door with their backs to the wall. Nelson reached over and knocked loudly three times on the door. "Police. Please open the door. We need to talk to Robert Johnson." He was certain there was no real Robert Johnson, nor did he believe anyone would be in the room, but he was hoping the person using the fake name had made his first mistake.

There was no answer. He knocked again.

"Police, open up!" Still no answer. He inserted the plastic key card.

When the small indicator light blinked green above the door handle, he turned the knob to open the door, still with his back to the wall.

"Police, we're coming in."

When nothing happened, he turned his head left and leaned toward the opening to take a quick look into the room before pulling back behind the wall. He signaled to Hunt and held up three fingers. He counted to three by holding up his fingers one at a time. On three, Hunt lunged through the door, sweeping the room with his Glock. Nelson stepped to the opposite wall and covered the other side of the room at the same time. Holding their guns in front of them with both hands, they quickly searched the closet, under the bed, and inside the bathroom until they were satisfied no one was in the room. They both saw the bed had been slept in, but there was no evidence that anyone had been in the room, other than a towel on the floor just inside the door.

chapter 21

As Tuesday dragged on, Peter grew more and more uncomfortable with the thought of the drugs in the trunk of his car. He kept his office door closed but finished little work. Though he had told his assistant that he was working on the marketing plan for Brickell Boats, when he looked down he realized he had been holding the first draft for several minutes without once looking at the pages.

Late in the morning, Peter sat through a half-hour meeting but rarely spoke. He had to get out of the office and decide what to do next.

He walked into Johnston Baynes's office and sat in one of two side chairs covered in a thick blue and green plaid fabric. He was aware of feeling positioned a little below eye level from John as the chairs forced anyone sitting in them to sit all the way back, something he was certain was no accident on John's part. Nothing was an accident with John, and Peter had learned over the years of John's use of psychology in meetings, such as where people sat and how to gain any little mental edge. He had noted that John always entered meetings a minute late if the purpose was to negotiate some disagreement. John would always place himself directly opposite the most senior person from the client group if it was their meeting, or he would put himself at the head of the table if it was his own meeting just to gain a tiny psychological edge. John was without a doubt the most persuasive man he'd ever known. What Peter knew of negotiating, he had learned from John. Now Peter needed to put that skill to its greatest test.

John removed his glasses and held them in one hand, looking for smudges on the lenses. He raised his eyebrows, which Peter knew was the unspoken but universal office language for the visitor to go ahead and say why he was intruding into someone else's workspace.

"John, I'm taking the rest of the week off unless you have something you need me for. My cousin Danny's here for a couple of days, my work is caught up for everything urgent, and I'm feeling a little burned out. Couple of days off might help," Peter said, trying hard to sound casual and matter-of-fact.

John watched Peter without looking away. Peter saw the worry spread across John's face as his forehead wrinkles deepened while he thought. "Sure, I don't have anything big this week. May need you to sit in on a new business meeting with that start-up cellular company early next week. A few days off might be good for you."

Peter nodded, letting the small dig from John pass. He didn't need a confrontation right now. And he couldn't argue that things had been going well for him at work. "I'll be around the house if anything comes up."

Peter turned and walked to John's office door. He looked back for a moment. He saw John had risen and was staring out the window toward the sidewalk below.

Peter was at the end of the hall when he remembered he needed to tell John he'd sent the Brickell marketing plan. When he walked back to John's office, he heard John on the phone leaving a message, so he stopped before he entered the door. He didn't know what to think when he heard John say, "Mary Beth, it's John. Please call me at work." Peter backed up and walked away before John could see him.

———

Gant sat across a large wooden desk from McNabb in the office at the back of the Best Price. His legs were stretched out in front of him and crossed at the ankles. Cigarette smoke swirled slowly above their heads, each of them with cigarettes resting on the overflowing ashtray in the center of the desk. McNabb had made a pot of strong French Market Coffee, and Gant neared the bottom of his second cup of the thick, black liquid.

"We might have underestimated whoever the hell it is we're dealing with," McNabb said.

"Yeah, but I don't get it. There were cops all over that place," Gant replied before he picked up his cigarette and took a long drag. He leaned his head back and sent a stream of smoke toward the ceiling before he sat up. "But when the cops left, they didn't have anyone with them. Looks like the guy with the coke got away clean."

McNabb nodded. "Had to be more than one. The guy I saw with the ponytail knew the cops were there before they came out of the elevator. He had someone watching. I couldn't tell if they signaled him from somewhere in the parking lot or if he had a radio or phone." McNabb thought for a second with his eyes closed, trying to remember details of the meeting. "Ran without saying anything else. Carried a heavy bag, from the way he held it, so I'm guessing it was my coke."

"How'd the cops know where to go? They were too far behind to be following you, and they were in front of me. If I'd been a few seconds earlier, I'd have been in front of them."

"Two possibilities. Either they're on to these bastards for some reason, or they have my phone or yours tapped. I'm sure he had the drugs in that bag. And by god we're going to get them back. I promise you that." McNabb reached for his cigarette smoldering on the rim of the ashtray.

Gant said nothing, just watched McNabb. He had never seen the man take things so hard. Ever since McNabb had the two street-level dealers killed the year before for selling a few dime rocks made with coke from some other supplier, it was as if he took everything personally. Gant knew it was important to keep personal feelings out of business. Every day he felt more and more like he had to get out, to get away from McNabb before the man made a mistake. McNabb jabbed at Gant with the short butt, emphasizing each word.

"And ... they're ... going ... to pay. What are you hearing on the street from our friends?"

Gant hesitated. He didn't want to get his boss stirred up any more than he was but decided telling him the truth was probably best anyway. "There's no new blow out there. Couple of our regulars have already had to go to old sources. Others are threatening to do the same. Can't really say much until we get back up and running. We need to get our supply going now. It'll be another three weeks before we have the next major shipment ready in Texas, and that'll be too late to keep these guys happy."

"Then let's make this thing happen now. I'm going to get the cash," McNabb said.

Gant sat up in his chair and cocked his head a little to the side. "Didn't think you would ever consider paying them."

"I don't plan to let them keep one damn cent. But they may be a little smarter than we thought, so we should have the money there next time. If we have to show the cash to make the deal, then we will. We'll worry about getting it back after we get the coke in our hands. Get two more men you can trust and have them ready to move fast. I'm working on a plan."

"What else do you need me to do?"

"First, we need to get a new message in the newspaper to set up a second meeting. Then get your men to buy four of those prepaid cell phones under phony names. We can't risk using our car phones again."

"I've got someone for that, William. But what makes you think they'll see the message or even want to talk again?"

"If I've learned one thing, it's how greedy people can get when they smell money. And there's something about nose candy that just makes people crazy."

McNabb crushed the small amount left of his cigarette in the ashtray and leaned back in his chair.

Gant sipped his coffee. He crossed his legs and noticed dust on his boots. He removed a white cotton handkerchief from his back pocket and wiped each boot, carefully polishing the toes to a glossy sheen. He watched quietly as McNabb leaned back in his desk chair and stared up at the ceiling. He knew the man was smart and usually worked out good plans that kept their risk low, but something about this situation had gotten to McNabb. He wasn't making good business decisions. Gant was now positive he should make some plans of his own. Something didn't feel right. He knew he'd made the right decision not to let McNabb's ego put him at unnecessary risk.

chapter 22

Peter looked at the clock above the kitchen sink. 12:15 a.m. He and Mary Beth had been sitting at the table since eight, after a dinner of steamed cabbage and smoked sausage smothered with Durkee's Sauce. They had been talking about better ways to contact McNabb next time. The dishes were piled in the sink where they'd rinsed and left them. The radio was tuned to the Jackson State University station, featuring a show on jazz classics. Dave Brubeck's "Take Five" provided background for the conversation.

"Can you be certain that McNabb isn't working with the police?" Mary Beth asked.

"I feel sure he's not, but I know we can't trust him." Peter leaned over the table on both elbows. "So how do we know when to go through with the deal? We have to make the next exchange foolproof."

"Just don't let him be in control of anything." Mary Beth reached back to pull the hair band off her ponytail and shook her hair down around her shoulders.

"I know that. But you know he'll try something. It's not like this is a lost diamond heirloom and we're getting a reward for finding the damn thing."

"That's not what I meant. You don't have to be difficult, Peter. I'm on your side, remember," Mary Beth snapped back. She crossed her arms over her chest as she turned sideways in the chair and propped her feet on the chair beside her. "I just meant you set up the swap where all he has to do is hand over the money and we hand over the drugs. Keep things simple."

Peter regretted being short with Mary Beth and tried to soften his tone, but like every conversation he'd had with her since leaving the Crowne Plaza, he always said something he regretted. "I'm sorry. I'm just nervous and tired. You're right. We just need to have a good plan where McNabb has no options and the police have no chance to get involved."

Mary Beth brushed the hair back from her eyes and rubbed the back of her neck. She didn't reply right away or look at Peter. He had noticed years before that when he said something hurtful to her she would often pause to let him realize what he had done rather than point it out. Then she'd change the subject.

"Right, we know now that both the police and McNabb are trying to find us. We have to stay so hidden that even if the police see us they won't be able to figure out who we are."

"Need to watch McNabb's house and business a little more and see if there's anything else we can learn about his habits." He stood and picked up her empty glass. He placed their drink glasses in the dishwasher and quickly loaded the other dishes from the sink. "I'm ready for bed if you are." He checked to be certain the back door was locked as Mary Beth walked to the bath to get ready for bed. While she was out of the bedroom, he removed his .380 from his pocket and slid the gun under the mattress on his side. He didn't want her to know he'd started carrying it everywhere.

Lying still under the covers, Peter noticed that Mary Beth wasn't breathing the deep, slow breaths he had loved ever since she had begun sleeping over at his apartment a year before they married. He knew she was awake, but he said nothing. All he could think about was what if she had been caught or hurt? Could he live with himself if his schemes got her in trouble with the law, or worse, got her injured or killed? Twice he started to say let's call it off, but something kept him from speaking.

He knew Mary Beth might be racing ahead with a plan in her mind. He admired her way of concentrating so hard that she shut out virtually everything. He knew she wasn't used to failing, having achieved so much academically, socially, and in sports all through high school and college.

He felt better as he thought of how methodical she could be once she set a goal for herself, like when she gave up a hard-won starting slot in tennis at Rhodes after her junior year to focus on her studies. She'd wanted to spend a semester of her senior year at the London School of Economics as part of the college's Study Abroad Program, and being on the tennis team would interfere.

It was that semester in London when they met. He had spotted her on just her second day there. She was standing in front of the library, trying to figure out how to read a map for the Underground. He had fallen in love with her before midnight. He was in the same program to study international marketing while she studied management. For the next six weeks, they were rarely apart and continued dating throughout the following spring semester. One or the other made the long drive between Memphis and Birmingham at least twice a month until they married on a hot afternoon in August just after graduation.

When Peter woke the next morning, the room was filled with bright sunlight and the smell of fresh coffee brewing. He rolled over to see the clock. It was a little after seven. He remembered that the lighted digits on the clock had shown 2:54 a.m the last time he had looked before drifting off. He pulled the covers down to his waist and yawned, wishing he could stay in bed for another hour. Sleep had been scarce in recent days.

Mary Beth was up. He slid on a pair of jeans and a sweatshirt. He could hear the shower running as he went down to look for the newspaper. Somehow the situation seemed brighter in the stillness of the morning, but he knew better. He decided that Mary Beth was smart enough to make him be careful. If they were in too much danger, she'd tell him to back off. He wasn't going to the office, so he had time to be patient. He'd wait until she brought up the subject to continue last night's discussion of what to do next. With that thought he put the night's fear behind him as he walked to the end of the driveway. He had a slight smile of resolution on his face, as if he knew something others didn't know. Although the temperature was still hot during the day, the morning breeze was cooler than he expected. Summer was fading into Fall.

———

Peter drove to the Amoco station near Northpark Mall. Using one of the pre-paid phone cards he'd bought at the new I-20 Truck Stop in Pearl the day before, he called Danny to let him know to come back at the beginning of the week. While Cindy got the kids dressed, he kept Danny on the phone half an hour explaining what Mary Beth and he had planned. The conversation was difficult as both avoided talking directly about drugs or the names of specific people. They agreed that Juice wouldn't be needed.

Peter drove the four blocks home and told Mary Beth he was heading out to pick up the drugs in case something happened and they needed more fast.

"You can't keep the drugs here, Peter. If someone figures out who you are, the last thing we need is for them to find that much illegal substance in our garage."

"No, not here. We just need a small amount here. But the rest of those bags need to be somewhere closer than where they are now. And besides, we can't keep on driving out to the same site over and over. Sooner or later, we will be spotted, and someone will get curious."

At the last minute, she decided to go along.

Thirty minutes later they were in north Madison County. When the pavement turned to red dirt, he slowed down to forty. The road narrowed and sloped toward a ditch on either side. The tires hissed on the damp soil.

When he arrived at Vernon Frank's pine farm, he stopped the car a short distance into the property. Getting out, Peter handed Mary Beth a pair of the surgical gloves and put on a pair himself as he set off toward where the drugs were buried. Five minutes later the toolbox was open on the ground beside the hole. He was happy to see that a heavy rain shower a couple of days before had no impact, and the inside of the tool kit was completely dry. Mary Beth groaned and rolled her eyes when Peter opened the box and looked up to say, "It's powder dry in the box." They were back in the Cherokee in less than ten minutes with the entire stash of drugs.

While Peter lifted up the back seat, Mary Beth put the toolbox in an opening under the seat frame and pushed the seat back down. He grabbed a couple of empty Coke cans, an old newspaper, and a sweat-stained Jackson Senators baseball cap and scattered them across the seat. The car looked its usual mess. He took both sets of gloves and stuck them inside a McDonald's bag from the back floorboard. He wadded up the bag and left it on the front seat to throw away at the first gas station he passed.

Peter headed toward the farm in Pelahatchie where he had kept a duck-hunting boat parked behind a barn that belonged to a friend at what had once been the friend's family home. The place was only seven or eight minutes from where Peter and Mary Beth lived, and no one was likely to be around. The farmhouse had been vacant since the parents moved into town several years before, and the barn was used mostly to store old furniture and rusty farm implements.

chapter 23

Mary Beth kept her door closed most of the day, telling everyone in the office she had a headache. No one bothered her. One week had passed since their attempted exchange with McNabb. The headache was real.

From a bottom drawer, she pulled a file of newspaper clippings on McNabb. She had copied everything she could find in her research at the public library archives. She again read through the stories of various drug busts from years before that suggested any tie to McNabb or his stores. Using a yellow marker, she highlighted all the names that appeared. Roy Gant was most often mentioned, other than McNabb who was never part of any drug bust but was usually identified as the owner of the liquor stores. Satisfied there was nothing new to learn, she placed the clippings back into the manila folder and stared across her desk. Work no longer seemed important, and writing reports of obscure legislators' voting patterns were of no interest.

She opened her email inbox and read down the list of senders, deleting several she knew were unimportant. She answered two from association members, urgent requests for information on tax legislation being considered for the next legislative session. She closed the email window and leaned back in her chair.

She noticed the 5x7 photo of Peter and her in a blue and green porcelain frame with glazed tropical fish jumping around the edges. She picked up the frame and thought back to the day the photo had been taken at Cedar Key. Mary Beth and Peter had rented a canoe and paddled out to a neighboring island. They had been thrilled to find Native American potsherds not far from the beach, and Peter had grinned like a kid as he used his fly rod to cast for small fish.

They had climbed through the tangled undergrowth of the island and felt like they had discovered the remains of a hidden civilization. She still had three bags of potsherds and shells from the trip, including several pieces of clay with intricate designs she sometimes ran her fingers across to imagine the young Indian girl who had carefully sculpted the patterns five hundred years before. When they had returned the rental canoe, Mary Beth handed her camera to the teenager in charge and showed him how to snap the shot. Peter and Mary Beth were pink from the sun, and their shorts and tee shirts were wet from paddling. Peter had his left arm around her. With his right hand he held up a small fish he had caught in the surf.

Thoughts of that trip filled with laughter and moments of shared delight had become her touchstone. Such memories made the feelings she and Peter once held for each other fresh in her mind. She wanted to get those feelings back. After the botched exchange in the parking garage, they had returned to a bitter pattern of stinging comments, but at least she and Peter were talking again. She spun her chair around and pulled up to her desk, taking out a pad and pen. Time to become more involved in Peter's weird scheme.

———

Although neither his heart nor his mind was in it, Peter had no choice but to attend the regular Monday production meeting at B&P for Financial Software Services. At least his energy level was up, probably from the two-mile run he'd managed to squeeze in that morning. Financial Software was a small client but one that paid on time and let the ad agency have a fairly free hand with the creative. He always paid special attention to the work of clients who trusted the agency to do its job. Peter mostly listened as the traffic manager flipped through job after job, explaining which ads were on deadline and which might need an extension. Peter said little and simply nodded most of the time. He was pouring his third cup of coffee and had his back to the group seated at the conference table when he realized his name was being called.

"Peter? Earth to Peter," the traffic manager said.

Peter turned quickly and looked at the woman calling his name. "Oh, yeah, sorry. I was just thinking about something. What did you ask?" He felt his face flush to the hushed laughter around the table.

"We need to know the size of that booth for the winter conference. Did you get an answer from the client yet? Last year the space was twenty by thirty, but we wanted to go twenty by forty this year if they will. Did they call back?"

Peter weighed his answer. He realized he should have called, but he had forgotten. "I'm still waiting on a call-back. I'll call again after the meeting and see what's holding them up. I'll get you an answer today."

Peter scanned the faces of everyone at the table, trying to read them, to gauge if they believed him. He could see that most sensed he'd not done his job, though certainly no one would publicly challenge him. He felt bad for letting down his team. He'd get his work done today, even though his thoughts were focused elsewhere.

Since the two major industry conferences were scheduled for January and February, they were nearing a critical sales period for FSS. Ad deadlines were late November. Normally, he would have been nervous and had dozens of questions and requests to his staff to work harder to get layouts to the client earlier. Today it struck him that most of this activity could go on just fine without him. Anyone could have made that call to the client, but Peter had always tried to put himself at the center of such relationships. Now it seemed silly and unimportant. The one thought he would keep from today was that the agency's work could go on without him.

Peter arrived home shortly before six, finding Mary Beth changing from work clothes to jeans and a t-shirt. After he changed out of his suit, they sat at the kitchen table and sorted through the mail. He made drinks of bourbon and Pepsi, which they sipped silently as they straightened the table to make room for dinner.

They finished a quick meal of chicken salad sandwiches on wheat that Peter had picked up from the New York Deli on the way home. He cleared the table while she rinsed the plates and placed them in the already half-filled dishwasher with yesterday's plates and glasses inside. Peter watched Mary Beth open her purse and remove a single sheet of paper, covered with hand-written notes. Just an ordinary evening in an ordinary household.

"I spent lunch thinking of what you said about preparing for the worst that might happen. I made a list of things that could happen and what we might do the next time." Mary Beth handed the paper to him. Nothing was ordinary or normal these days.

He read the notes as he walked into the den and sat on the couch, taking what was left of his drink with him. He switched on the table lamp and finished reading the list. He smiled. Mary Beth was good at contingency planning. She had used a problem-solving technique he often used for client marketing, which was to build scenarios of what could go wrong and then develop solutions.

Mary Beth sat patiently, arms folded in front of her. He sensed something different in her attitude from the fact that she had spent so much time working on something she had expressed her doubts about just a few days before.

His eyes went back to the top of the list:

PROBLEM: At the hand-off M tries to steal the package. Maybe even tries to kill us.

ANSWER: Meet in a place where you can let them know someone is watching with a gun pointed at them. Meeting place has only one easy way in (we can watch who comes near), but there are multiple ways out. Set up a way out that will be hard to follow if we have to run. Don't give M time to set up an ambush.

PROBLEM: Police follow M to hand-off
ANSWER: Cover the entrances and use the radios. Run if anything looks wrong. Set up a diversion to make it look like you ran one way, but go the other way. Meet in a place you would normally go anyway, so if the police stop you, you have a reason to be there.

PROBLEM: M realizes it's not the real merchandise.
ANSWER: Make the packages look exactly like the real thing. Take a real package or two on top in case he opens it.

Peter was surprised to see that Mary Beth's first scenario had included a gun. She had been so opposed to Peter taking a gun the first time, finally agreeing that it would be all right for Danny to cover Peter using his rifle. "Are you sure about the gun? You were uncomfortable about using one before."

She pressed her lips tightly together and nodded slowly. "If we're going to try again, I'm not going to let some drug dealer kill us."

Her cold look startled Peter. He wondered if he had tapped into a side of her he never knew, and he wasn't sure if a calculating, cold side of her was something he liked. He knew they needed a gun, but he had expected to be the one to argue they needed real protection.

For the next three hours, they went over every idea they could think of that met all the conditions Mary Beth had described. Malls and shopping centers had too many entrances to watch. And too many people. The mall parking lots covered too much area to watch. Office buildings would be too hard to get out of without being seen. Remote places in the country might work, but they wanted a location more public for safety—and they needed pay phones nearby.

The hotel parking deck at the downtown Crowne Plaza had been a good location but wouldn't work again. After another hour planning how they might watch entrances, what they should wear as disguises, and how they might get away, both were ready for sleep.

They agreed Peter would scout small parking lots and old buildings the next day on his way to work. After Danny arrived in the evening, they'd finish the plan and contact McNabb again.

chapter 24

Roy Gant sat calmly with the engine of his Cadillac running to keep the air conditioning on high as he watched Harry Ramsey walk out of the Jackson Police Department central lock-up after his bail had been posted by someone Gant had paid. He saw Ramsey pause to look up at the clear blue sky. The fresh air and sunshine must have felt good after living with the faint urine smell common to every jail cell. A smell Gant was too familiar with. He blew his car horn, and Ramsey walked the two blocks to where Gant waited.

Without exchanging pleasantries, Gant spoke first. "How much do they know?" He pulled out into traffic and didn't look at Ramsey as he drove down South State Street. The traffic was light, and the car managed to catch several traffic lights green.

"I don't think they know much, but I think you have a problem in Texas. They asked me about names from Texas I never heard of." Ramsey ran his fingers through his long, greasy hair to push some loose strands back from his face. "Don't worry. You know I didn't tell them a damn thing. Nothing."

Gant thought about what the man had said, wondering if Ramsey was really the leak that had tipped off the police or if there was a problem with the supply chain in Texas. "McNabb wants to talk with us."

"Why me? I don't know nothing."

"He just wants us to figure out where the leak came from. Maybe you can help. He's meeting us at the barn."

Ramsey had been with Gant to the farm five miles outside Byram once before to meet with McNabb. After a fifteen-minute drive, Gant pulled his Cadillac up to a gate and handed Ramsey the key. "McNabb must not be here. Open the gate, will you? And close it behind us. No need to lock it, he'll be here soon."

The heavy car's tires spun, and the rear end fishtailed slightly in the soft mud as they went down the rutted road. A sudden shower had turned the dirt road to muck.

Gant drove his car inside a huge barn with unpainted wood sides faded to gray and shut down the Cadillac's engine. The barn was empty except for a John Deere tractor with a front-end loader and backhoe attached, parked halfway inside the opening at the far end of the barn. He hoped Ramsey hadn't noticed the slight steam rising from the still-hot tractor engine as rain splashed onto the engine from the roof drip-line.

Gant liked the location that was a quick drive from downtown yet isolated from Jackson's urban sprawl. Densely wooded stretches of hardwood trees bordered the farm on both sides for several miles. They could bring three cars inside the barn and be out-of-sight from the road. The barn was surrounded by a twenty-five acre hay field cut low to the ground. No one could approach without first being seen.

The two men got out of the car and walked toward a picnic table sitting directly beneath the hayloft. Neither said anything.

Ramsey sat on the weathered pine bench of the table, his legs stretched out in front of him. Gant put one foot up on the bench and casually leaned over with an elbow resting on his knee. A faint car noise could be heard on the highway. When Ramsey leaned back and looked away toward the front gate to see if it was McNabb, Gant quietly slid his .25 automatic from his boot and pointed the small pistol at the back of Ramsey's head. He eased the hammer back with his thumb, trying to silence the hammer as it locked in place.

Ramsey heard the tiny click and dove forward just as the gun exploded behind his head. His movement caused the small caliber bullet to graze his skull instead of leaving its deadly energy deep in his brain. Still, the bullet managed to open a two-inch wound across the top of Ramsey's head, and he fell face forward onto the soggy ground.

Ramsey was still conscious. He rolled over onto his side and rose halfway, propped on his right arm. A mixture of horse manure and dirt caked the side of his face. He reached his left arm toward Gant in a feeble effort to protect himself. He mouthed the word, "Why?" as he looked into Gant's eyes.

Gant's lips were pressed tightly together. He moved his head slightly from side to side as he pointed the gun at Ramsey's heart and squeezed off three rounds. The arm went limp as the man fell back and was still. Gant leaned over and put two more rounds into the side of Ramsey's head just above his ear. Satisfied, he reached in his pocket to feel for the tractor key.

Mary Beth spooned eight heaping teaspoons of French Market coffee into the brown paper filter of the Mr. Coffee. She liked the first cup of the morning to be strong.

As she stood at the kitchen window and waited for the coffee to finish, the sun turned from soft orange behind the thick pines to a harsh, near-white light. The rays filled the pale blue kitchen with a contrast of bright spots and hard-edged shadows. She walked to the front yard and found the morning newspaper under an azalea bush near the driveway. She removed the rubber band and stuffed it into her pocket.

She stood at the breakfast table, flipping through the newspaper, looking only at headlines. The city council continued its circus. City business had halted when four members walked out on Tuesday's meeting. Councilman Simpson vowed to amend every motion and stop all council business until action was taken on his motion, which was to pass a resolution that the mayor's declaration of a midnight curfew was racist. Mary Beth had long ago given up hope that the political polarization of Jackson would change, but reading about it in the paper still made her sad.

As she scanned the pages, she thought about McNabb. On a hunch, she quickly turned to the classified section and read down the Personals. There it was.

"Peter. It's McNabb," Mary Beth yelled from the kitchen. "He didn't even wait for us to contact him again."

Peter had finished his shower and was pulling on a pair of jeans when she ran into the bedroom. She held out the newspaper and pointed to an item near the bottom of the page.

SWM, 45, SEEKS SWF, 35-50. REDHEADS ONLY. I'M STILL INTERESTED. WOULD LOVE TO SEE YOU AGAIN SOON.

They walked into the kitchen where Danny stood pouring a cup of coffee. Peter handed him the paper. Mary Beth thought Peter was too quiet. He said nothing as he walked to the table and stood waiting for Danny.

After Danny read the ad, he said, "Okay, the moment of truth is here faster than we planned. You guys really up for another try?"

Mary Beth realized that all three seemed somehow braver after getting away from a close call the first time. All were ready to try again, though Peter had only nodded when she asked him. He seemed distracted and withdrawn.

They made a list of things they needed. Mary Beth called in to work and left a message on the overnight answering machine that a family emergency had come up and she would be out for a couple of days. The emergency wasn't life threatening, she said on her message, so no one should worry.

Taylor Nelson smelled the faint, sickly sweet stench of sewage as he walked down the sidewalk for an early lunch. The stink was gone in a moment as a breeze kicked up from the other direction, replacing the odor with the smell of fresh asphalt and auto exhaust. A moment later the delicious aroma of freshly baked bread filled his head. Car doors slammed all around him, and he heard a car horn a block away. He knew others thought of such sensations as pollution and noise, but to him they were smells and sounds of activity and excitement.

Having grown up in a small town of less than twenty-five hundred people, he felt like Jackson was a real city even if the people who moved there from Washington, Dallas, or Atlanta laughed about Jackson's slow pace and small size. He loved walking its streets at lunchtime, seeing busy people hustling back to their offices, watching the red-cheeked young faces so plentiful in a capitol city.

He met up with Sleepy Hunt, and the two walked through the front doors of Keifer's Deli. Both men ordered the special, a hamburger with curly fries, and sweet tea. They took their trays and sat outside at a small plastic table with a large umbrella partially shielding them from the mid-day sun. The other two outside tables were empty, though one was covered with two trays and an assortment of wadded napkins, sandwich paper, and empty paper cups.

Nelson took a big bite of his hamburger and washed it down with tea. "Joe said McNabb and Gant haven't used their cell phones since the deal at the parking lot. Must have figured out how we followed them."

"Yeah, I checked a little while ago," Hunt said. "Still nothing. And they had been using them several times a day, right up until things went crazy at the Crowne Plaza."

"Let's step up the surveillance. We can't rely on the phones now, even if we can get the tap on McNabb's liquor store telephone. Set up a rotation on Meadowbrook Road. McNabb always leaves his neighborhood using Meadowbrook. Let's pick him up there. And get someone back on Gant. If they plan to do another deal, they'll do it soon."

Nelson looked at his watch and realized he had half an hour left. He

pulled a short Baccarat cigar from his pocket. "A perfect half hour smoke."
He held the fat five-inch cigar up to his nose to smell the spicy aroma.
"And mild enough for day time. Something's about to happen for us in
this case, so I'll just consider this smoke an early celebration."

As if on cue, a breeze lifted the napkins and sandwich paper on the table
next to him and sent them fluttering down the red-brick sidewalk like
oversized confetti.

chapter 25

Danny slid his hands under a large cardboard box with Georgia-Pacific's blue logo printed on the side. The box was filled with ropes, pulleys, eye bolts, and assorted tools Peter had gathered and tossed into the box that morning. Danny removed the box from the back of the Jeep and placed it on the back seat of the Ford he and Peter had purchased for nine hundred and fifty dollars in cash earlier that day after finding it in the classified car ads. They'd also paid someone cash for a Dodge sedan in good running condition and parked it behind an office building not far from Peter and Mary Beth's house.

Fifteen minutes later the two were downtown. As Peter drove them past the empty Marx Building, he said, "This used to be a thriving part of downtown. Lots of lawyers, accountants, and small businesses were around here. When I saw the building yesterday, I knew this was the spot."

He circled the block before parking in a narrow alley behind the office building and out of sight of any car passing down the street. An empty furniture store's back doors opened into the alley opposite those of the Marx Building.

Danny removed heavy bolt cutters from the box of tools and walked to the large metal back doors of the former furniture store. The afternoon sun was still high enough to scorch the alley, and Danny felt the stored heat rising from the concrete loading platform as he stepped up on it. After a quick last look around, he placed the sharp edge of the cutters on the chain that ran through the door handles. Squeezing as hard as he could on the long handles of the tool, the link split in two with a loud snap. He replaced the link with a well-used, weathered lock from the box of items he'd brought.

When Danny saw Peter struggling to open the door of the Marx Building, he walked across the alley, pressed the tip of a small pocketknife blade into the bolt, and slid the bolt back a fraction of an inch. The gray metal door swung open immediately.

"Wasted childhood," Peter said, pushing past Danny into the deserted hallway.

"If tomorrow goes right, I'd say it wasn't so damn wasted, you butthole."

Both men laughed quietly as they searched down the dark hallway for stairs. The building was well kept, without the usual assortment of cardboard boxes, old desks, and broken glass that characterized vacant downtown buildings.

They found a room just off the corner overlooking the alley. They could see a window from the furniture store almost directly across from where they stood.

Danny sorted through the box, removing a pulley, a roll of duct tape, and a large self-threading eyehook. He walked back downstairs and crossed the alley to the furniture store where he let himself in using his key on the lock he'd added to the chain. Once inside, he immediately noticed the acidic smell of urine and realized that homeless men or crack heads had already found some other way inside. He saw signs of recent human activity, including several Pabst Blue Ribbon cans and the rags of a makeshift sleeping bag. Every few steps, he placed a strip of duct tape on the floor, marking his route up the stairs.

Danny found the room three floors up, opened the window, and saw Peter across from him. While the windows weren't exactly at the same level, the drop from the Marx Building to the furniture store was only a few inches. The building still held heat from the late summer weather, and sweat ran down his spine, wetting his shirt in places.

Peter leaned forward with his hands on the windowsill and grinned. "We can do this. I know you thought it was silly, but what do you think now?"

"You're right. I do think it does look kind of … let's just say theatrical. But it could work."

Within five minutes they had rigged a pulley between the two windows.

"We need to get out of here," Peter said across the alley as he threw tools back into the box. "We've got to get ready to move the boat down the river tonight."

———

Glancing at the freshly painted directory sign by the front steps of the four-story red brick building, Gant noticed that the tenants of the Shelton Road Building were mostly attorneys and financial consultants, a term that to him simply meant insurance and mutual fund peddlers. He followed McNabb inside through ten-foot-tall glass double doors.

They walked to the elevator through a bright lobby of gleaming white marble, decorated with a single seven-foot plastic palm tree. McNabb's accountant kept one small office on the third floor. The wiry old man's only clients happened to be the string of liquor stores, convenience stores, and pawnshops owned by McNabb. Or owned by companies that were owned by companies that were owned by McNabb.

Gant was a step behind McNabb as they reached the door at the end of the third-floor hallway. A small black sign with white block letters read Winkler & Assoc., LLC. McNabb tried to turn the handle, but the door was locked. He knocked, and Gant heard Winkler's voice, "Yes?"

"It's me. Open up," McNabb answered.

Winkler opened the door just enough to see who stood there, and when he saw it was McNabb, he opened it all the way. McNabb walked past him through a cloud of cigarette smoke, waving his hand in front of his face. Winkler looked at Gant and motioned him inside. Then Winkler took a quick look down the hall before closing the door and turning the handle on a huge dead bolt.

McNabb sat in one of two well-worn red leather Queen Anne side chairs that faced a large oak desk, the leather seats and arms showing thousands of tiny cracks from sitting years in a dry office with no care. Gant walked to a window and stood waiting, saying nothing, casually looking outside toward the parking lot.

"Did you get it all?" McNabb asked.

"Well, why the hell do you think I had this place locked up like Fort Knox?" Winkler asked, the use of expression in his voice costing him a sudden dry, hacked cough. "Of course I got it."

Gant snickered to himself. Winkler was the only one who talked to McNabb like that and got away with it.

Gant looked around the room to see if he could spot the reason for so much smoke. A large clear glass ashtray sat on Winkler's desk with cigarette butts piled to overflowing, one still smoldering. He stepped over to the desk and crushed the butt with his thumb.

Winkler walked to a small closet with a metal door and a security lock with a numbered keypad. He punched in four numbers and removed a large burnished leather briefcase from beneath a stack of files.

"It's all there," Winkler said as he placed the open briefcase on a chair in front of McNabb. "It wasn't easy to get, either. You need to get this money back to me as soon as you can. Absolutely within a week. If not, it'll cost you a lot more than you want to know."

McNabb reached in and grabbed a stack of hundred dollar bills neatly bundled with a strip of paper. Gant noted that the bills weren't new.

McNabb smiled. He held the bundle in his left hand and fanned through the bills with the thumb of his right hand. Gant had seen before how money always seemed to fascinate McNabb and make him seem almost giddy. Especially untraceable used bills.

Tossing the money back into the briefcase, McNabb sounded light-hearted as he spoke to Winkler. Too light-hearted, Gant thought.

"Oh, I'll get it back soon. You can bet the farm on it."

Someone already did, Gant thought as he followed McNabb to his car. Gant left in his own car to spend some time at the office in back of the Best Price, lining up a couple of men to be ready when he got McNabb's call.

━━━━

Peter parked his car and trailer behind the Jackson Academy baseball field and unloaded his Kawasaki Mule. He'd purchased the off-road utility vehicle with bonus money two years before as a reward to himself for a good year. He looked at his watch. The sun was down, and it would be dark in fifteen minutes. He drove the Mule slowly and without lights until he was far past the row of large, brick homes that backed up to the thick woods bordering the Pearl River. The dirt road was once used to reach the city's old waterworks near the river. In less than five minutes, he was bumping along another rutted road that meandered along the riverbank where he had last seen a small fishing boat that someone kept there.

He parked when the road curved away from the river, taking the last fifty yards on foot through the tall oaks and sweetgum trees. He found the metal boat leaned against a large oak tree at the top of a steep clay bank that had been crumbling a few feet at a time for years and tumbling into the river. Twisted tree roots faced the sky, and long trunks disappeared under the water's surface from where the river had undercut tree after tree.

He could feel the sweat on his back as he flipped the boat over and eased the bow into the water between two tree trunks. Using an old yellow nylon rope hanging from the eyebolt on the bow, he tied the boat to a large exposed root. He retrieved the small outboard motor and gas tank from the bed of the Mule and hooked them up.

He found a thick growth of honeysuckle covering the top of a large oak tree that had fallen, and he steered the utility vehicle into the middle of a lush tangle of vines, making a path that seemed to close up behind him.

Someone would have to be looking carefully to discover the Mule here. He grabbed a large flashlight from the seat.

Peter pushed the boat adrift as he stepped onto the front seat and climbed to the back. After three pulls the engine fired. He switched on the spotlight, gunned the engine, and turned the nose of the boat down river. A chill made him realize his shirt was soaked through.

Peter shined his light ahead to check for floating logs that could flip the small boat. He saw a set of large reddish-orange eyes glowing along the edge of the river. Gator, a big one. He slowed the boat as he went past to take a good look and saw the creature near a sandbar, only its eyes and the ridges along its tail sticking up from the water in the shallows. The gator was at least ten feet long. Before he reached the Lakeland Drive Bridge a mile downstream, he saw three more alligators.

He recognized a steep clay bank on his left and thought of the two times he'd been there to run trotlines, catching lots of catfish, including one that weighed more than ten pounds. He trailed his hand in the water and was surprised at how warm the river was. The thought made him wish he had taken the time that summer to set out lines.

When Peter arrived at Woodrow Wilson Bridge twenty minutes later, Danny and Mary Beth were waiting. They tied the boat to a piling beneath the bridge and drove toward a pay phone they had picked out earlier. Everything was ready for the next meeting with McNabb.

Taylor Nelson sat on his couch holding a Diet Coke as he scribbled a few thoughts onto the back of a blue junk mail envelope he hadn't opened. It helped him to write down the facts and look at them as a group. The local news had gone off an hour before, so he had the television on CNN, but he wasn't paying attention. He was trying to piece together what his team knew about McNabb's activities lately. Something wasn't making sense, so he wanted to go step-by-step and figure out what they were missing.

From their tap using the cell phone clone and what Joe had overheard, Nelson knew that someone was trying to make a deal with McNabb. He wrote:

– attempted deal

– in public place

– obvious disguise

– no drugs on street

– no backup for McNabb?? (Not like him!)

– we've been seen, they know we're watching

– how are they communicating?????

– only an amateur would set up the deal in a parking lot

– no drugs on street means what? (he's not a dealer!)

– why no backup for McNabb?

– deal happen too fast for McNabb? (did we just miss them?)

– McNabb will be ready this time.

– drug supply on the street seems low.

– next deal will happen soon.

Nelson underlined *soon* three times and sat back on the couch. It wasn't the first time he'd been close to catching men doing big deals, and if he didn't make something happen soon, he might find out too late that the deal was done. He flipped open the Yellow Pages, picked up his phone, and dialed the Best Price Liquor store.

"Best Price, can I help you?"

"Yeah, uh, Joe Graham is my cousin, and I just came in from Natchez, and he said to call him here if I was ever in town."

"Yeah fine, just a minute. What's your name?"

"Just tell him it's his cousin Gene," Nelson said, using their pre-arranged code name. Nelson held the phone for nearly a minute until he heard someone pick up.

"What's up, Gene? You in town?"

In case anyone else was listening on another extension Nelson chose his words carefully. "Hey man, it's me. Listen, I'm in town working for a couple of days, so I thought I'd call. Want to get a beer after work?"

"Sure, that'd be fine. How about we meet at The Cherokee a little after nine? I get off by then if it's not too busy here."

"Great. Listen, you know that other friend of mine I've been trying to catch up with?" As he spoke, Nelson circled the words "McNabb will be ready this time" over and over on the paper in front of him.

"Yeah."

"He must have changed his phone number or something. I can't get up with him. If you see any of his friends, would you let me know? I know some of them shop there. I think he's about to move, and I need to find him first."

"One guy he hangs around with was in here earlier tonight. I'll let you know if I see anyone else and can find out what he's up to these days."

"Great. Look, I'll see you after work."

chapter 26

With his plain-toe, solid black cowboy boots propped on the gray metal desk in McNabb's office, Roy Gant waited alone for a call back from one of his men. He was enjoying the only art he owned, the fine stitching that outlined a large cactus on the side of his boots. Never one for fancy clothes, he did consider himself a connoisseur of cowboy boots. And he knew price wasn't always the best way to judge a good pair of boots. One of his favorite pairs only cost fifty-five dollars in Mexico, but they were handmade and fit like a second skin. While his Dan Posts were certainly not the most luxurious, he always favored them for everyday wear over his Tony Llamas.

He preferred sensible boots. Plain toe, though he did like nice stitching. One solid color. No fancy decorations, except his special-occasion Tony Llamas with lizard skin toes and a silver accent tip. He knew his friends in Texas called them Gringo boots, but he still preferred them for special occasions.

The cell phone on the desk in front of him rang.

"Gant."

"We're set," the voice said, not bothering with any polite formalities. "These phones will be on. I just want to make sure we understand one thing. We need to be very clear on our instructions."

"Yeah?"

"We're to finish this matter completely. Those are our instructions? And a dime bonus if we leave no loose ends?"

"Absolutely. No loose ends. And immediate payment. I'll call soon," Gant said as he hung up.

He checked his watch. McNabb had told him it wouldn't be long now.

He'd decided to wait until at least nine to make his nightly trip to the bar in case McNabb called again, but he was more than ready for a beer. This time they would all be prepared, and his two top guys knew not to get drunk until the job was over.

———

Peter and Mary Beth sat in the front seat of the Jeep with Danny in the back. They parked in front of the single pay phone in the lot of the BP station on the frontage road just down from the Northside Drive exit and watched to see if anyone was paying any attention.

"Pay phones are about gone," Danny said.

"Yeah," Peter said. "Everybody will have a cell phone soon, and they'll go away like clip-on ties."

Mary Beth said, "Like TV dinners and Harvest Gold appliances."

Danny said, "Like rabbit ears and dickies."

"Okay, okay," Peter said, not really irritated. "Can we just focus on what we're doing?"

Mary Beth and Danny laughed.

The pay phone hung on the side of the store and couldn't be seen easily by the clerk inside. So many cars pulled up in a day no clerk would remember any one particular person using the pay phone anyway. The store bustled with customers, and every gas pump had a car in front. No one would pay Peter any attention.

"I'm calling," Peter said as he put on a baseball cap and stepped from the car. He dialed McNabb's home number. McNabb answered on the third ring.

"Hello."

"You said you want to talk. Do you know who this is?"

After a hesitation, McNabb spoke, "Yeah, I know. I don't want to talk this way."

"I'll call you at the same place as before in ten minutes. You're late, it's over. You're followed, it's over."

"I'll be there."

Peter put the phone down gently even before McNabb could hang up. He drove three blocks to another pay phone at the end of a small retail strip of stores to wait the ten minutes for McNabb.

Gant's new cell phone rang. He read McNabb's number on the little blue screen. "Yeah."

"They called. Everything set?"

"Since half an hour ago. Everything's in place." Gant grabbed his pistol from the top of the desk and slid the weapon into his belt.

"I've got to get to the same phone fast, but I need to make damn sure I'm not being followed. I'll drive to Nick's and go in like I'm having dinner. Meet me in the alley. Now."

Less than five minutes later, Gant parked in the dark alley behind Nick's and waited with the motor running. The back door had a large red sign on the handle, indicating an alarm would sound if opened, but the door stayed propped open most of the time so waitresses and busboys could go outside to smoke cigarettes. McNabb walked out the door, into the alley, and got into the car.

"Get to the Amoco Station on Northside Drive. You only have a couple of minutes."

Good thing it's only two miles, Gant thought. Nothing like cutting it close.

Jordan Hunt was staking out McNabb's house. He called Nelson at home when McNabb left alone and drove to a nearby restaurant. "You said call if he moved. He's inside Nick's. I'm not sure what's going on."

"Did he meet anyone?" Nelson asked.

"Not outside, but I haven't gone in. It's a small place, and he might see me. It doesn't seem like anything much, but who knows."

Nelson held the phone and thought for a few seconds. "He might just be having a drink. Or he might be up to something. We need to risk it. Try to get a look at who he's with. You said he only got a quick glimpse of you before, so he shouldn't recognize you."

Nelson hung up, and the phone immediately rang again. He assumed Hunt had forgotten to tell him something. "Yeah?"

"This is Joe."

"I thought you were Sleepy. He just called a second ago when McNabb left his house."

"This may fit then. I'm in the can, so I've only got a minute. Gant was here. I was hanging around in back to clean up the stock room, trying to listen at the door. I heard a cell phone ring. I couldn't hear him good, but I heard him say, 'Yes sir,' which could only be McNabb. He wouldn't call anyone else sir. Then he tore out of here."

"Well, then, we don't need to meet after work. Check in with me, though. Something may be up from the way McNabb's acting. He left his house alone and went to Nick's. Usually when he goes there, it's with his wife for dinner."

Nelson hung up and then called downtown to the department night desk. He learned that the clone cellular phones of McNabb and Gant hadn't been in use at all. Damn it, Nelson said to himself, realizing McNabb must have new cell phones.

———————

Waiting to call McNabb, Peter stood with the telephone receiver in his hand and pretended to be talking so that no one else would come up and use it. He watched fast-moving, rust-colored clouds sail low overhead, reflecting the glow from the hundreds of lighted parking lots, gas stations, and retail store signs in Jackson. The breeze felt good as the heat stored during the day rose from the asphalt beneath his feet.

To kill time, Peter read the names and numbers scribbled around the interior of the telephone booth. He imagined each one could tell stories both interesting and pathetic.

Peter looked at his watch. He picked up the quarter and dime he had placed on the brushed metal counter and dropped them into the slot.

The phone rang ten times and Peter was about to hang up when he heard someone pick up the receiver.

The voice sounded flat and cold. "I'm here."

"What happened the other day at the parking lot? You were followed," Peter said.

"Possible, but I'm not certain. Maybe you were followed. Obviously you weren't alone either. You knew the police were there before I did," McNabb said. "I won't let you set me up like that again."

Peter realized McNabb was trying to throw him off guard. "It wasn't me. So, were you followed or were they listening to your calls?"

"What difference does it make? I'm followed a lot," McNabb said, all-business sounding. "But don't worry about the phones or a tail. I've taken care of those. Let's get to business."

"What you got in mind?"

"I'll make the trade, but I'm not bringing that much money alone. And not at night. I'll have the money in the morning."

Peter wasn't expecting demands. He had imagined this conversation many times, but each time *he* had control, *he* directed the transaction. When he spoke, his teeth left small marks beneath his bottom lip from biting down hard as he concentrated. "You bring one person. I'll bring one. Be at this phone at 7:30."

But McNabb was not finished. "Listen, you have something I want. I have something you want. Fair enough. But if you try to rip me off, *you will pay.*"

Peter could tell McNabb wasn't just tough talk.

He had been in many difficult negotiations with CEOs of large corporations. He had seen the spectrum of corporate scare tactics. He had seen calm tough guys and loud tough guys. He had seen mean and nasty tough guys. And he had met the quiet, vicious type. But he had never heard anything more convincing or more chilling than those three soft-spoken words from McNabb.

He felt himself shiver. In his own roughest-sounding voice, he said, "Be there at 7:30. I'll tell you where we can meet. Bring your guy, but I'll know if you're followed. If the cops show up again, you'll never see this merchandise." Peter hung up and walked back to the car.

He told Mary Beth and Danny about the one guard he agreed to. He didn't tell them how cold-blooded McNabb sounded.

———

Peter sat up in the bed and pulled a beige, summer quilt down to his waist. The room was dark except for the faint bluish glow from a streetlight that created an outline around the curtains. His tee shirt was drenched and twisted around his body from tossing in his sleep. The cotton shirt stuck to his skin as he tugged on it. Reaching up to brush his hair back, he found his scalp completely soaked. He had been dreaming about Christopher, about going to Christopher's apartment after he was dead, and that the police arrived there before Peter. In the dream, a policeman stood in the doorway, and all that Peter could see around the policeman was Christopher's hand. In the dream, the hand was reaching out. But in reality, Christopher had died alone. In his addiction, his baby brother had ended up dying alone.

The house was still and dark, and Peter heard no sounds from outside.

Propping up on one elbow, he saw the lighted numbers on his bedside clock. 2:48.

He lay back with a sigh, his head sinking deep into the pillow. When he rolled over onto his side facing away from Mary Beth, she spoke softly, "Are you all right?"

He rolled back over to face her outline in the dark. "Yeah, I just woke up from a dream. Did I wake you?"

"I've been awake for an hour." Mary Beth turned toward him and propped herself on her elbow. Their faces were inches apart. "Peter, I promise this is the last time I'll ask, but are you really, really sure we're doing the right thing? What if something goes wrong like the first time? We were lucky, you know."

"I'd rather say we were ready last time. We will be this time, too. It'll go fine. We've thought everything out. Bet, this is the only way I can feel like I did something right for Chris. Maybe even for us. I want one more chance."

Mary Beth lay back and faced the dark ceiling. "I guess we all want one more chance."

He could tell her eyes were open. Her words were barely loud enough for Peter to hear. The distant sound in her voice at that moment made him wonder if they were both talking about the same thing.

"It seems like things get more dangerous every time we talk to McNabb. I want to go along. I really do. I can see what this means to you, but at some point we have to be realistic about how much risk it's worth."

He knew what they were doing was way out of character for her, for both of them. "If it doesn't work out this time, I'll give it up."

Neither spoke for several minutes.

Mary Beth spoke up first. "I feel like Mary Beth is gone now and some other person has taken over her body. A few weeks ago, I only worried about how to get you to schedule a vacation, or what we'd have for supper."

"I know. But I can't roll back the clock either."

"Now I'm spending every waking hour wondering how to make a good disguise, or if it's morally right to shoot at a drug dealer if he tries to kill us. Nothing seems real, and I'm scared we won't like who we are when this is over."

Peter looked toward Mary Beth. He slid his hand over and rested it on her belly. "We haven't changed. Maybe we've seen a side of life that's hidden most of the time, but I don't want to get to the end of my life and look back wishing I'd had the guts to fight back, to do something because it was the right thing to do."

"I know that's important to you. In some small way, fighting back makes us feel like we've done something for Chris. But I feel like I've lost something that I can never get back."

Mary Beth rolled over and put her head on his shoulder, molding her body as close to him as she could. His eyes were open. He thought about when he'd overheard John leaving her a message. He wanted to ask her about that, but he couldn't bring himself to do so.

"Promise me one thing," Mary Beth whispered, her mouth inches from his ear.

Peter was silent.

"If we get the money, we don't keep any of it. Tell me again that's how you feel."

"This isn't about the money. It's never been about the money."

Peter didn't know when he drifted off to sleep, but the alarm going off at 5:45 brought him instantly awake. He swung his feet over the bedside and stood up.

By six o'clock, all three sat drinking coffee at the kitchen table. No one even mentioned breakfast as they went over the plans one last time.

As they were leaving, Danny said, "Hey guys, relax. You look nervous as a whore in Sunday School."

chapter 27

Gant leaned back in his chair, his arms crossed over his chest and a Camel cigarette idling between the fingers of his right hand. He watched to see how the man he had chosen for an important job would react to McNabb, and vice versa. The air in the small back office of the Best Price was warm, and a thin ribbon of smoke hovered motionless overhead as the three men sat talking. The slender young man, who preferred to be called T.J., sat calmly and looked directly at McNabb's face as McNabb made his wishes clear about getting back both his money and his drugs.

"We'll show the money. Even put it in their hands if we have to. I don't care. But once we get our merchandise back, do whatever it takes to tell the world you don't mess with me like this. I want those bastards so full of holes you could spit right through them." McNabb reached over and crushed a cigarette out, as if emphasizing what would happen to those who challenged him.

All three held cups of coffee, but only Gant and McNabb smoked. Gant had told T.J. to say little and talk only when McNabb asked him a question. He hoped T.J. would replace two dead men no longer available to help Gant with the dirty jobs sometimes required. This job would be a test by fire of whether or not McNabb would allow T.J. into the small inner circle that actually met him. Most of the work these days was handled between Gant and his contract guys who never met McNabb.

"Are you ready to ride in the trunk?" McNabb asked T. J., cocking his head to the side as if expecting an odd answer.

Gant observed T.J.'s perfect skin and expensive haircut as T.J. sat still and upright, looking only at McNabb. His black slacks, blue button-down dress shirt and polished black Cole-Haan loafers were a stark contrast to the jeans and flannel shirts almost universal to the guys Gant hired. If he didn't know better, he'd probably think the guy was gay. Or maybe a graduate student from some well-off family. Even the long blonde hair was styled like that of a carefree college student. It wasn't the look of most of the hired guns Gant usually used, but he had used T.J. before and knew he would be good for a job that required someone smart but ready to be both ruthless and fearless.

Despite being only in his late twenties, T.J. had proven his worth. Gant had used him to kill two drug dealers who had tried to take some of McNabb's business. They were dead within three days of the contract, the bodies left in public places. As far as Gant could tell, the police had no witnesses and no ties back to them. Impressive work.

T.J. nodded and answered, his tone respectful and his gaze not turning away from McNabb. "Yes sir, I've already taped the trunk latch of the Cadillac to keep it from locking and run a loop of rope through the trunk lid brace to hold it closed. Mr. Gant has told me what you expect."

Gant admired a young man with such confidence but somehow without the cockiness that usually came with youth. This one might survive, he thought.

"All right then. Roy will call your cell phone when we're ready to make our move. Sit tight. But when you come out of that trunk, I want to see the devil's agent of death. Roy tells me I can trust you to be that."

Gant was pleased when T.J. said nothing more but simply looked McNabb in the eye and nodded. No bragging. No bravado. His quiet self-assurance obvious.

Turning to Gant, McNabb said, "Roy, I don't know what they're planning, but I have a feeling there could be more than the two of them. Do you think we have enough men?"

"With two cars to box them in and the three of us in their face, I think they'll be dead in thirty seconds."

"Well, let's hope your men are as good as you say. We better go." McNabb looked at his watch. "They'll be calling in fifteen minutes."

Gant stood and motioned for T.J. to follow him outside. McNabb also followed. Gant checked the street to make certain no one was watching them. As T.J. climbed into the trunk, McNabb asked him what he carried in the cloth bag.

"It's a Winchester pump twelve gauge, twenty-four inch barrel, loaded with five rounds of number one buckshot. I've got another five rounds on a stock ammunition holder and ten more in my pocket. This here will seriously rip somebody up, sir." T.J. reached both arms around to the back of his belt under his vest and pulled out automatic pistols in both hands. "And if that doesn't work, these twin Glock 23 forty calibers have police clips. In five seconds I can get off about twenty shots. I've got four more clips loaded and ready. Same thing lots of police tactical guys use."

———

Peter stopped the Ford in front of the Texaco on High Street at 7:25. There were cars at most of the pumps, but no one stood near the telephone booth. He put both hands in his pockets so no one would notice the latex gloves he wore. He waited in front of the phone for five minutes, and then dialed the pay phone for McNabb.

Peter had sent Mary Beth across the Interstate to watch McNabb from closer, knowing that no one would connect him or Danny with Mary Beth parked in the lot of a convenience store more than a hundred yards away.

"Do you have the money?"

"I have it. You got the merchandise?"

"I have it all with me. Here's what you need to do."

"I'm listening."

"Leave your car there. Then ..."

"Wait a minute. I want my car with me."

After a moment of hesitation, Peter decided to gamble. "Then this discussion is over. Goodbye." He held the phone for a moment to see what reaction he got.

"Wait. Tell me what you have in mind. Then I'll decide."

"Fine." Peter tried to sound unconcerned, as if he were merely telling someone directions to the mall. "Take the money with you and walk behind the gas station. Cut through the hedges. There's a Dodge parked there with the key on the top of the driver's side rear tire. I want you to take that car. You got a problem with that?" Peter waited. He could tell McNabb was thinking.

"Yeah, okay, but you better not be screwing with me."

"This is just to get the police off your ass, and to make sure you don't have any surprises for me in your car."

McNabb said nothing in response, which made Peter realize maybe McNabb *was* hiding something in the car. He felt a chill at the thought. "There's a two-way radio in the glove box. Turn it on and leave it on the channel it's on now. Cut through the back road behind Hooters and get on I-55 South at Meadowbrook Road. Call on the radio when you get off at the High Street exit. And don't forget, we're watching you right now. We'll be watching you then."

Peter hung up before McNabb could say anything else.

　　　　　　　　———

Although Mary Beth couldn't hear McNabb's words as he leaned over and spoke to Gant through the car window, she saw McNabb was irritated from the way he shook his head and waved his hands as he spoke. He turned and walked quickly toward the back of the Amoco Station. Gant started after McNabb with a briefcase in his hand. Mary Beth felt her heart rise up into her throat. It's working! That must be the money. They're going to do it.

As soon as Mary Beth saw McNabb and Gant drive out of the parking lot, she pulled into the traffic on Northside Drive and veered onto the entrance of the interstate to drive south just ahead of the entrance McNabb would be taking. The traffic was steady but moving well for rush hour. The congestion had thinned enough to let her maneuver if needed but not be noticed. As she moved into the middle lane with cars passing on her left, she called Peter. When he answered, she used their pre-arranged signal in case anyone else happened to be scanning the radio channels. "Hi honey. Just wanted to let you know we're on our way to meet you. Everything went well."

"Great, see you soon," Peter said.

Mary Beth slowed to just over fifty-five miles per hour, which she thought wouldn't be noticeably slow since she was pulling a trailer. She had gone only a mile when she saw the Dodge coming up behind her on the left, just as planned. As the car passed, she saw McNabb talking on the radio. She sped up to keep pace with the car, now some two hundred yards in front. As they neared High Street, the same street she knew Peter had traveled only minutes before, the Dodge moved over to exit. Mary Beth closed the gap to one hundred and fifty yards. She was relieved to see that no other cars were exiting behind the Dodge. That meant McNabb would have only Gant with him at the exchange. Although she was prepared to get behind McNabb and slow someone down if needed, she had been dreading the idea of trying to block the path of one of McNabb's guys.

chapter 28

Even though Peter had been expecting the call, he started when he heard McNabb's voice on the radio. Danny, in the front seat next to him, didn't move.

McNabb's tone sounded so cold Peter felt fear turn to acid in his stomach. "What now, Boy Scout?"

He waited for a second and willed his voice to sound calm. "From the exit at High Street go west five blocks past State Street, then turn south on Mason Avenue."

"Where are we meeting?"

"You'll know soon enough. It's an old office building. I'll radio again when you get near the building."

Peter slipped the radio into his shirt pocket as he neared the meeting spot and turned into the alley. He parked the Ford right outside the rear door of the furniture store to give the appearance he waited inside that building. As he got out of the car, Peter pulled out the two black masks Danny had bought and handed one to Danny. Danny held the mask, and then looked at Peter, slowly shaking his head.

"I know. It's too much. Just forget it," Peter said, and each stuffed a mask back into his pocket.

Danny quickly removed the lock he'd previously put on the chain that ran through the back door handles of the furniture store and hid both lock and chain under a rotted cardboard box a few feet away. He opened the trunk and removed one-by-four boards Peter and he had spiked with nails, piling them behind a clump of weeds halfway down the alley. Then he turned and sprinted toward the corner of the building where he squatted behind a stack of old wooden shipping pallets, a large blue garbage dumpster hiding his right side. He could watch the entire alley through the spaces of the pallet boards.

Peter arrived upstairs in the opposite building. His chest heaved from carrying the heavy sports bag that held the fake and the real drugs. He waved at Danny from the window, and Danny signaled back that he could see Peter and everything was ready. Peter watched Danny remove the heavy pistol from his waistband and place the gun in front of him on one of the pallet boards.

Seeing the gun gave Peter the urge to run from the room and drive away, but he knew it was too late. If they were careful, the swap would soon be over.

Peter radioed McNabb. "Okay, you there?"

"We're here," McNabb answered, his voice faint.

"Turn left onto Farish Street, then turn at the first alley on the right. Go to the rear of the furniture store."

"I'm only three blocks away."

Peter waited at the window, standing back far enough to be hidden. Two minutes later he saw Gant drive slowly into the alley and stop the Dodge next to the Ford, facing the loading dock of the empty furniture store.

"Come inside the building right in front of you," Peter said into the radio.

McNabb and Gant entered the building through the big double doors as instructed. Peter saw Gant pull a pistol from his waistband and hold it at his side as he scanned the building windows. He had a briefcase in the other hand. McNabb carried a second briefcase.

Peter again spoke into the radio. "Do you see the tape on the floor?"

"Yeah. I see it. What kind of bullshit is this? Just tell us where you are."

"This is no trick. We're just making it safe and easy for both of us. Just follow the tape up the stairs. We'll be through with the trade in two minutes, and we can both get out of here." Peter tried to sound calm and reassuring, but sweat trickled down his sideburns onto his jaw.

"Listen asshole, you better play this straight."

"I told you, just go up the stairs. You'll see me when you get there."

Peter stepped closer to the window to watch Danny. Danny peeked around the corner of the building in case McNabb had someone following nearby, and then ran as quietly as possible across the loading dock, knowing he had no time to waste. That's good, Peter thought. If there's no one following, we can make the exchange and get out of here. Danny pulled the chain from beneath the box and slipped the links through the handles on the double doors McNabb and Gant had entered. He locked it with the old lock he had brought, trapping the two men inside. He jumped off the platform next to the Dodge Gant had parked and opened a pocketknife. He pushed the knife into the front tire on the passenger side of the Dodge and did the same on a rear tire. Peter heard a faint hiss and hoped McNabb couldn't hear it.

Danny grabbed the spiked boards he had left in the weeds, then ran down the alley and placed the boards across the road, kicking gravel and dirt onto the boards to hide them. He ran back to his post behind the dumpster to watch for anyone following McNabb. Peter realized he had been holding his breath as he watched, fearful that McNabb and Gant would see Danny, but the building across from him remained quiet. Everything was going as planned.

In the stairwell, Gant walked just behind McNabb with his pistol ready. He turned his head side to side, peering down each hallway, watching for someone to appear from behind a corner. McNabb took the cellular phone from his pocket and held the phone side-by-side with the radio as he spoke. On the drive downtown, Gant had called T.J. on the phone to say what was going on with the radio and to make sure T.J. would keep absolutely quiet. McNabb knew the man would figure out the rest as he drove in their direction in McNabb's car. Gant had also called his other men, who were converging on the location, and he gave them instructions to stay two blocks away but be ready to move. All three cars should now be only moments away, waiting for his signal.

"We're at the room with the tape, so where are … oh shit, what is this?" McNabb said.

Gant looked up when McNabb yelled. He saw the rope and followed it with his eyes across the alley until he saw a man standing in the building opposite them. The man wore a red cap and ponytail.

"This is ridiculous," McNabb yelled across the alley.

"Look, just send across the money, and I'll send your merchandise at the same time. That way we know there's no trick," the man yelled back.

"How do I know you've got the stuff?" McNabb asked.

"How do I know you do?"

"Put a bag in the pouch and send it over," McNabb demanded.

"Fine, but you send over a stack of money at the same time. That's the way this works."

Gant looked at McNabb for instructions. McNabb motioned with his head for Gant to bring the briefcase. He sat the briefcase on the floor, removed a stack of one hundred dollar bills, and stood up waving the money in his hand. He placed the money in the bag on the rope. He saw the man in the hat hold up a package, then place the package into the other canvas bag. They each tugged on the rope to exchange packages. A flock of pigeons swooped down between them and then were gone as suddenly as they appeared.

When the cocaine reached Gant, he handed the package to McNabb. McNabb looked the package over and then held it out. Gant pulled up the leg of his jeans and slid a long, thin folding knife from his boot. He opened the knife with one hand and jabbed the blade into the package. He removed the knife and touched his finger tip to the white powder that stuck to the blade. The powder felt slick and almost oily in his fingers. He removed a small rock, crushed it between his fingers, rubbed the cocaine on his gums, and then sniffed a knife tip of the powder. He nodded to McNabb that it was the real thing.

McNabb turned to the window and shouted across the opening, "Let's do it."

Gant kept glancing over to watch the man in the red hat place the taped bundles into the pulley contraption while he loaded the money into the other bag. When the bags were loaded, they repeated the process and completed the exchange.

As Gant hurriedly tossed the bags into the two briefcases, McNabb stepped to the side of the window and dialed the man in the first car, telling him to close in on the west end of the alley behind the building. Gant left the two cases sitting open while he dialed T.J., telling him to drive into the alley from the east end and cover the rear of the other building. He stopped in mid-sentence and reached for one of the bags with a quizzical look on his face. His eyes grew bigger as his face turned red.

"Check another one," McNabb shouted, dropping to his knees and picking up a bag in each hand to look at them closely.

Gant quickly kneeled down and sliced the knife into a bag. He touched the powder to his tongue and instantly spit. "Baking soda!"

"You punk, you're dead!" McNabb screamed through the window at the man whose ponytail flew behind him as he ran from the room. McNabb pulled a small automatic and fired two shots into the window of the building across from him.

Not waiting for McNabb, Gant yelled into the phone as he took the stairs three at a time. "Go to the east end of the alley. Kill the son-of-a-bitch."

Danny had smiled to himself as he watched the two men pulling on the rope like they were hanging laundry from a high-rise clothesline. He could hardly believe Peter's plan might work. Drug dealers were actually paying. Looking up caused him to notice how blue the sky had turned, but sudden yelling put him on alert. He grabbed his pistol and heard two shots come from the window on McNabb's side of the alley.

When he heard Peter screaming from inside the building to get the car, he started running. Just as he reached the Ford, lead pellets from a shotgun blast whistled past, and the backseat window beside him exploded. He turned in one motion and fired two shots wildly from his pistol as he dived in front of the Ford and scrambled around to the other side, shredding the skin on his elbows. Two more loads of buckshot ripped into the Ford's front fender, making the car look as if someone had stabbed the metal repeatedly with a pencil.

From the end of the alley, a young man with straight blonde hair ran across the gravel lot directly toward him. The man held a shotgun level and pointed in Danny's direction. Another shot from the man slammed into the car, the sound exploding overhead. Danny rose to a crouched position behind the front end of the car, his back pressed against the fender and his head down, waiting for the guy with the shotgun to close the distance between them. He had one chance. When he heard gravel crunch just on the other side of the car, he took a breath and brought his pistol up in front of him. With both hands tightly gripping the weapon, he spun as he rose and fired three quick shots at the man only steps away. Fire leapt from the barrel of the shotgun. This time the pellets were so close Danny felt as much as heard the deadly load whiz past him. The man doubled over, and the shotgun skidded a few feet ahead of him onto the dirt as he grabbed his stomach and fell forward.

Danny yanked open the passenger side door and crawled across to start the car. He was backing up when Peter opened the back door, tossed in the bag, and dived into the back seat head first.

"Go! Go! Go!" Peter climbed over the seat to the front.

Danny backed in a wide arc around the man lying on the ground, rocking back and forth with his hands turning bloody as he held them pressed to his belly. The spinning tires threw gravel across the alley. Just as he yanked the gearshift down into drive, the front windshield shattered.

Danny looked over at the furniture store and saw Gant's pistol sticking through the bars of a window on the first floor. As if in slow motion, he watched shell after shell arc from Gant's big automatic. The two double doors to the building were being rattled like an earthquake as McNabb frantically tried to open them enough to squeeze through, but the chain did its job.

Danny heard several more metallic hammering blows and repeated explosions as bullets pounded the car. Both front passenger windows shattered from a single bullet passing through the glass.

Behind them, a white Camaro turned down the alley, creating a tornado of dust, its tires spinning, struggling to find traction. The Camaro hit the spiked boards, shredding tires and slinging the boards backwards as the car fishtailed down the alley before it slid solidly into a loading dock and stopped.

Danny pressed the accelerator to the floor. The Ford's tires screamed as they gripped the pavement. He didn't see the Chevy truck until it slammed into the Ford's driver side door.

chapter 29

Gant heaved a rusty, grey desk chair through a side window, showering the sparse grass beside the building with glass shards and splintered wood. He climbed through the opening and jumped the six feet to the ground with McNabb close behind. They ran around the building to the Dodge, only to find both tires flat on one side. Gant saw the Camaro crashed into the side of a loading dock a half a block down with its tires flat, too. The driver had already left the Camaro and rounded the corner on the run.

When Gant looked back down the alley, he saw someone on the ground. Though he couldn't see the face, he recognized the black slacks and blonde hair. Even from this distance, he saw a large pool of blood spread across the gravel. T.J. wasn't moving.

McNabb still held the briefcase with one bag of real cocaine and several bags of baking soda while Gant carried the other.

Gant touched McNabb on the arm lightly and said, "We got to go, William. We got to go now."

He saw McNabb was frozen and uncertain, staring down the street as the truck chased the men who had stolen his drugs ... and now his money, too. He said nothing and didn't react to Gant. He clenched and unclenched his left fist.

Gant gripped McNabb's arm and spoke more firmly. "William, just walk away. We'll find these guys. The cops will be here any minute."

The furniture store sat in a rundown part of town in a section without much traffic, but only three blocks away the streets were filled. Gant knew to head toward the activity in order not to stand out. He put his hand on McNabb's elbow and started escorting him forward.

Saying nothing, they walked quickly but not fast enough to catch anyone's attention. At the end of the block, they turned toward the Federal Building. Gant noticed several people coming out of shops and peering around corners. Halfway down the second block, he heard sirens as two police cars came into view. They walked on as if nothing were out of the ordinary.

"William, I think I can get a car from my buddy over at the Firestone store on Pascagoula Street," Gant said. "I'll call when I'm on the way."

McNabb just nodded.

They split up, and Gant turned south at the next street while McNabb walked into the Federal Building with his briefcase.

———

The drug task force reporting to Lt. Taylor Nelson sat around an eight foot oak table with stacks of manila files, dog-eared yellow legal pads with hand-written notes, and an assortment of coffee cups. Nelson had already asked his men for the latest information and any theories about what might happen next. Hunt had finished telling about McNabb's strange late evening visit to Nick's Restaurant.

"I think we need to come up with a new surveillance plan," Nelson said.

Before anyone could answer, a uniformed officer opened the door without knocking and leaned halfway in. "Sorry to bust in, Lieutenant, but we're getting all kinds of calls about gunfire downtown and a car chase. We've got a car that just arrived on the scene where the shootout might have started. Looks like one guy's dead in the alley behind the Marx Building. They said we needed to let you know if something out of the ordinary happened. Even for Jackson, this seems a little weird."

Nelson felt as if the air had been sucked out of his lungs. He sat straight up and practically shouted, "Where?" His sixth sense meter was set on high for anything a bit unusual, and this registered off the charts.

"The last I heard, there was a car chase going east toward Rankin County," the officer said.

"What are they saying?" Nelson asked.

"At least three calls reported a series of gunshots. Two other calls came in immediately afterwards from the same area about a truck ramming a white car. A cell phone caller said he was at a traffic light at Silas Brown and West Street, about to pull into the intersection, when a white car came through the red light doing at least sixty with a white Chevrolet truck ramming it from behind."

As if they were one body, the men ran to two cars in the lot and started toward Silas Brown Road.

———

"Take my gun," Danny shouted at Peter.

Peter was turned halfway in the passenger seat, looking out the back window at the Chevrolet truck that had already smashed in their driver's side door and now was repeatedly crashing into their Ford from the rear. Peter saw blood running down the left side of Danny's face from hitting the window. Despite blood covering the side of his head and a deep gash above his left ear, Danny kept both hands on the steering wheel as he weaved around the busy downtown traffic.

Peter reached over and pulled the pistol out of Danny's belt. He turned in his seat and watched the truck right on their bumper but was uncertain what to do.

"Just shoot right through the window! Do it! Shoot out the back window," Danny screamed over the straining engine and the squealing tires.

Peter started shooting, and the back window of the Ford became a web of cracks, with intermittent holes throughout. When the gun stopped firing and merely clicked on empty shells, Peter sat back into his seat.

"Get the quick loader," Danny yelled. "It's in my front pocket."

Peter opened the cylinder and dumped out the six empty shells, took the loader, and slid the bullets it held into the back of the cylinder to reload. Danny swerved around a minivan at a red light just as Peter turned and pulled the trigger again. The motion caused him to shoot wide of the truck behind them. The truck came around the minivan and began to close the gap.

"Peter, we're only three or four blocks from the river. We need to stop him now if we want to get to the boat without him right on us."

Peter leveled his gun with both hands and aimed at the left side of the truck windshield. He wished he'd brought his small Beretta .380, which he knew he could shoot better, and cursed himself for leaving his best gun under his mattress. He'd told himself he wasn't a gangster, wouldn't get in a shootout, and didn't need a gun. Even now, when it was clear he was fighting for his life, something wouldn't let him aim at the driver. He fired only close enough to try to make the man back off. He fired again and missed the truck behind them. He fired two more shots and blew a hole in the middle of the truck's windshield, but the driver didn't slow down as Peter expected and instead pulled beside them on Danny's side. He could no longer take a shot without firing too close to Danny.

"Give me the gun," Danny said, reaching over.

The truck smashed hard into the left side of the car, forcing Danny to put both hands back on the steering wheel to keep from veering off the road. Side-by-side, both vehicles approached the bridge at Silas Brown Road just as a car came toward them from the other side. Danny grabbed for the gun as both vehicles neared the bridge. Pointing the gun out the window with his left hand, he fired off the last two shots at the truck's front right tire, only inches away. The car approaching from the other direction reached the end of the bridge and swerved at the last moment.

Peter couldn't tell if the sound came from the tire blowing or from the truck pounding into the left rear side of the Ford, but he heard metal grinding against the guard rails and realized they were turning sideways on the bridge. Both vehicles skidded off the end of the bridge and toward the drop-off above the river. He reached up to brace himself.

The Ford rolled down the steep embankment past the bridge. His grip came loose, and he felt himself slam against the door window, upside down. Since neither Danny nor Peter had taken time to put on a seat belt, both were tossed around the inside of the vehicle as it rolled over before stopping on its side where the dirt road circled down to the river. The truck, whose front bumper had momentarily locked with the back bumper of the Ford, had slid sideways and flipped over.

As soon as the car stopped rolling, Peter struggled to get out. He was on top of Danny and began trying to get off him without putting all his weight down. Blood was splattered everywhere. Danny wasn't moving. The windshield had popped out most of the way, so Peter lifted both legs as he lay on his back and kicked against the remaining glass. The mat of shattered glass came out of its rubber and chrome seal and lay on the ground like a thick, shiny quilt.

Peter switched off the engine before he crawled out on his hands and knees and looked back at Danny. Danny didn't move. Peter feared he was dead but then noticed Danny's chest expanding slightly.

Peter knew not to move someone after a wreck, but the man in the upside-down truck was only a few feet away and might still be after them. Others would be close behind. He had to get Danny and leave the area. He grabbed Danny by the front of his shirt and tried to drag him out of the car through the open windshield. But when he tried to reach with his left arm, Peter couldn't use it, and he felt a sharp pain near his left shoulder. He saw a lump poking out and realized his collarbone was broken. Blood stained the front of his shirt, but he couldn't tell where it was coming from or if the blood was even his. Using his good right arm, he tried dragging Danny again but managed to move him only a couple of feet. He felt a searing pain in his rib cage on the right side.

Peter slumped to his knees on the riverbank. He heard police sirens and judged them to be only blocks away. He looked at his boat and knew he had only seconds to act. Words he'd heard a hundred times as a child echoed in his head. He repeated them out loud. "Be a man, Peter."

Rising to his feet, he grabbed Danny's shirt and dragged him toward the boat. Moving a couple of feet at a time, he pulled Danny to the riverbank. He leaned all his weight against the boat, pushed the bow halfway into the river, and staggered back to the Ford for the money. He didn't see the bag at first but picked up Danny's gun. Then spotting the bag nearby, he grabbed it, limped back to the riverbank, and dropped everything into the jon boat. He pushed the boat into the river and tied it below the slope of the bank. He pulled Danny the last few feet to the boat, stepped in, and reached back to grab Danny's shirt. With one last heave, Danny slid over the side of the embankment and dropped the eighteen inches into the boat. Peter pushed off and began drifting downstream just as two police cars stopped on the bridge, sirens blaring.

Peter pulled out the choke and yanked on the starting cord. The motor started briefly but died. He pulled the cord again and again but didn't have enough strength to generate the speed needed to start the motor. He gasped from the exertion, and his shoulder ached like nothing he had experienced in his life. "Be a man, Peter," he said again, his breath coming in gasps. He pushed in the choke, took a deep breath, and pulled hard on the cord. The engine started. He flipped the gearshift forward and turned upstream. As he emerged from beneath the bridge, he saw two plain-clothes police officers, guns drawn, approaching the wrecked Ford. One saw him and shouted. "Stop! State agents."

You'll have to shoot me, Peter thought as he gunned the engine. He was a hundred yards from the scene within seconds. Looking back, he saw an officer standing on the riverbank, staring at him, holding a red cap and ponytail.

chapter 30

Mary Beth drove toward the bridge at Silas Brown. She had heard nothing on the radio and had no plan, but she felt she should at least go in that direction.

From a block away she could see two police cruisers and an unmarked car on Silas Brown, blocking both ends of Woodrow Wilson Bridge. The police cars all had their blue lights flashing, and traffic began to back up. Several cars pulled to the side, their curious drivers milling around in groups of three or four, chatting. Pieces of metal and glass lay scattered on the street. She was sure Peter had time to have been to the bridge and now be in the boat. Something had gone dangerously wrong if Peter and Danny had gone to the backup escape route. She wanted to drive closer but feared that, pulling the trailer, she'd be unable to turn around and leave. Mary Beth sat in her car, observing the scene. Now wasn't the time to fall apart. She had to think straight.

She parked two blocks from the bridge and mingled with the others who'd stopped to see why the police cars blocked the road. Although she couldn't tell exactly what was happening, it didn't appear as if anyone had been arrested. She was almost certain she'd heard the faint sound of an outboard motor when she first stopped and lowered her window.

An ambulance arrived on the scene minutes later, lights flashing its garish signal of misery across the tree-lined road and its siren moaning that someone was in pain. Mary Beth pressed to the front of the crowd and glimpsed a man being loaded onto a stretcher. It wasn't Peter or Danny. The attendants seemed to have no urgency about transporting the man from the scene. She took deep breaths and scanned the scene beyond the ambulance but could see little of the scene across the river.

After waiting a few more minutes to make sure no other men were being loaded into ambulances, she returned to the Cherokee and drove toward the backup rendezvous at Jackson Academy baseball field. There was nothing else to do. She could only hope Peter and Danny got away.

———————

Peter kept the throttle twisted in his hand to full speed as the arrow of the small boat's wake cut through the smooth water of the Pearl River. The boat left long continuous waves rolling onto each shoreline. He saw no sign of another human for the two-mile stretch that took him upriver toward the bridge at Lakeland Drive. Above him, red oak, willow, sycamore, and sweetgum branches reached over the narrow river. Their leaves had lost the deep green of summer and now had hints of crimson, purple, and orange. He weaved back and forth, avoiding limbs from trees whose roots had given way to the gradually widening river. He tried to stay in the deepest part of the shallow river. Only once did he hit a submerged log, causing the foot of the motor to kick up nearly out of the water. He knew he was lucky the sheer pin had held.

Peter heard sirens for the second time as he steered the boat around the cement pilings supporting the Lakeland Drive bridge. He realized the police intended to cut him off. But he would be long gone before the first police car drove behind the office buildings beside Lakeland Drive and onto the sandy road leading under the bridge. The police officers would only see the last remaining waves from the boat wake bouncing from bank to bank until the river's surface was smooth again.

Peter knew he was near the spot where he'd left the Mule utility vehicle. He slowed the boat, found a small cut in the bank, and nosed the bow between two stumps. When the boat touched the bank, he gunned the engine enough to slide two or three feet onto the shore. He tossed the bag with the money and the coke onto the shore, using only his right arm. His left arm hung limp at his side.

He bent over Danny, who showed no signs of waking but was still breathing. A large lump had grown on the left side of Danny's head above his ear. His hair was matted with blood, and more blood continued to ooze from the wound.

He spoke to Danny and shook him gently by the arm to see if he would wake up. No response.

Peter grabbed Danny again by the front of his shirt and pulled him over the side of the boat. He climbed back into the boat and removed the gas cap from the tank. Unhooking the hose, he lifted the red tank over the side of the boat and allowed the river to fill the tank with water. When it felt full, he released his grip and watched the red container sink. He used his good hand to loosen the brackets holding the motor, then lifted it with his good arm and dropped it into the river. He pulled the plug from the bottom center of the transom, and water started gushing into the boat. Noticing the pistol on the floor of the boat, Peter picked the gun up and hurled it as far downstream into the river as he could. Then he ran up the embankment, found the Mule, and drove back down to Danny.

The jon boat was now three inches deep in water. Peter eased the Mule against the bow and pushed it into the current. It began a lazy circular motion out toward the middle of the river. Peter hoped the metal boat would sink within a couple of minutes, but at least the river would carry it downstream and make the task difficult for anyone searching for where he had gone ashore.

Peter had difficulty breathing and realized that he made a slight wheezing sound when he took a breath. His ribs burned as if someone had stuck him with a hot brand. He had little strength left and knew he had to get help fast. He struggled just to walk.

He tried one last time to lift Danny into the bed of the Mule. He slumped to the ground when he realized he didn't have the strength. No self-admonishment would make the difference now. Danny needed medical help fast. Peter stood and tugged Danny's shirt front. He managed to drag him a few feet behind a mound of beach-like white sand where he couldn't easily be seen from the river. He took the loaded sports bag, walked some fifty yards away, and thrust the bag beneath a tangle of vines. He climbed into the Mule. "I'll be back with help in a few minutes. Just hang in there, Danny."

He steered the Mule down the well-worn path toward Jackson Academy as fast as he could without having the bumps jar him so much he'd pass out from the pain. He removed the radio from his pocket and decided to try to contact Mary Beth. He changed the channel to five, the code to ten, and pushed the talk button, "Are you there?"

Within seconds he heard a weak signal, as if Mary Beth was close to the limit of the radio's two-mile range. The voice he heard was filled with relief and fear.

"Yes, I'm here. What happened? Are you guys all right? I was so scared. I saw the ambulance and didn't know what was going ..."

"Wait," Peter interrupted. "Just tell me if you're at our backup place."

"I'm only a couple of blocks away. I've already circled by twice, but I didn't want to stop. I'll be there in 30 seconds," Mary Beth answered. The urgency in her voice was obvious.

"Just meet me there, and don't talk on the radio anymore." Peter's side was now a roaring fire, and each bump of the Mule fanned the flames higher.

From the edge of the woods behind the baseball field, he saw Mary Beth as she turned into the parking lot. She stopped beside the Mule, facing the opposite direction. A dust cloud drifted forward in front of her car. She threw open her door and took three steps toward the Mule. Peter didn't attempt to stand up. He wiped feebly at the blood on his face. He held his left arm close to his stomach.

"Jesus, Peter. Where's Danny?"

"McNabb's man chased us down, and we wrecked at the bridge. Danny's knocked out, but I got him into the boat and brought him up here. We've got to go get him. I think I broke my collarbone, and I can't lift him by myself." He didn't mention his ribs.

"Where is he?"

"He's on the river bank where I had the Mule. You drive. Come on, we've got to get to him before the police come up the river."

Mary Beth climbed into the driver's seat of the Mule after Peter walked around to the other side. "Just pull this lever back to put it in gear and press the gas."

"I know. Hang on."

It took them seven minutes to reach Danny. He hadn't moved. Mary Beth opened the tailgate on the Mule bed and backed it next to Danny. Peter froze and held his hand up. Mary Beth stopped. A helicopter.

"We've got to get him up now!" Peter yelled.

Mary Beth grabbed Danny's arms, as Peter grabbed Danny by the front of his shirt, lifting him into the cargo bed. Mary Beth shut the gate and latched it. Danny's legs dangled over the top.

"Go! Let's get away from the riverbank" Peter jumped into the passenger seat. "Wait. Stop." He jumped out before the Mule had even moved and ran toward a thicket. He grabbed the sports bag and threw the bag into the Mule. "Okay, let's go."

Just as they came around a curve, they heard the helicopter passing behind them low over the river.

"Pull under that tree." Peter pointed at a large, red oak still thick with leaves. The helicopter passed behind them without slowing.

After the helicopter disappeared up the river, Mary Beth drove back to the Jeep and pulled alongside. She opened the back passenger door and backed the Mule as close as she could. It required several tugs of a few inches each to move Danny onto the back seat. Danny moaned when they moved him, but he didn't wake up. Mary Beth put the sports bag in the rear cargo section of the Cherokee and covered it with an old blanket and jumper cables.

Peter climbed into the passenger seat, leaned back, and began to realize how hurt he was. He knew the throbbing was more than bruised ribs. The pain felt like an ice pick in his side. "We need to get Danny to an emergency room. And me, too."

"What will they say?" Mary Beth asked. "Will they report this to the police?"

"I don't know. We need to tell them we had a car wreck. No ... a motorcycle wreck. Some stranger brought us in. That's all. And you can't wait around. You have to hide the bag. Go by the house first and let's unhook the Mule. It's on the way and won't take us more than sixty seconds. You can't be driving it around in case they see us with it at the emergency room. The cops might begin to put things together."

———

Mary Beth turned into the parking lot of University Medical Center's Emergency Room.

"Just drop us off. Then disappear before anyone realizes who you are," Peter said.

"What are you going to say?"

"I'll just explain that we had a motorcycle wreck when a tire blew out. I'll sign to pay for all hospital charges so the hospital won't get worried and ask too many questions."

She parked near the door and leaned on the horn. A male ER nurse with weight-lifter's arms and a flat-top haircut came to see what was happening. He ran to the car when Peter got out, covered in blood.

"Don't worry about me. You'll need a stretcher for my friend. We had a motorcycle wreck," Peter slumped near the back door of the Cherokee. The nurse opened the door and began checking Danny, who lay motionless.

"What happened? Has he been unconscious since the wreck?"

"We had a flat tire and lost control. This woman saw it and stopped to help. He's moaned a little but hasn't said anything."

"Were you wearing helmets?"

"Uh, yeah, of course we were." Peter stood up to look at Danny.

The nurse reached into the back of the Cherokee, felt for Danny's pulse, and ran back inside to get help. Peter stood and watched as the first nurse and another attendant returned with a stretcher. They also brought a young, female nurse who stood in front of Peter and looked into his eyes.

"Can you walk? Step over here out of the way and sit down."

Peter turned toward the glass double doors of the emergency room. The female nurse grabbed his arm and helped him walk slowly inside. Peter collapsed and slid to the floor as he reached the doors. The nurse held his arm and let him down as gently as she could.

Peter looked over at Danny. He was on a stretcher. Three people were around him, poking and prodding different parts of his body. They'd put a large white collar around his neck to hold his head steady. The male nurse held up an IV bottle for Danny, but he was not looking at him. He was facing the parking lot, his gaze focused on Mary Beth's car as she drove away.

chapter 31

Mary Beth wanted to go back to the hospital, but she knew she could help Peter and Danny more by staying away in case the police found out about them. *Stay calm*, she kept telling herself. *You're in charge now. If something has to be done, only you can do it.*

Only minutes later, she pulled the Cherokee behind the weathered barn at the farm in Pelahatchie. Peter had solved this problem for her. The drugs and the money would be safe here. The sun was high, creating deep shadows with hard edges beneath the pecan trees that surrounded the barn. No one seemed to be around, and the closest neighbor was nearly a quarter of a mile away. She grabbed the sports bag from the back of the Jeep and walked inside. She had only watched Peter walk into this barn to hide the drugs and had not come with him, but everything was as he had described it. At the far end sat several old bales of hay and a faded Massey Ferguson tractor with two flat front tires. In one corner, she noticed a stack of old lumber, rolls of tarpaper for roofing, and windows someone had saved from an old house. It was obvious from the dust and cobwebs that the materials had been sitting there for years. She squeezed herself behind the stack of thick rough-sawn pine boards and removed one board that looked as if it had fallen from the pile. She saw the bag that Peter had left and found just enough space to hide this bag next to it. She placed it on the ground and put the old board back on top. No one could see the two bags unless the entire pile of wood was moved.

Driving back toward town, she spotted a pay phone outside the Pelahatchie Bay Trading Post, a combination bait shop, gas station, and restaurant on Pelahatchie Creek, which flowed into the Ross Barnett

Reservoir. She parked in front of the restaurant and used the pay phone to call the University Medical Center. She asked for the room of Peter Brantley. Her heart stopped when she was told no one by that name was listed. She glanced at her watch and realized it had been only fifty minutes since she left Peter and Danny at the ER. They wouldn't be admitted into rooms yet.

She entered the convenience store side of the Trading Post and noticed an odd mixture of items on a series of shelves. Soda crackers and various cans of Vienna sausages and potted meats lined a shelf above stacks of white bread. On nearby walls, gray peg boards held tiny plastic bags of fish hooks, lead weights of every size, red and white bobbers, and assorted spools of fishing line. One entire wall was devoted to plastic worms in every color and length imaginable. Another held minnow buckets, bright orange life vests, and ropes of various thicknesses. The coolers along one wall were filled with several kinds of beer and brightly colored red, green, and orange soft drinks with names Mary Beth had never seen. She found herself staring at the items, uncertain of anything other than the need to make time pass as quickly as possible. She knew she was on the edge of losing control, but she had to be strong.

She walked to other side of the building to the dining room and sat down. An attractive waitress with beautiful, silky, long red hair spilling over her shoulders walked up to the table and slid a food-stained menu and a glass of water in front of Mary Beth.

"Can I get you something?"

Mary Beth turned away too quickly when she saw the woman was missing several teeth on the upper right side of her mouth. The mouth seemed so oddly out of place in contrast to the flowing red hair and smooth white skin. "Coffee, please," Mary Beth managed, not making eye contact.

Despite all their planning and contingencies, something had gone wrong. She knew there was a chance the police would be notified or somehow figure out that Peter and Danny were involved in the wreck at the bridge, but she didn't know if the hospital was required to report anything or whether the police could prove their involvement even if they somehow figured out what had happened.

She sipped from the coffee cup she held in both hands and realized the coffee was cold. She didn't know how long she had been sitting there holding the cup. The waitress walked by with a coffee pot as she worked her way around the row of booths along the large front glass windows.

"Warm-up?"

"Yes, thanks."

Mary Beth held out her half empty cup and nodded, momentarily glancing up into the woman's eyes.

"Let me bring you a fresh cup. That one has to be cold as long as you've been holding it. You all right?" There was kindness in the woman's eyes, as if there was an unspoken understanding.

"Sure, I'm fine."

Putting down the coffee cup, Mary Beth pulled a napkin from a little plastic holder shaped like a hay wagon, exactly like the one that always sat on her grandmother's kitchen windowsill when Mary Beth was a little girl. She wiped under each eye. She placed three one-dollar bills on the table before she walked outside to the pay telephone again. She guessed it had been nearly an hour since she last called.

Mary Beth exhaled audibly when the hospital operator rang the call through to Peter's room without comment. Peter answered on the third ring, his voice heavy and slurred. "Hello."

"It's me. How are you? What's happened?"

Peter spoke slowly and barely above a whisper. "Danny's in a coma, but they say his vital signs are good. I have a punctured lung and four broken ribs. And my collarbone is dislocated. But I'll be fine."

Mary Beth swallowed hard to try to talk but couldn't seem to find her voice. Finally, she said, "I'm coming down there."

"Mary Beth, we'll be fine. I think they believe the story about the motorcycle wreck. But they wonder why you left so quickly. The doc asked me who you were. I said I don't know."

"I need to be there."

"You should just go home. There's nothing you can do here. And I don't want them to connect you with bringing us here."

"I don't care. I'm coming down there now. I don't think anyone from the ER even saw me, and the ER staff won't be coming into your room."

"Just don't go near the emergency room and don't use the Jeep. Use the other car. And I need you to call John at work and tell him that Danny and I had a motorcycle wreck."

"I'll call Cindy, too, and tell her about Danny. I put the package in a safe place."

"What?"

"I'll tell you about it later. I'm coming down there now. We need to talk about some details. John and Cindy will want to talk, too, and everyone will be asking questions. This situation won't go away Peter. We have to control it."

"Okay, you're right. We'll figure out what to do if we need to do anything … and Mary Beth, despite things not going exactly right, we did what we started out to do. As soon as we find out Danny is out of danger, I think we'll feel good about what we've done."

Mary Beth didn't think Peter even believed the words himself. "I don't think so, Peter. I don't think so at all. But we should talk about that later, not on the phone. I just pray that we haven't gotten in so deep there's no way out. I love you."

"I love you, too."

chapter 32

When Roy Gant arrived with his boss at a white two-story apartment building in South Jackson, he parked in the far back parking lot protected by an eight-foot wooden fence. He backed his Cadillac between a Tracker bass boat and a small utility trailer. Only a few scattered cars sat in the lot, and no one was outside. He wore the dark wire-rimmed sunglasses he'd favored for years.

"I'll get the shit," Gant said to McNabb. He opened the Cadillac's trunk and removed two large briefcases containing several tightly taped packages of cocaine, or something meant to look like cocaine.

They walked to a sparsely furnished apartment, with only a couch, kitchen table with four chairs, and a double bed. There were no pictures, no clothes, and no homey items. A bottle of Johnny Walker Black and two glasses sat alone on the wooden table.

"You sure no one else knows of this place?" McNabb asked, his voice angry and abrupt.

"Never told anybody about it. Only time I ever come here is to repackage merchandise into smaller bags for our street guys. You were right, William, about a day would come we needed this place."

"Well, just check the shit and get the word on the street that we'll pay big for anything that helps us find those sons-of-bitches." McNabb paced back and forth across the living room in front of the heavy curtains blocking the view from outside the window. "I don't give a damn what it costs. It's personal now."

That's what scares me, Gant thought, but he said nothing. He placed the bags in a row on the table, along with the two he had already opened.

Once again, he used his knife to remove a small amount of the powder. From a small shaving kit bag he had retrieved from the kitchen, Gant retrieved a tiny glass vial. He placed a small amount of the powder into the vial from the bag he thought was real, and then added a few drops of a chemical from another small vial to see the chemical reaction. "This one's very pure coke."

One by one he tested the remaining bags, each time growing more agitated as it became clear that none except the first contained more than baking soda.

Muttering softly, McNabb stalked around the room. "I'm going to kill those bastards. Nobody does this to William McNabb." He turned and swung at the sheetrock wall, leaving a hole the size and shape of his fist.

Gant was cramming the fake packages into a grocery sack when his cell phone rang. He looked over at McNabb and shrugged his shoulders to indicate he had no idea who might be calling. "Gant." He listened but said nothing for several seconds. "Can you get the names?" Gant continued to listen, nodding his head as he did. "Yeah, okay. Call me back when they get in a room. I'll need the number. Thanks. I owe you. There's good money in this if it turns out to be the guys we want." He pressed END and slid the phone back into the front pocket of his pants. He turned to McNabb. "Remember my nephew I told you worked at the ER at University? My sister's good-looking kid with the crew cut? I pointed him out to you once."

"Yes, what is it?"

"He's the one I called earlier to watch for anything unusual. It might be nothing, but two guys pretty beat up from a wreck were brought in."

"Well, hell, Roy, lots of guys get in wrecks," McNabb said.

"But usually they come to the ER in an ambulance. Some woman just dropped these guys off in her car and split. Didn't even leave her name. And there's one more thing."

"Tell me something good."

"She was driving a Cherokee."

———

Nelson, Hunt, and Graham spent the afternoon trying to track down McNabb and Gant. Their informants knew nothing. The three detectives now sat around the coffee table at Nelson's home in Belhaven, the sliding door open to let the thick cigarette smoke escape into the late afternoon heat.

Soon after forming his task force squad, Nelson began bringing his men to his house after work for a couple of beers, thinking the camaraderie would help build a strong team. The house became a regular and natural meeting place soon after. But today they drank coffee instead of beer. The sun fell behind the trees but still left diagonal shafts of light like spotlights on various points in the lush back yard thick with St. Augustine grass.

"Where in the hell do you think they are?" Nelson stood at the open patio door, watching squirrels chase each other around the back yard.

"I don't know," Graham answered. "Hard to believe neither the two men nor their cars have shown up at home, the Best Price, or any other usual hangouts."

"Any ideas about next steps?" Nelson asked. He walked over and sat down in an overstuffed chair, letting out a loud sigh.

"Well, they're not on the run. I say we just sit on their houses and wait," Hunt said. He leaned forward to pick up a large white mug of steaming black coffee.

"Damn it, what in the hell is going on?" Nelson asked, but it was more of a statement than a question.

"The guys from Vice say they've seen the dead guy from the bridge in the Downtown Club a lot," Hunt said. "They know he's connected to Gant, but they don't have anything on him. His sheet is full of smalltime stuff, first busted for pot when he was nineteen, a couple of assaults in bar fights."

Graham picked up a file from the coffee table and browsed through the papers inside. "Looks like he did short time in County for receiving stolen goods. Nothing big."

"Anything on those cars from the bridge?" Nelson asked.

Hunt nodded as he answered, "We tracked down the registered owner of one. Says he just sold it for cash this week to a white guy with a red hat and a ponytail."

Nelson shook his head. The description was the same as the hotel clerk remembered about how the man looked. And the same as Sleepy saw during the first incident at the hotel. Nelson knew it was no accident that so many people remembered the exact details of the hat and ponytail. Mention of the hat and ponytail made him recall a conversation he'd had a few weeks before about police work. He'd explained how some robbers evaded being identified by wearing something eye-catching to keep a frightened person from looking at what they actually looked like. Something the victims couldn't ignore, like dark glasses or a bright jacket —or a red hat. He remembered saying a red hat. He didn't mention his thoughts to his men. "What about the guy shot in the alley?"

"Still alive," Hunt said. "Critical, over at University. We've got a uniform sitting on his door to call if he wakes up, but it doesn't look good."

"What do we know about him?" Nelson asked.

Graham answered. "Guy's been working out of New Orleans but lists his home as Bay St. Louis with his parole officer. A bad dude. Twice arrested for armed robbery. Two years at Parchman, same time as Gant. Looks like they met there. Suspected in Louisiana for a hit on a drug dealer. Here's the interesting part, L.T."

"Tell me something good."

"The hit on the drug dealer in New Orleans. Same M.O. as those two hits here. Identical work."

"Now that's the best thing I've heard. Might not be a perfect tie to McNabb, but it's a start. If he wakes up, get in there and talk. We need that link to McNabb. It'll be through Gant, but that's fine. Joe, are you still scheduled to work at Best Price tonight?"

"Yeah, I'm the late duty, seven to ten. I've got to head that way soon."

"Well, let's keep that going. McNabb will have to show up eventually. I want to know if he got his hands on the cocaine. I'll be surprised if we don't start hearing of a lot of fresh flake out there soon."

When his men left, Nelson poured the last swallow of his cold coffee into the sink, rinsed the cup, and placed it back into the cabinet. He peeled off the plastic seal of a bottle of Jacob's Well bourbon that had been sitting on the counter. He unscrewed the black top and poured two fingers into his favorite tumbler, a heavy plastic glass with fly-fishing lures sealed into the plastic. He swirled the liquid around the glass and took a small sip, feeling it burn his tongue.

He knelt in front of his stereo and switched the settings to play an album. He usually played CDs but was in the mood for one of his older jazz albums on vinyl. He listened to jazz when he wanted to concentrate. He carefully slid out the recording of Thelonius Monk and placed the record on the turntable, plugged in a set of headphones, and sat down. He slowly sipped the whiskey, letting the heat build in the back of his mouth before swallowing. When he exhaled he could taste the blend of corn, sugar, and charred oak he had come to love. He lay back on the couch with his eyes closed, listening to a bebop version of *Smoke Gets in Your Eyes*.

Something new was beginning to bother him. He wanted to believe it couldn't be true, but he'd learned to doubt coincidences.

chapter 33

With the white, sterile hospital blinds closed, Peter couldn't tell if the light in his eyes was from a streetlight or if it was morning. He was on his right side facing the window when the nurse walked in carrying a tray loaded with small white paper cups containing pills, as if she were serving little capsules of hors' d'oeuvres. Peter turned over and rubbed his eyes, trying to focus through the remnants of the pain pills he had taken the night before for his broken ribs. Mary Beth dozed in a chair next to the bed. She had gone home at midnight but couldn't sleep and had slipped back into the room around five in the morning.

"Good morning," the nurse said as she walked to the blinds and opened them, allowing in the soft light. She looked at Mary Beth sitting in the same chair she had been in for hours the night before. "You're back already?"

"I just got back a little while ago." Mary Beth sat up and stretched her arms above her head, forcing the sleepiness out through her fingers.

"I checked on your friend. He's not out of his coma. He does have a pretty massive concussion, but the doctor says there doesn't appear to be swelling around his brain, and that's good. They also found he had a bad fracture of his left leg. He's likely to need surgery but not with a concussion. You're both lucky to be alive, you know." She handed Peter a small cup with three pills as she reached over and poured a cup of water from a pitcher on his bedside table. "Take these."

The nurse pushed up the sleeve of Peter's hospital gown and wrapped the blood pressure gauge around his arm. She motioned with a thermometer that looked like a glue gun for him to turn his head, and she placed the device in his ear for a few seconds. A couple of minutes later, she was out the door.

Peter leaned forward and spit one of the pills into his hand. It was a white hydrocodone. He sat up on the side of his bed and faced Mary Beth while he wrapped the pill in tissue and tossed it into the trash. "I'm not taking the pain killers so I can think. Let's talk about our story. What have you told anyone?"

"Nothing. I haven't said anything."

"Me either. So far no one has asked any questions about the wreck, other than the doctor asking what had happened. I told him I was driving and hit some gravel. Crashed into a ditch."

"That's all I told John and Cindy," Mary Beth said, as she walked to the window and opened the blinds.

"We need to keep the Triumph out of sight, and we'll have to get rid of it as soon as we can."

"Unless someone goes in the garage, I think it'll be fine," Mary Beth said.

Peter began thinking about the many hours he had spent keeping the old Triumph running and in perfect condition. Although he rarely rode the motorcycle anymore, he'd gotten the bike years earlier when he was first out of college and began making what seemed at the time like a lot of money. He had always wanted a motorcycle, but Mary Beth was scared of them, and he found himself driving it less and less. The bike stayed parked in the garage mostly, but it was polished and well-tuned.

"I called John again," Mary Beth said. "He said he'd come by first thing this morning. And I expect Cindy sometime early. She said she was getting her mother to take care of the kids."

"Just be sure she doesn't go into the garage. You might even want to put that old tarp over the bike. If by some chance Cindy sees it, we'll need to explain that I had gotten a new one."

"I'll run home and do that. Cindy was asking a neighbor to get the kids ready for school so she could leave early and be here before noon. She can stay for several days, but she'll stay down here mostly."

Peter said nothing for a few seconds. He was thinking about his partner John. He wanted to ask Mary Beth about why John had called her, but now wasn't the time or place.

———

Mary Beth spread blueberry cream cheese on half of a toasted bagel and glanced at the morning paper. The hospital cafeteria wasn't crowded, but a few people were seated at several tables. She sat near a group of nurses who were drinking coffee and all seemed to be talking at once.

As she read the newspaper and finished half of the bagel, Mary Beth couldn't help but overhear the nurses talking about how police had sat outside a patient's room all night until he died. The conversation was in hushed tones, so Mary Beth could hear only occasional words and phrases. When she heard something about a car chase, she immediately stood up and took her tray to the window. She wanted to get to Peter's room as soon as she finished buying a few things from the hospital gift shop. She felt certain the dead man had been the one chasing Peter and Danny.

She browsed quickly through a tiny shop located just off the main lobby, looking for items she thought Peter might need. She picked up a *People* magazine, two rolls of Butter Rum Lifesavers, and two packs of Dentyne gum. She placed her purchases on the counter while she looked through her purse for money. She laid a ten-dollar bill on the counter and glanced around as she waited for the clerk to ring up the items.

She was looking at a rack of artificial flower arrangements lining the glass wall along the front of the shop when she noticed a man in jeans and cowboy boots walking past in the hallway. Something seemed familiar about him. The clerk said something, and Mary Beth turned back to listen. She realized the man was Gant!

"I'm so sorry. I forgot. I'm late for something." She left the items on the counter and grabbed her ten as she stepped quickly to the door to peek down the hallway. Gant was rounding the corner toward the elevators. She heard the faint click of his boots on the hard tiles.

As soon as he was out of sight, she ran down the hallway in his direction, hoping the squeaks of her tennis shoes on the waxed floors didn't cause him to look back around the corner. When she reached the stairwell, she yanked open the door and ran up the stairs two at a time. She was out of breath by the time she reached Peter's floor. She opened the door of the stairwell a few inches and looked down the hallway. No one was there, so she ran toward Peter's room, shutting the door behind her.

"Peter, Gant's here!" She rushed around his bed and stared back at the door, afraid that any moment he'd crash through it, gun drawn.

"What do you mean here? On this floor?" Peter sat up, alarm evident in his voice.

"I don't know. I saw him walking to the elevators on the first floor, but I ran up the stairwell. I don't know where he was going for sure, but he must know something. Why else would he be here? What are we going to do?"

"He can't know who we are, Mary Beth. Maybe one of his men is here. The guy who chased us wrecked, too. There could be other reasons he's in the hospital."

"Peter, I think that man died last night. I overheard nurses talking about it a few minutes ago when I was eating breakfast in the cafeteria. I was coming to tell you that. What if Gant does know who we are?"

"Damn it," Peter said, lying back in the bed.

"Look, he can't know what I look like," Mary Beth said. "I need to go out and see if he's looking around this floor. Or Danny's room."

Peter hesitated and seemed to be struggling with an answer. She could see from the look on his face he didn't want her to go outside the room. He rubbed his fingers on his chin. His eyebrows wrinkled as he concentrated.

Mary Beth knew she had to do something. "I'll just walk down to the nurses' station. If he's not on this floor, I'll do the same on Danny's floor. Then I'll come right back." She didn't wait for a response.

She opened the door a crack and peeked out. She didn't see anyone. She stepped forward and reached back to close the door. As she stepped into the hallway, a man hidden by a large arrangement of various kinds of cut flowers in several colors nearly bumped into her. "Oh!" She jumped back a few inches before she realized the man wasn't Gant. She felt her face glowing red.

"Pardon me," the elderly man said, smiling. "Didn't mean to scare you, young lady." He stepped to the side.

She tried to smile. "It's all right. You just startled me," The gentleman nodded and walked on. She continued down the hallway to the nurses' station. After circling the station and looking for any sign of Gant down all four hallways that converged at the station, she took the elevator up to Danny's floor. She walked the length of the sixth floor hallway, pleased to find the hall crowded with nurses and a group of women and children overflowing into the hall from the waiting room. She decided to walk back to Peter's room after not seeing Gant.

Just as she was almost to Peter's room, she heard the faint sound of hard shoes on tile. The same sound she'd heard when Gant walked by earlier. The tapping echoed down the hall from near the elevators. She had to look. She walked quickly toward the elevators, hearing the elevator bell just before she reached the alcove where the elevators were located. Holding her breath, she turned the corner only to see the doors closing. No one was there.

She entered Peter's room. She found him sitting up in a chair with his shoes on. "I didn't see him. Maybe he's here for some other reason," she said, not really believing it. She wondered if Peter thought he could somehow fight off Gant if he entered the room.

"He has to be here for something else. How could he know about us, especially this fast? Not even the cops know," Peter said, but he didn't sound convincing either. "We'll just have to keep our eyes open while we figure out what to do."

But Gant does know. I know it, and you know it, Mary Beth thought.

———

Mary Beth sat on the corner of her bed and slid off her shoes, letting them fall to the floor. She crossed her legs and leaned forward to rub her arches one at a time, using both hands to work out the kinks that always started in her feet when she was stressed. She was tired, but as the day had dragged on, her anger had begun to replace weariness. She was disappointed in herself for her part in Peter and Danny getting hurt, but her resentment toward McNabb and Gant was building. Nothing in life would ever again be simple. Peter was hurt. Danny was in a coma. And now they were forced into an elaborate web of lies to friends, family, people at work, Peter's partners, and everyone they were close to. She also carried in her heart her own lie to Peter, her involvement with another man.

Then there was the fear. Fear of getting caught. Fear for Danny's life. Fear that she had forgotten some small detail that would lead the police to her door. Fear of what she and Peter had become.

But above all, there was now the very real fear of being hunted down by McNabb. Now that she had seen Gant in the hospital, she knew she had to do something. Peter didn't say much, but she could tell he was alarmed. She knew she had to assume the worst and that Gant was close to figuring out who they were, or knew already.

The tears she'd fought back several times recently were gone. She'd always hated crying and told herself she was done with it. Now a seed of anger replaced her tears, and from this seed was sprouting the idea that she had to take control. She had to find a way to make sure she and Peter wouldn't have to spend the rest of their lives looking over their shoulders whenever a stranger passed on the street or the phone rang and no one was there. And there was no time to wait, to plan, or to think the situation through the way Peter would.

She took two pillows from the bed and sat in a small space between the bed and the wall, hugging one pillow as she sat on the other. She sat that way for an hour as she thought through her plan. When she was satisfied the plan could work, she got up to get dressed.

After slipping on a pair of blue jeans and a t-shirt, she walked to the kitchen and looked for a page of hand-written notes Peter had made. When she found it, one entry caught her attention. "Gant leaves liquor store every night at six — goes to Downtown Club." Earlier she noticed Danny had left his wallet and a tiny black book filled with addresses and phone numbers on the kitchen counter. She thought nothing of it when she first noticed the wallet there, but now realized that Danny had perhaps known better than she and Peter what trouble they might find themselves in. He wouldn't have left his wallet by accident.

She picked up the little book and walked back to her bedroom, flipping through the pages. A small bookmark caused the pages to open to a specific entry that caught her eye. A moment later, Mary Beth realized Danny had marked this entry for her or Peter to find. The address book opened to an unsigned note Danny had written, saying simply, "Call Juice if anything goes wrong." Beneath the note she read Juice's phone listing.

She sat on the side of the bed and wondered if she should involve yet another person. Peter might not agree, but he was in the hospital and could do nothing. The danger was real. She dialed the number from the book.

After four rings a young woman answered, sounding as if she had been asleep. "Hello."

"May I speak to Juice?"

"Who?" the woman asked.

"Juice ... oh, I'm sorry," Mary Beth said, trying to remember his real name. The thought suddenly popped into her head that Danny had said Juice was trying to get everyone to call him Nick, since no one wanted to buy a house from someone named Juice. "Nick, may I please speak to Nick?"

"Hold on," the woman said, sounding a little annoyed and not attempting to hide her irritation. She could hear the woman calling out for Nick, telling him some woman wants him. "Can't you even get your girlfriends to wait until I'm gone to call?"

"Yeah, this is Nick."

"Juice ... Nick," Mary Beth said with obvious hesitation, not knowing what to call him. "It's Mary Beth Brantley. Peter's wife. We met once a few years ago at Danny's house."

"Sure, I remember you, Mary Beth. What's up?" The apprehension in his voice was evident.

"Danny's been hurt. He's unconscious and has some broken bones. And Peter's in the hospital, too, but he'll be fine. I know you don't know me well, but I didn't know who else to call."

"You did the right thing. Now tell me what's happened."

"Danny's often talked about you, and I know you two are close friends," Mary Beth said, hesitating for a moment. "I need your help."

"It'll be fine. Tell me what's happened. I'll help. Just start at the beginning."

Mary Beth stayed on the phone for another half hour. Juice asked few questions, mostly just listened. Mary Beth felt she had to risk telling him everything. She told Juice what she was planning.

"I'll be in Jackson by early tomorrow. Don't do anything until I get there, okay? Please. I mean it. I'm on my way, but you need to wait for me to get there," he said.

"I can pay you twenty thousand dollars to help." She wondered if the offer was the right thing to say.

"This isn't about money."

She smiled for the first time in more than twenty-four hours, hearing those words for the second time. She hung up and decided to try to sleep. As she walked around turning off lights, she heard a neighbor's dog start barking, but that wasn't unusual. She checked the lock on the back door and switched off the kitchen light before walking to the front of the house. As she reached to turn off the front light, she noticed a car stopped in front of the house next door with its headlights still on. The front porch light was on at the house, but no interior lights were on, and both cars were gone.

Just as she was beginning to think the car shouldn't be parked there with her neighbors gone, the vehicle slowly drove past her house. She watched as the car turned the corner and disappeared into the darkness. She thought she had seen one man alone in the car.

She couldn't go to sleep, the sound of Gant's boots on the tile floor of the hospital echoing in her head.

chapter 34

"We found the house," Gant said as he climbed into McNabb's car, not bothering to say hello. He slid the seatbelt over his shoulder and snapped the buckle into place. He knew McNabb wasn't in the mood for small talk.

"Is it them?"

"Looks like it. Here's what we know. Two guys were brought to the hospital by a woman, saying they'd had a motorcycle wreck. One's from here. Lives out in Ridgeland. Other one seems to be from out of town."

The late afternoon traffic on Lakeland moved slowly, so McNabb turned down a side road into a residential area of modest brick homes with tiny new trees in the front yards. "Can we move on them now?"

"They're not going anywhere. One's in a coma and the other has a broken shoulder. I got a good look at the guy in the coma. Hard to tell with his face all swollen, but he could be the guy I shot at in the car. I'm just not sure yet, so I didn't think there was any rush."

"I want to know if they're the sons of bitches with my money! Don't tell me there's no rush."

Gant felt his face heat up. He turned his head to look out the window and took a deep breath before he spoke. "William, the house isn't easy to watch in that neighborhood, but I have a guy driving past once in a while. There's no way to park nearby without having a neighbor see. It's best if we take a day to be sure we know what's going on." Gant paused briefly to see if McNabb would challenge his idea to go slowly. "There's a wife there. No kids we can see any sign of. I say we watch first. Then we go in and have a little chat with her. She'll tell us what we need. I'll handle it myself tomorrow night, after midnight. Tonight my guy will get close for a look at how to get inside the house. They do have an alarm system."

McNabb was still silent. Gant looked over at him, waiting to see if McNabb was satisfied with the plan.

"What about the other guy? The one with the shoulder. You didn't see him?"

"I went past his room three times, but his door was shut. I didn't think I needed to hang out there. His name is Peter Brantley. Some kind of advertising executive." Gant reached into his pocket and pulled out a cigarette. He placed it between his lips and flicked his lighter but held the flame away from the tip for a moment. "There's one more thing."

"Well what is it?" McNabb said, not bothering to hide his irritation.

Gant didn't like the way McNabb had begun talking to him lately. But he decided to ignore the tone for the time being. He knew it wouldn't serve him well to argue with McNabb right now. But it was one more moment that made him think his plan to get away from McNabb was the right thing to do. And while he hadn't said so outright, Gant knew that McNabb blamed him for the entire deal going bad. "I had my guy go to the house and take a quick look around. It was daytime, so I told him not to go inside the house. But he did get inside the garage."

"And?"

"There was a motorcycle there. He said the bike didn't look like a junker. It looked perfect."

"What's that mean?" McNabb said, a harsh edge in his voice.

If he had to do all the thinking he ought to be the boss. But Gant knew to keep his opinion to himself and his feelings pushed below the surface. Prison had been a valuable education in survival. He took a deep breath and fought back his anger, answering in a matter-of-fact tone. "It wasn't wrecked, for one thing. These two guys claimed they were in a motorcycle wreck, but the motorcycle is perfect. Now why would two guys be on one motorcycle if they had another one at home? These have to be our guys. Tomorrow night we'll know for sure after I have a little chat with the wife."

———

Sitting in a straight-back chair, Mary Beth raised one leg in front of her and slowly pulled a sheer black silk stocking over her foot and smoothed the material over her freshly shaved leg. The stocking reached her thigh, where she snapped the garters to pull it tight. Turning her head, she caught her image in the mirror behind the door and realized why men always seemed so excited by stockings and garters. She felt as if her consciousness of the world had reached a new level and that whatever naïve view of the world she once held was now wiped out forever.

With a foot up on the seat, she ran one hand down her leg from her knee along the side of her thigh and up to the black lace panties. She turned slightly to see the deep cleavage created by her bra. The dark outlines of her small nipples were visible through the lace. She rubbed her nipples with the palms of her hands and turned sideways to see if she could see them take shape through the soft fabric.

She had worn the garter and stockings along with the high-cut panties and push-up bra only once before. She smiled, remembering the incredible sex she and Peter had enjoyed after that Halloween party. She had attributed the passion of that night to the alcohol both had consumed. Seeing herself now in a different light, she realized it might have been more.

She pulled on a short black leather skirt and a tight red blouse with a deep V in front. The skirt covered the black underwear, though the dark stocking tops could clearly be seen when she sat with her legs crossed.

She removed from a shopping bag an expensive blonde wig with short curls, purchased that afternoon, and pulled the wig over her head. She repositioned the wig until she was satisfied the hair looked natural and then pinned it in place. Next she removed a new pair of four-inch heels covered in black satin from their box and put them on.

She leaned toward the mirror and applied heavy charcoal eye shadow with a bit of silver at the corner of her eyes.

Standing in front of the mirror, she posed to see if she could look comfortable and natural. She pulled the chair in front of the mirror and practiced sitting, crossing, and uncrossing her legs to see how much she could show and how to control giving someone just a quick peek.

She sprayed perfume behind each ear and picked up a large purse. She went through a checklist of the items she had already placed in the purse, including a small pill from Juice, a wrapped package of cocaine, and a smaller bag Peter had brought home earlier with just a few teaspoons of the powder. She thought about Peter's pistol he'd said was under the mattress, but she knew she couldn't use a gun. With one last glance in the mirror, she walked into the living room where Juice sat on the couch.

He stood up when he heard her walk into the room. "Wow," he said quietly as he stood and turned toward her. "This will work."

In his hand was the sports bag he and Mary Beth had retrieved from the barn that afternoon, with only four fewer kilos than it originally held at the Greyhound station.

"I'm ready." She opened the front door and walked outside to the garage. She was all business now, and the sooner they got started the better. Seeing no neighbors outside, she opened the garage door. "It's under that tarp."

Juice pulled back the canvas cover Mary Beth had placed there earlier and climbed on the big motorcycle. He strapped on the blue helmet that had been hanging from the handle bars. He pressed the starter, and the engine echoed off the walls of the garage. He waved Mary Beth on, and she pulled out of the driveway in her car, Juice following.

Fifteen minutes later, she pulled off to the side of a rural road next to a steep incline. She got out and looked both ways for any traffic. "How does this look? I think this is about where Peter told his doctor he had a wreck."

"Yeah, this is a good place," Juice said.

She stood beside her car with the door open as Juice bent over the front tire of the motorcycle. He pressed a knife into the tire, making a long slit, and then pushed a large piece of broken Coke bottle into the cut. He switched off the engine, turned the key back to the on position, and rolled the motorcycle down the hill. The bike flipped end over end, bits of metal and plastic flying off, and came to rest at the bottom of the embankment. He banged the helmet on the pavement a couple of times and tossed it down the hill beside the smashed motorcycle.

Juice climbed into the car with Mary Beth. "Let's get out of here before someone sees us."

Mary Beth drove into the parking lot of a nearby Chevron station and parked on the side near two pay phones. She removed a scrap of paper with a telephone number from her pocket and dialed. The phone was answered after one ring.

"Yeah, I want to report seeing a motorcycle on the roadside that looked like a wreck," she mumbled.

"Yes, may I get your name please?" the young woman from the sheriff's office asked. "Was anyone injured?"

"I don't have time to get involved. Just go out to Highway 17 near mile marker twenty-seven. You'll see it." She hung up when the young woman asked her name the second time.

"Thanks for thinking of doing that with the motorcycle," she said as they drove. "Do you think the hospital will report Danny and Peter as having a wreck?"

"They might. They keep all sorts of records because of all the lawsuits these days."

The sun had set, but it wasn't completely dark when Juice drove into the Downtown Club parking lot. Mary Beth was in the seat beside him. The horizon behind the trees and two-story warehouse buildings that made up the skyline for this part of town still glowed a bright orange.

"That's his car," Mary Beth said immediately. "Do you see anyone that might be following him?"

"Hard to say. Let me scope it out for a few minutes." Juice drove through the parking lot to the vacant lot next door and backed his Blazer into a spot beneath a large old sycamore tree. From there he scanned the parking lot. "I don't think he's being followed."

The tree's long limbs formed a canopy that shielded Juice's car from the glow of three mercury streetlights just coming on along the front of the parking lot.

Mary Beth flipped down the visor on the passenger side and checked her makeup. "Well, this is it. Wish me luck."

"Be very, very careful," Juice said. "You don't need luck. You have to be smart and not take extra chances. Once you're inside, you have to stay in control. You'll be working without a net in there. I'll wait right here for fifteen minutes. If anything feels wrong, anything at all, just walk out and we'll get the hell out of here. If not, I'll go take care of planting the bags. I'll be gone forty-five minutes at the most and then park right here again."

She started to get out of the car, but Juice grabbed her arm. When she turned they were eye-to-eye.

Softly but sternly, Juice said, "Mary Beth, this guy won't play games with you. If he figures you out, you'll get hurt. Don't take unnecessary chances. I've been around a lot of people with coke. People selling it, people buying it. People sniffing it, shooting it, smoking it. Anything you've heard good about cocaine is nothing but a lie. Everything bad you've ever heard is true. My buddies call coke the white lie."

Mary Beth was surprised by the gentleness of Juice's hands when he took both her hands in his and leaned forward just inches from her face. "Nose candy makes good people into bad people and bad people into assholes. I have to say one more time that I don't think this is a good idea. I don't think Peter would like it. And Danny wouldn't ever want you to do this for him. Are you sure you have to do this?"

Mary Beth shrugged. "Believe me, I'll be careful. I have to do this. To make sure no one comes after us. They may be on to Peter and Danny, but they don't know about me. I have to do something now ... before they do."

"If you're going to do this, I'm going to help. But understand that once you sit down at that guy's table and start things rolling, there's no easy way out. Do you have the coke? And the GHB?"

"Everything I need is in my purse." She leaned over and hugged him. "Thanks, Juice."

———

Juice unfolded the map Mary Beth had drawn on a sheet torn from a legal pad and studied the drawing as he sat at a traffic light on North State Street. He passed University Hospital on the right as he drove north. Seeing the hospital made him wonder again what Peter and Danny would think if they knew what he and Mary Beth were about to do. He had been in enough dangerous situations to know something unexpected always happened. He hoped he would be able to deal with the situation when it did.

He put the map on the passenger seat and drove toward the strip shopping center. With luck, he would find McNabb's car there, thus avoiding a return trip later that night to break into the liquor store as a backup plan, though he knew he could do the break-in easily if it came to that.

Two minutes later, Juice cruised down the front of the shopping center past the Best Price store Mary Beth had shown him that afternoon. He turned right past McRae's and circled behind the store. He smiled when he saw McNabb's car on the street. He looked left at the back alley and, as Mary Beth had warned, saw a man parked in a white Taurus. Obviously a cop. Juice smiled to himself, pleased that Mary Beth had learned so much detail about what the police were doing. For a moment he wondered how she'd learned so much.

There was no way to get to McNabb's car without being seen. Juice circled back though the parking lot and pulled into a slot between two cars in front of the shopping center. He got out and walked into the department store, noting that the security guard—in a white golf cart with an amber flashing light on top—was at the far end of the parking lot, talking and laughing with two men on the sidewalk. The guard wasn't paying much attention to his work. After three minutes Juice walked back to his car.

He stopped and lit a cigarette, providing him a moment for one final look around to see if anyone was nearby. The guard was still in his conversation. When no one else appeared interested in him, Juice pulled out a package of Black Cat firecrackers and laid them beneath the car parked beside him. Twisting together the fuses at one end, he forced the cigarette through the tangle of fuses so that the glowing tip would ignite them in a couple of minutes.

He drove around the block to park on a side street behind the shopping center, hidden from view by a light green clapboard house on the corner. If he cut diagonally across the alley, he was only a few seconds walk from McNabb's car.

He had just parked and rolled down his window when the popping sound started. The cop sprang from his Taurus with his gun drawn half hidden at his side and quickly moved around the corner. The instant the cop was out of sight, Juice ran toward McNabb's car, making no pretense of being someone out for a stroll. In his right hand was a McRae's Department Store shopping bag. Inside the bag was a thin, flat metal bar to help him unlock McNabb's car, along with a sports bag full of cocaine. He lowered the bag to the pavement beside him before he slid the metal bar down the driver's side door window and under the rubber seal. He felt the metal connect with the lock and tried to force the mechanism to the side. Nothing happened. It had been several years since he had used the device to break into a car. He never had been good at it, and he had only stolen one car. But he had stolen dozens of tape players and radios from cars before deciding there were safer ways to make money. He felt the metal slide into place and suddenly the lock popped up on the door. He opened the door and reached inside to push the trunk button.

Opening the trunk, he tossed the sports bag inside before leaning over and pushing the bag past the spare tire and against the springs of the back seat. If McNabb opened the trunk, he would have to bend over and look under the trunk lid to see the bag. Juice closed the trunk and locked the car door. He turned and walked away, holding the shopping bag as if he'd finished making a small purchase. When he was no more than fifty steps from the car, he saw the cop come walking quickly back around the corner. Juice didn't look back but simply walked to his car and drove back to the Downtown Club.

chapter 35

Mary Beth stood in the doorway for a few seconds as her eyes adjusted to the dark room. The Downtown Club was hazy with smoke from cigars and cigarettes. A dozen or so men gathered around the pool tables in back or slouched on the bar stools. She saw only two women, seated with one man in a corner booth. Most of the men looked like the type who were there for a quick beer on their way home from the nearby welding shops, auto parts warehouses, and used car lots.

She saw Gant sitting at a table past the end of the bar, near three pool tables. As she walked slowly behind the row of bar stools along the right side of the room, the noise grew a bit quieter. She found a stool near the end of the bar, not far from Gant's table. The bartender flipped over his shoulder a small white towel he had been using to wipe freshly washed mugs and walked over to Mary Beth.

"Yes ma'am," he said, lifting his eyebrows as if asking an obvious question.

"Vodka. Rocks. Double," Mary Beth said just loud enough for Gant to hear. She opened her purse and removed a pack of Virginia Slims, a Bic lighter, and a twenty-dollar bill. She placed the twenty on the bar. She took out a cigarette and was about to light it when the bartender reached into his shirt pocket for matches. He lit one and held the flame a few inches in front of her. She leaned forward toward the match without bothering to reach a hand up to the front of her blouse, allowing the bartender a good look where she had left an extra button unfastened. She smiled when he realized he had been caught looking. She acted as if looking was expected and appreciated but wasn't to be acknowledged. The bartender turned and began pouring a drink and, a few moments later, set the drink in front of her on a thin napkin.

She could see herself in the mirror behind the bar, beside bottles of Jim Beam and Jack Daniels Bourbon, Taaka Vodka, Gilbey's Gin, and a pyramid of glasses stacked upside down. Above the mirror, bumper stickers of all types were stuck to the wall, some brown from age. Ski Mississippi. American by Birth, Southern by the Grace of God. Wallace for President. Gun Control Means Using Both Hands. Problem with My Driving? Call 1-800-EAT-SHIT. Work is for people who can't fish.

She looked in the mirror and pretended to find something wrong with the makeup around her eyes. She turned toward the bartender as she stood up and clutched her purse. "Where's your ladies room, Sugar?"

"Back in that corner, behind the pool tables."

She picked up her drink and walked toward the restroom, taking a route close enough to Gant for him to smell her perfume. In the restroom she leaned toward the smudged mirror as she opened her lipstick. She twirled the tube, and then slid the end between her lips from left to right, coating both lips at once with a thick red color. She checked her wig, took a gulp of vodka, and swished the liquor around her mouth to make sure she had the smell on her breath. Then she spit the vodka into the grimy sink and poured out the rest while holding her fingers over the ice. She refilled the drink with tap water and walked back to her bar stool. She sat and sipped the water for ten minutes before downing the last few drops.

She slid the glass across the bar and caught the bartender's attention. "Another, please."

The bartender dumped the ice in the sink, picked up a fresh glass, and filled it with ice and a double vodka. He put the glass on a fresh square napkin and slid the drink in front of her. He picked up a five-dollar bill from the ten and five from her change.

Mary Beth slowly sipped the vodka, thinking that a couple of sips might even help relax her a little. In the mirror she checked to see if Gant watched. When she was sure he was, she put her elbows on the bar and crossed her legs, allowing the tight skirt to slide up her thigh enough so that the top of the stocking peeked out just a little. She rocked sideways on the stool and pulled the skirt lower. She knew the effect had been good. Gant was practically staring now. He didn't realize she was watching him in the mirror.

The bartender served a couple of beers at the other end of the bar before he wandered back down in front of Mary Beth. She spoke first. "What kind of stuff you got on the jukebox?"

"Oh, you know. The usual. It's a pretty good selection. Dwight Yoakam, Kenny Chesney, Toby Keith, Jo Dee Messina, Confederate Railroad. Some older stuff, too. George Jones, David Allen Coe, Willie Nelson. Here, I'm buying if you're flying." The bartender took two dollars from the tip jar and handed the bills to her. She reached for the money, knowing the two dollars were just to see her walk across the room and bend over the jukebox.

She smiled at him as she stood up and grabbed the money. "Anything you want to hear?"

"Whatever you like is fine, Sweetheart."

She sipped her drink as she walked to the jukebox, swaying her hips. She mostly picked slow songs. As she bent over to punch the numbers and letters, she knew every man nearby was watching her and hoping the skirt would ride higher up the backs of her thighs.

On the way back to the bar, she stopped off briefly at the ladies room again, repeating her earlier move of pouring out the vodka and replacing it with water. She walked past Gant and sat sideways on the bar stool, giving him a quick view between her legs as she swung around to face the bar. When she crossed her legs, she let the skirt ride up a little higher than before. From Gant's viewpoint, the stocking tops would be clearly visible.

Mary Beth sipped her water for another fifteen minutes. Occasionally she spoke to the bartender, who always seemed to wander back to her end of the bar immediately after he served customers at the other end.

Just as she finished the second double water, the bartender slid a drink in front of her. "Compliments of the gentleman over there." He tilted his head toward where Gant was sitting.

"I don't usually take drinks from strangers," she said, speaking slowly and trying to sound just a bit drunk. She smiled a little, but tried not to come across too easy.

"Hey, it's up to you," he said and stepped back, standing farther away than before and not attempting to keep the conversation going as he had tried earlier. She could tell Gant wasn't someone the bartender wanted to compete with for a woman.

She let the glass sit on the bar for a minute, and then took a deep breath, picked the drink up, and turned in her seat. She held the glass up toward Gant in a mock toast and took a sip. Gant picked up his beer and returned the toast, leaning back in his chair with his legs crossed and his boots reflecting the colored bar lights. She turned back around to face the bar, but let the skirt slide up another inch so that the stocking top and just a fraction of the garter showed. She sat that way for a couple of minutes before she tugged on the skirt and again pulled it down over the side of her leg.

For another ten minutes she sipped her drink only casually and cautiously watched Gant, not wanting to appear too eager. She wondered if Gant was used to waiting out new women he met. When the bartender returned from checking his customers at the far end of the bar, she asked him to take Gant another beer. When the bartender delivered the beer, she stood and walked to the table.

Several men nearby, who had no reason to be hopeful about their chances with the whore in the short leather skirt, looked disappointed nevertheless as she sat down.

"Mind if I join you? I hate to drink alone."

"Please do," Gant said, halfway standing and reaching to help with her chair. He didn't appear surprised to see her.

"I'm Casey. What's your name?"

"Everyone calls me Gant. I don't think I've seen you in here before."

"No, you ain't seen me here before. I just moved into town. I split with my old man in Hattiesburg and moved up here to try something new." She tried not to pour on the country too much. She wanted to sound uneducated, not stupid.

"Well, you might like it here. Just about everybody comes in this bar is a regular. We don't see many new people here." He added, "Especially any as good looking as you."

Gant seemed smart. She knew he was venturing a safe compliment to see where it might go. She just smiled and didn't act offended.

It worked. He grew a little bolder. "Are you meeting someone here?"

"No. Just wanted to get out of that little apartment and have a drink around some people. Not that I know anybody around here." Mary Beth fumbled in her purse, acting a bit drunk as she removed her cigarettes. "Had the opposite problem back home. Knew too many people. Every time I went out down there I ran into one of my ex's sisters or his drinking buddies." She shook out the last cigarette, crumpled the package, and tossed it onto the table. She held the cigarette between her fingers, leaning toward Gant while holding the cigarette in front of her face. Before leaving home she had emptied the pack of all but three cigarettes so she could run out easily. "Light?"

Gant reached into his pocket and pulled out a Zippo lighter. She noticed it was worn from years of use, brass showing at the corners where there had once been shiny chrome. He flicked his thumb across the little wheel, and a flame appeared on the first try. She leaned over, allowing her blouse to swing open and giving Gant the same clear view she'd given the bartender.

"Thank you, Sweetie." She took a long drag on the cigarette and tilted her head back as she blew the smoke into the air above her head. *Damn, this tastes good,* she thought, surprised she was ever able to quit.

Gant said nothing, merely nodded slightly as he slid the lighter back into his jeans pocket and crossed his legs. His own cigarette sat burning on the ashtray. She noticed his boots were polished to a fine sheen, which fit with the extra starch in his shirt and the pressed crease in his blue jeans.

She leaned forward to talk. She made up as little personal history as she had to and tried to steer the conversation back to Gant. He said little about himself. Only that he helped someone manage a string of liquor stores and that he had grown up in the Delta before moving to Jackson twenty-five years earlier.

She sipped the vodka drink, trying to allow the liquor to melt the ice and water itself down. She reached in her purse and pulled out four one-dollar bills. "Honey, do you mind getting me some smokes? Virginia Slim 100s?"

Gant accepted the bills and walked toward the cigarette machine near the front door. As soon as he walked away, she reached into her purse, removed the small pill Juice had given her, and placed it on the edge of the table. She casually looked around. It seemed no one was watching closely. She crushed the pill under her glass and brushed the powder into her palm. She moved her hand over Gant's beer as if reaching for the ashtray and dropped in the powder. Then she slid two empty cans into her purse. She picked up her own drink and walked to the restroom, once again repeating the switch of water for vodka. She reached up and fluffed her hair a little, leaving it slightly imperfect. She opened her lipstick and ran it across her lips, coloring both in a single stroke.

Gant was already waiting back at the table with the new pack of Virginia Slims. When she took out a cigarette, he held the lighter for her again. She took a drag, tilted her head back, and downed the last swallow of water. Gant held his beer up to the bartender and made a circular motion with his finger extended to order another round. Then he downed his beer and, she hoped, the pill. Juice had told her he had no experience with the pill many used as a recreational drug, but it was also known as the Date Rape Pill and was very powerful when combined with alcohol. He said the man who sold it to him in Birmingham claimed it worked in only a few minutes. Juice told her to be careful and watch for signs that the pill was taking effect because once it did she had to get Gant out of the bar quickly —or she might not be able to get him out at all.

Mary Beth leaned back in her chair and again held up her drink in a toast to Gant. "Here's to new places and new friends."

She placed the drink to her lips and pretended to take a big swallow as she leaned back and crossed her legs. Gant was taking a long drink of his beer, but she saw him look down just as she crossed her legs. She shifted in her chair so the leather skirt rode up. She knew Gant could see above the stockings to her garters.

A pool table was open behind Gant. She uncrossed her legs and momentarily held her knees three or four inches apart as she slowly leaned forward. Gant could see the insides of her thighs all the way to the lacy panties. In a low, husky voice, she said, "Want to play pool?"

"Sure," Gant said, smiling.

She walked to the table, wobbling slightly. She could feel the three quarters she had stacked inside one of her shoes on her last trip to the ladies room. The quarters made her walk unbalanced. She had seen the trick on a spy show on the History Channel.

Gant put quarters into the pool table and racked the balls. "You want to break?"

"Sure baby," she said as she began applying chalk to the cue stick.

Gant walked behind her as she bent over to make the pool shot. The cue ball made a crisp, loud crack as it sent the triangle of balls spinning around the table, though no balls went in.

"Good break. Bad luck," Gant said, seeing how hard she had hit the cue ball.

"Yeah, my old man used to take me to play a lot." The story was partially true, and she knew she could back up the statement with her play. She and Peter used to play often after they bought a pool table for the den.

Neither she nor Gant played well. She made a couple of easy shots to show she had played before, but she intentionally missed several shots to buy time and to flash Gant until his interest in her could build to a peak. She could see Gant was enjoying watching her bend over and stretch to make shots. She allowed everyone around to see plenty of leg and lots of cleavage when she leaned forward to study each shot. Finally the game was over when Gant sank the eight ball after she had moved the ball so close to the hole that to miss the shot would have been obvious. Gant was beginning to appear drunk.

"I get bored real quick. Let's go have another drink." She tossed her cue stick on the pool table as she walked back to their chairs. Gant followed.

For another twenty minutes she managed to carry on a conversation. She mostly asked Gant questions about Jackson, places to eat, other clubs, all of which he answered with short sentences. She noticed he was having trouble concentrating. She was certain the pill was beginning to take effect.

It was now or never. She could feel her heart speed up and reminded herself Juice was right outside on speed dial if she needed him. She forced herself to smile when running for the door was what her brain was yelling. She scooted her chair closer to Gant and leaned into him, putting her hand on his knee and letting her fingers trail lightly down the inside of his leg. She knew he could smell her, despite the smoke and stale beer. "Do you like to dance? Is there somewhere we could go? I'm tired of this place."

"I don't like to dance." Gant was slurring his words now, giving Mary Beth a little more confidence. "But we can go somewhere else if you want to."

"Then drink up," Mary Beth said. Gant tipped back the nearly full beer he had just ordered and drained it. She stood up, squeezing Gant's thigh before removing her hand. "Let's go."

Gant was up in a second. He dropped several bills on the table, and the two of them walked outside. The entire place grew momentarily quieter as it had when she walked in. She heard a hushed comment about Gant's getting lucky, followed by muffled laughter.

"Where's your car, honey?" she asked. Gant motioned toward his El Dorado. She almost sighed with relief when she saw Juice parked in the spot where he said he would be.

You have to be good at this and you have to be strong, Mary Beth told herself as she walked across the parking lot. When they reached the car, she spun around and leaned back against the driver's side door. She grabbed the front of Gant's shirt and pulled him to her as she put her arms around his neck. In his eyes she could see a mixture of confusion and desire. The pill was slowing Gant, but he managed to put one hand down to her skirt to feel her thigh through the leather. She rubbed her palm down the front of Gant's pants across his zipper, knowing that he couldn't think straight once she had him completely aroused and drugged at the same time. She could feel him begin to grow hard, so she cupped him through his jeans, closing her eyes as she did and talking herself through it. *Just get through it. It's almost over.*

She allowed him to push up her skirt, moving his hand away once he had felt the silk panties. His other hand was around her neck. As he bent toward her to kiss her, she could smell the alcohol on his vinegar breath and the acrid bar smoke that had saturated both their clothes. She turned her head at the last second, pulled his head forward, and put her mouth to his ear, kissing it lightly. "Not out here, Baby. Let's go somewhere private," she whispered, her lips moving against his ear.

Mary Beth thought she saw Juice sit up in his seat as she looked ahead. She hoped he was holding the thirty-inch wooden Louisville Slugger bat he had placed on the seat next to him when they had left the house earlier. Gant's hands moved over her body, but she stopped him before he could feel under her clothes. "Let's get in the car for that, darlin'."

After Gant found his keys, she unlocked the doors. She had to help Gant into the driver's seat and went around to the passenger side. She dropped the keys onto the floor.

"Where're my keys?" Gant asked, with the sentence coming out as one long word.

"It's all right, Baby. Let's just sit here." Mary Beth turned in the seat so she could scan the parking lot. She reached over with her right hand and fondled him lightly, pretending to work his zipper. "Let me take care of you first. Just sit back and relax."

Gant leaned back, let his arms fall to his sides, and closed his eyes.

She left her hand in his lap, rubbing the outside of Gant's pants just enough to keep him occupied and his eyes closed. She looked around the parking lot at the cars as Gant grew still. She continued moving her hand slightly between his legs. As far as she could tell, no one else was around. Gant's head slumped to the side.

"Hey Sweetie, are you awake?"

No reply from Gant. She shook him by the shoulder. Still no response.

She put on latex gloves from her purse and began working as quickly as she could. She picked up the keys and wiped them with a scarf, then placed the car key in the ignition. She removed the large wrapped kilo package of cocaine and threw it into the floor on her side where it would be clearly visible from outside the car. Next she opened a small plastic bag of cocaine and placed it on the center console. She found a small mirror and wiped it clean of prints. Taking Gant's right hand, she pressed his thumb and fingers onto the glass. She put a teaspoon of the cocaine on the mirror, along with a short McDonald's straw she had cut in half, and placed them all on the console next to the bag of drugs.

She pinched a small amount of the cocaine between her thumb and finger and forced it into Gant's mouth. She was careful not to use too much, taking just a tiny bit that Juice had told her would be enough to show cocaine in Gant's blood. She sprinkled cocaine powder onto Gant's top lip and down the front of his shirt.

From her purse, she removed two Bud Light beer cans she had taken from the table inside, knowing they had Gant's fingerprints on them. She turned both cans upside down and shook the small remaining liquid onto Gant's shirt. She threw one can on the floor and placed the other between Gant's legs on the seat.

Headlights startled her as a pickup truck parked nearby. Two men got out. The man on the passenger side saw them in the car. She leaned over and put her arms around Gant, pretending to kiss him. She heard the two men laughing as they walked inside.

She turned the key and the engine started immediately. Sliding over in her seat so she could reach the gas pedal with her left foot, she put the car into reverse. Checking to make sure no other occupied cars were around, she began backing across the parking lot.

When she reached the paved street, she continued across the road into the parking lot of a NAPA auto parts store on the opposite side. She steered the car toward the front door and slowed slightly as she neared the glass. As the car hit the door and the glass shattered, she removed her foot from the gas. The car stopped with its trunk two feet inside the front of the store. The engine was still running. Immediately she heard deafening alarms go off. Gant was slumped against his door, his head to the side and partially out the open window. He certainly looked like a passed-out drunk.

Mary Beth reached for her purse and found the contents had spilled onto the floor. She opened her door and stepped outside, then leaned in and scooped up her makeup, keys, and wallet. She removed her gloves and crammed them into her purse.

She walked quickly across the parking lot toward the bar, using every bit of her self-control to keep from running. She went straight to the pay phone just inside the front door and dropped a quarter and dime into the slot. When the 911 dispatcher answered on the second ring, Mary Beth said, "Hey, some drunk just ran into the building across from the Downtown Club. You should send the police." She hung up and took the side exit out of the bar.

chapter 36

Parked a block away from the Downtown Club, Taylor Nelson sat in his Lumina on the night's early first surveillance shift, watching Gant making out with a Downtown Club whore. When the car backed across the street and just kept going into the glass front of the NAPA store, Nelson spoke out loud to himself, "What in the hell?" Before he could decide what to do, a short-haired blonde in a tight skirt stepped out of Gant's car and hurried back into the bar, tiptoeing through the rocky parking lot in high heels. For a moment he thought her walk seemed somehow familiar, but he couldn't place the blonde hair. When Gant didn't get out of the car, Nelson had to check on him. He called for uniformed officers as he drove to the front of the auto parts parking lot.

When he walked up to Gant's car, he realized Gant was unconscious. He didn't think the car had been going fast enough to hurt Gant, and he couldn't imagine he'd had time to drink himself this drunk. He reached in the open window and felt for a pulse on Gant's neck. It felt strong. Before he could investigate further, a police cruiser roared down West Street with its lights flashing. He stepped back from the car and held out his badge as the uniformed cops skidded to a stop in a black and white cruiser in front of the El Dorado.

"Lt. Taylor Nelson with the Drug Enforcement Task Force. Looks like he passed out," he said to the first uniformed officer to walk up, though somehow he doubted it. "I was driving by and saw him back all the way across the street from the parking lot over there. Female with him ran back to the bar. Short skirt, red top, blonde curly hair. Can't miss her." As far as he was concerned, this was just a traffic accident and DUI, nothing the Task Force should handle. He decided to wait around and watch to see what happened, so he backed up a few steps and let the uniformed officers do their jobs.

One of the cops just stared for a second, obviously wondering about the coincidence, but he said nothing. The other cop walked up to Gant and checked his pulse, shining his light down the front of Gant to look for blood or other obvious injuries. "Hey, buddy, you okay?" There was no response.

He opened Gant's eyelids with his fingers. "He's totally out. Looks like he's just drunk. I don't think he's hurt." He shined the flashlight into the interior.

"Holy shit! Look at this," the officer said to Nelson and the other uniformed officer who had walked up. He shined the long black flashlight onto an open bag of white powder, then on a mirror and straw lying on the console. And finally they saw the kilo of cocaine on the floorboard.

Now it was Nelson's case.

———

Mary Beth sat low in the seat beside Juice and watched over the dash. She removed her wig and shook out her own hair, glad to be herself once again. She reached out and touched Juice's arm just as he put the Blazer in gear. "Wait. Can we watch?"

"We should get out of here. That first guy who walked up had a badge. May have seen the whole thing. You said they'd been watching this guy. He may have been following Gant."

She felt her stomach become a knot as Juice pointed out the officer in plain clothes who had been watching, but she wanted to know what would happen. She couldn't take her eyes off the plain clothes officer. "Well, just watch for a minute. I want to see him arrested."

Juice shook his head as he put the car back in park. "At least put these on." He handed Mary Beth an Atlanta Braves baseball cap and a white sweatshirt from behind the seat.

As she slid the sweatshirt over her head, Mary Beth had a feeling of déjà vu. She said nothing, but she felt no surprise at what was happening to Gant.

The two uniformed officers opened Gant's door, and paramedics lifted him out after affixing a collar to hold his head. They laid him on a stretcher. When they frisked him, one officer held up a small pistol he found inside Gant's boot. The two officers each removed their cuffs and fastened them to his wrists and the side bars of the stretcher.

When one of the police officers turned and started walking toward the front door of the bar, Juice turned to Mary Beth. "We have to go. They may know what you look like. Slide down in the floor where they can't see you."

A crowd of several men and two women came out the front door to see what was going on, attracted by the flashing blue lights. Two cars pulled into the parking lot at the same time. Juice drove away.

"I think you can sit up now," Juice said when they were two blocks away and no cop cars were following them. "Damn, lady, you're good. Remind me not to piss you off."

———

Juice drove Mary Beth home to change clothes before they went to the University Medical Center. She listened to the answering machine. "This is the Hinds County Sheriff's Department. We've recovered a wrecked motorcycle registered in the name of Peter Brantley. Please call us immediately."

She called back and explained who she was. The woman who answered then transferred her to a deputy who asked her to start over. She again explained that there had been a wreck and someone had taken her husband to the hospital. She told the deputy she had been so upset she didn't think about reporting the accident herself and assumed that had been taken care of when Peter had been admitted to the hospital. She also told him she only had a general idea of where the wreck happened. The deputy took the information and said he would come by the hospital to complete a report the next day.

She changed from her short skirt and pulled on a pair of jeans. In the bathroom she washed off the heavy makeup and dug through her purse for her lipstick. The lipstick wasn't there. She dumped out the entire purse, frantically sifting through the items.

"Juice," she yelled.

He came running through the bedroom.

"Are you all right?"

"Yeah, sorry, I didn't mean to sound so alarmed. But I think my lipstick's in Gant's car. I spilled my purse. I thought I found everything."

"Hey, it's all right. They won't know whose it is. Don't worry about it. Are you sure you didn't leave anything they could trace? You got your wallet and all?"

"Yeah, it's all here."

"Then don't worry about it. Even a fingerprint won't help them unless they have yours on file. You haven't been arrested have you?"

"No!" She punched Juice's arm.

"Then what could it possibly hurt?"

On the way to visit Peter, Mary Beth decided to tell him everything, but not today. Well, at least everything she and Juice had done. They went straight to Peter's room. Mary Beth walked in first. Peter was awake.

"I've been calling you," Peter said. The unspoken question of where she had been and a bit of irritation was obvious.

She hugged him, trying not to hurt his ribs, kissed him on the forehead, and smoothed back his hair. He had eaten everything from the plastic hospital plate except a square of green Jell-O.

"I had a lot of errands to catch up on. Guess who's here," she said and turned toward Juice, who walked up to Peter's bed.

"Juice, hey man. What are you doing here?" Peter asked, a confused look on his face.

"Mary Beth called and told me you guys had a little problem, and I wanted to come over to help if I can. I hear Danny's not doing so well."

Mary Beth was happy that it hadn't occurred to Peter that she had met Juice only once years before and certainly did not know him well enough to have his phone number. Though the medications weren't keeping him in a total fog now, she could see he wasn't thinking clearly.

"Juice came over to help me with the motorcycle." She did not want to risk saying too much, still spooked by all of the events and never knowing when a nurse might come in.

"What do you mean?" Peter said.

"We had to stage a wreck." She gave Peter a moment for this information to sink in. "Juice knows everything. He agreed we had to make it real for the police. Just in case."

Peter looked at Mary Beth for several seconds before speaking. "Yeah, that was a good idea." He looked over at Juice with gratitude in his eyes. "Thanks for coming, Juice."

Mary Beth kissed Peter on the cheek and put her lips close to his ear. She had to tell him what was happening. At least some of what was happening. "Your bike is gone, honey. Please don't be mad. We rolled it down a hill. It's all smashed up. We set it up to look like a wreck, and then we talked with the sheriff's department. They think you had a wreck and someone brought you here."

Peter listened in silence before he nodded slowly.

She could see he was thinking. Perhaps trying to decide if he liked Juice being in on things. Or maybe he was questioning if he truly liked destroying his motorcycle. He really loved that bike. She spoke low in his ear again. "Peter, we had to stage the wreck for your alibi." She hoped to help him understand they'd done the right thing.

"I'll leave you two alone," Juice said. "Where's Danny's room? I'll at least try to get someone to tell Cindy I'm here and see if I can do anything for her."

"Six fourteen. Take the elevator at the end of the hall up to the sixth floor. Six fourteen is on the left when you get off," Mary Beth said.

As Juice reached the door, Peter looked at Mary Beth, then called out, "Juice."

"Yeah man?" Juice said, standing halfway out the door.

"Thanks for coming. And thanks for helping Mary Beth."

"De nada, bro. Just wait 'til you get my bill." Juice turned and left before Peter could reply.

Mary Beth was glad Peter sounded like he was beginning to understand how Juice had helped. As she looked at Peter, she felt closer to him than she had in years. This was the man she remembered, the one she had fallen in love with so many years before.

Mary Beth pulled her chair close, leaned over Peter, and put her head on his good shoulder. She wanted to get in bed with him and cuddle up. There was so much she wanted to tell him, but she thought more talk should wait until he came home and they could talk with more privacy. And less pain medication.

Peter seemed satisfied with what she and Juice had done but remained quiet as they lay there together. She guessed he was sorting out what all had happened.

Finally, Mary Beth decided she should tell Peter at least part of what they'd done. "We put drugs in Gant's and McNabb's cars. We called in a tip and got Gant busted." Mary Beth could see the light of approval in Peter's eyes. He gave her a smile.

"And tomorrow," she said, "we'll do the same to McNabb."

chapter 37

Just after 6 a.m., Mary Beth woke up and hurried out to get the newspaper. There was a photo of Gant on the front of the Metro section under the headline "Police seize cocaine and cash." There was also a photo of the kilo of cocaine along with two shotguns, two handguns, a switchblade knife, and $500,000 in cash the police had seized.

She felt a chill run down her spine when she saw the guns and read they had been in Gant's car. She also knew Peter would have to hear the entire story now. The article explained that Gant was on parole after serving five years of an eight-year sentence for selling marijuana to an undercover cop in a huge sting that netted twenty-one people in four counties. There was no mention of a mysterious woman being with Gant when he had wrecked his car. The cash had been found in a secret compartment in his trunk.

Juice stood in the kitchen, fully dressed, looking through the pantry when she walked back into the house. "Good morning. I thought I'd make some coffee if I could find it."

"Here, I'll get it. Read this. Is Cindy up?" Mary Beth held out the newspaper and pointed to the story about Gant. She dumped French Market Coffee into the filter without measuring and poured water into the Mr. Coffee.

"I haven't seen or heard her. Damn," Juice said as he saw the headline. "I guess you busted his ass. This is great. It says he's on parole. That could help us with the other guy. What'd you say his name was, McNatt?"

"McNabb. Do you think they can get him to turn on McNabb?"

"It's hard to say. These guys are loyal. But he's also facing a lot of years for someone his age. He may not get out until he's an old man if he doesn't cooperate. I'd say there's a good chance he'll try to do something to get a break."

She frowned. "I'm not going to take a chance that they can get him on their own. I think we need to give them a little help. They've been after McNabb a long time."

Juice looked up at Mary Beth with a puzzled look. "I'd say you gave them a hell of a lot of help already. How do you know so much about them being after McNabb?"

Mary Beth heard Cindy walking down the hall and put a finger to her lips. Happy not to answer, she reached over and flipped the newspaper to the Sports section just before Cindy came into the kitchen, rubbing her eyes.

"I don't smell coffee yet," Cindy said, smiling. She was wearing a long t-shirt and jeans but no shoes. "I've got to have some to get going."

"I'm just putting it on. Did you sleep well?"

"Yeah, I slept a little because I was so tired. But I just can't sleep the night through in a strange bed or when Danny's not there."

Outside, a cardinal whistled near the window where Mary Beth had recently filled two bird feeders—one with sunflower seeds and one with thistle. Mr. Coffee gurgled and sent out the roasted nut smell of brewing coffee. As the first direct rays of sunlight streamed through the pine trees and into the kitchen, the three of them sat at the table, saying nothing.

After breakfast, Cindy dressed first to go back to the hospital to check on Danny. As soon as Cindy left the house, Mary Beth pulled the three-inch thick telephone book from a kitchen drawer and found the listing for Crime Stoppers. She wrote the number on a small pad and tore off the page, placing the paper in her jeans pocket.

Calling to Juice in the study, she said, "I'm ready to call Crime Stoppers, but I don't want to call from here."

"Where do you want to go?"

"I'm going to call from the mall. Do you think this plan will work?"

"Don't know why it won't. With the lead you give them, they should be able to get a search warrant. Someone was watching the back of that liquor store just like you warned, so they're on to McNabb. And you said Gant had been at McNabb's store several times."

Juice drove while Mary Beth rehearsed her story. They pulled up in front of the mall, and she walked to a pay phone outside the front door. The mall wasn't open yet, so there was no one around.

Someone answered after three rings. They provided Mary Beth a number she could use to identify herself. She launched into her story. "See, I was checking out rental space downtown a few days before for a little antique shop I want to open. I saw this empty building and walked down an alley to look in the window. It's an old furniture building. I saw two men stuffing something into a carrying bag, like the ones people use for their workout clothes. It scared me to death. When I saw the picture of this man Gant in the newspaper, I recognized him right off. The packages of drugs in the picture this morning looked just like what I saw the men stuffing into the bag. Then I peeked around the corner and saw the men getting into a white Lincoln Town Car. I got part of the license number because I could tell this was something that didn't seem right. It was JVB twenty-one and either five or six. I got too scared and didn't want to call in, but when I saw how much those drugs were worth I decided I should."

She answered several other questions, including descriptions of the men. She gave a perfect description of McNabb and said she was positive about Gant from the picture in the paper.

———◆———

At just after 10 a.m., there was a knock at Peter's door. Mary Beth answered before Peter. "Yes?"

A man in khaki pants, a white short-sleeved shirt, and green striped tie stuck his head around the door. "Good morning. I'm Detective Stanley

Hunt. I'm sorry to bother you folks, but I've got a hospital report of wreck victims where there's no police report. Do you mind if I ask what happened?"

Mary Beth cleared her throat slightly before she spoke, forcing herself not to look over at Peter. She smiled. "Oh, I'm sorry. The sheriff's department knows about it and they're doing a report now. They've recovered my husband's motorcycle."

She noticed the detective's look of disappointment and the slightest drop of his shoulders. "Do you know why there's not an accident report already?"

"Oh, I guess it's just because some nice woman passing by brought in my husband and his cousin, but no one else saw the wreck. Then the sheriff's office called, so we didn't think we needed to do anything else. I'm so sorry officer, did I do that wrong? I just didn't know what to do."

"No ma'am, that's fine," the detective said. He looked toward Peter as he backed out of the room politely. "I hope you get better soon. Sorry to bother you folks. I'll get what I need from the sheriff's office."

———

Nelson and his entire task force had been meeting for an hour, comparing notes on McNabb. Spread on the table were several large plastic bags with various items inside and labels describing where they came from.

Nelson held up a clear plastic bag containing a red hat and fake ponytail, twisting the bag around and looking at it from every angle. He put the bag down and picked up a smaller bag, noticing a lipstick tube inside. "Has this been printed?""Yeah, they dusted it, but it only had one partial thumb that was any good. We didn't get any hits," Graham said.

Nelson opened the bag and held up the tube. "Gentlemen, let me teach you about the fine police science of women's lipstick." He was faking his

British literature professor's accent. "Each one may be as individual as the woman. I've made it my life's study." He was only partially joking because it was true that he was fascinated by the many techniques women used to apply lipstick, and he always noticed the shapes and angles of the lipsticks of the women he knew.

There was laughter around the table.

"For example, there's the basic slant, which you see most often, though a precise woman can get the slant to reach a fine, thin edge for painting perfect lips. There's the Hershey Kiss shape for painting puckered lips. It's rare. But there's also a double slant for the busy woman who does two lips at once, showing that she has a lot of poise but not a lot of time. Also a bit rare. Then there's always the flat lipstick, for the boring woman."

More laughter.

"Let's see what we have here," he said to his men, as he opened the lipstick tube and twirled the tube. He grew quiet, just stared at the lipstick, studied its shape. A rare double slant. The men sat quietly around him, grinning at each other and waiting for a great punch line. Nelson simply sat there. His face became vacant as if his mind were somewhere far away.

Before he could say more, his administrative assistant opened the door a few inches to say he had a call from a sergeant in charge of Crime Stoppers.

Without taking his eyes off the lipstick, he waved her off with his hand. "Take a message, will you, Joyce."

"He insisted you would want this call, something to do with McNabb."

Nelson looked at her and hesitated before he pointed at the phone to let her know to transfer the call. The room grew even quieter than before. He closed the lipstick and stood the tube on the table in front of him.

The only movement was from blinds swaying in the breeze from the window, open to let out the cigarette smoke. The Police Department was a non-smoking building, and Nelson hated cigarette smoking despite his personal love of good cigars, but two of his men smoked, and he thought it more important to support them as a team. He pressed the conference call button on the phone. "This is Nelson."

"Hello, Lieutenant. I hear you guys have been after McNabb for months."

"We're as far up his ass as we can get without looking out through his eyes."

"Well, I have something you might want."

"We're listening. What you got?"

"Just got a tip about a possible drug deal someone saw. One of the cars described was traced to McNabb through a license number, so I thought your team should be brought in."

"Does it look like enough for a search warrant for McNabb's properties?" Nelson asked, as he reached over and pushed the button to raise the volume on the conference phone.

"Oh yeah, we can go with this. Good description, good detail. They described what sounds like a lot of coke being loaded into McNabb's car exactly where we had that shootout downtown. They matched his personal description to a tee, and gave a positive ID on Gant from his photo in the paper."

Nelson ended the call from his friend on the Crime Stoppers detail, saying, "I'd kiss you if you were here. Thanks. We'll need the transcript."

"You got it."

Nelson pressed the off button on the telephone. All the men around the table sat up. This was good news.

"All right," Nelson said. "This could be the break we need. Joe, where are we on the warrant for Gant's apartment?"

"It'll be served within the next hour."

Nelson and his men sat motionless around the conference table marked by dozens of cigarette burns around the edges. For a few seconds, they let the situation soak in, and no one said anything. The men waited for Nelson.

Nelson leaned forward, nodded a few times, and put both hands palms down on the table. He met every man's gaze. "Guys, we may have him. Sleepy, call Judge Whitmore and see about a search warrant for McNabb's Town Car, his house, and the office at Best Price. We have records of that car being at both places that day, so maybe they'll include all three."

Joe Graham cocked his head and lifted his hand a couple of inches. "L.T.?"

"Yeah, Joe?"

"So, if this is really it, we hit them hard? The whole list? With everything we got?"

Nelson looked around the room, scanning over the dozens of notes, mug shots, and surveillance photos tacked on the cork boards lining one wall. "I think this is the day we cut the head off the snake. Tonight we collar every one of these sons-of-bitches we can find," he said, pointing with his eyes and the tilt of his head toward the board of mug shots. "If you got anything planned, you better call home and talk sweet. It's going to be a long night."

chapter 38

Mary Beth pulled out her desk chair and placed an open cardboard box on the seat. She scanned the office that was nearly empty now, signs of her time here packed away. She was saving the desk for last. The blank walls looked older than she had expected. Yellow rectangles where pictures had hung showed how the wall paint had faded without her noticing. A box in the corner contained a stack of empty manila folders, a stapler, scissors, a chipped coffee mug with a logo of the Fraternal Order of Police Hattiesburg Lodge #55 crammed full of old pens that she would leave for the person who sat here next. Not much of a legacy, she thought, though it didn't make her sad to think it. She was happy to be moving on with her life, happy to be leaving Jackson behind. This felt right.

Five years in this office, she thought, and in an hour every trace of her would be gone, packed away or thrown out, half of it destined for a thrift store or a garage sale. She reached over to turn off the computer, now wiped clean of every email and personal photo, but the phone rang before she could shut it down. Fifteen minutes later, Mary Beth hung up the phone with John Baynes and went back to packing her desk, trying not to think about the call. She clenched her jaws to force the emotions beneath the surface and tried to focus on the box on her chair. She had said little during the call. Mostly she listened as he confessed why he'd been so upset the past few months. She wanted to explain her behavior, but knew she could never tell him what had really happened. She hoped he would accept her vague answers and simply let things drop. He and Peter had been friends for too long, and she didn't want that to end.

She finished clearing her desk of the last photo of her and Peter at the

Grand Canyon, three personal books, and the souvenir coffee mug from
Mississippi Power that she loved and decided to keep. A utilities company
cup. Not much of a keepsake. She looked around the small office one last
time. Would she miss it after today?

The last six weeks had seemed unreal, like a nightmare. At first she had
juggled working every day while sitting at the hospital at night with Peter.
Constantly looking over her shoulder whenever someone walked up
behind her. Peeping out the curtains when a car slowed near the house.
When he had come home after a few days, she had juggled working and
running home again and again to check on him. Danny had remained in
a coma, coming around in degrees, so Peter was taking hard his role in
Danny's injuries. And having Cindy live with them hadn't made Peter's
guilt easier. No matter if it was the lie of the motorcycle wreck or the
unmentionable truth of the getaway car wreck, Peter had to live with the
fact that he was the cause of Danny's great pain. And she had to live with
the fact that she was a part of it, too. And who knew if it was really over?
She had been a willing participant, against her better judgment and
knowing the odds were against them. She was beginning to believe life
might return to normal and that no one was after them.

Mary Beth packed the last of her personal things from her desk into a
cardboard box. The other four overflowing boxes were loaded in her car.

She sat down one final time in her chair and faced her computer screen.
She wished she had turned it off earlier, but there it was waiting for her to
do what she had been dreading since she and Peter had made the decision
to leave Jackson. Leaving was not that simple, as much as she wanted it to
be. One loose end remained to be dealt with, or she could never make a
clean break with this phase of her life and start over. She opened her Draft
file, found the unsent email she had struggled with, and held her hand
over the computer mouse as she reread the draft for the tenth time. She
couldn't send it. Finally, she deleted the three-page email and started over:

I know I don't have any right to ask this, but please meet me. What I want
to say should be in person, not in an email, as you once told me. 4 p.m.
The library, of course. MB

She took a deep breath and clicked SEND. The email disappeared. She
willed herself to smile. Time to move on. She hadn't even rolled her chair
back from the computer when a response came back. She opened the
email immediately and saw the simple reply: Leaving now.

———

Mary Beth parked near the entrance to the library. The small Bradford
pear tree growing in the triangle of dirt at the end of the row of parking
spaces was already turning colors, and she remembered how beautiful the
tree had been the previous fall when the leaves changed from green to
gold and red.

She walked through the magazine section, straight back to the microfilm
room where they had often met the previous winter and spring. As she
neared the door, she saw Taylor Nelson already there, seated in the same
chair at the same table where he'd sat the first time they met, each of them
going through old microfilm to research newspapers cataloged years
before. She wondered if he picked that chair on purpose. She stopped
and looked around before entering the room. Seeing no one else, she
closed the door quietly behind her and sat next to him right where she
had moved over to talk the first time they were alone in the room. He rose
half way as she sat, but he said nothing.

"Thanks for coming," she said, and felt silly for saying it.

"Did I do something wrong?" he asked, his voice soft.

"No. What happened had nothing to do with you. It's something I can't
explain. I can't talk about it. Please understand. I wanted to see you. You
know that."

Nelson looked into her eyes, and she forced herself not to look away.

He sat back and crossed his arms. He sat that way for a few seconds before he smiled and nodded. He took Mary Beth's hand and asked, "Why meet me now? Anything that might have been was over weeks ago. I know a lot more than you realize."

She looked down at their hands and wondered what she had been thinking. Why was she here? This much potential for danger was never a smart move, and her attraction to him made no sense. He was not the type of man she had ever been drawn to, nothing at all like Peter. But in his presence, she felt a deep connection she couldn't deny. Deeper than just physical. And that knowledge was something she was going to have to live with. She looked at his hands rather than into his eyes. "You gave me something I needed at a hard time in my life. You listened to me. And you made me laugh. I learned a lot from you. But all the time I was dying inside."

"So you *were* unhappy. I didn't get that wrong."

"I was unhappy. But I never stopped loving Peter. I tried to tell you. I mean, you never seemed to need to know that. You seemed so in control, like you never really wanted more."

He looked at her and nodded and never looked away. "It seemed like more than that to me. A lot more. And I did want more."

She put her head down and was silent for a moment before she looked up, directly into his eyes. "You're right. Maybe it was something bigger. No, not even maybe. You felt my kiss. That's the only time I've kissed another man in twenty years. I am not saying I didn't want it." She had plenty on her heart to say, but giving voice to it would not take this in the direction she knew it had to go.

The door opened, and a young man who looked like a college student started through the doorway. When he saw their chairs facing each other and their heads close together, the young guy smiled, backed up, and closed the door.

Before she could go on, the man staring back into Mary Beth's eyes spoke. "Look, I was never comfortable about you being married. I never wanted to ruin anything for you. And you tell me you love him, so that's that if you mean it. I'm not someone who goes after married women. This just happened. But either way, I care about you. You made me feel things I hadn't felt in a long time."

She sat up in her chair. "Then you'll know why this is the last time we'll meet. I'm ... we're ... moving away. I just wanted to say thank you for being there when I needed someone. I'm sorry. So sorry. I never meant to mislead you."

"But just to cut me off like that. No contact. No anything. I was worried about you."

"Some things in my life I can't explain. You have no way of knowing what I've been through." She knew she should not add this, but she wanted him to know. "Or what you've meant to me."

"Actually, I do know."

She stood up, not certain what he meant.

Nelson stood and took her in his arms. She did not resist. She felt comfort in the strength of his embrace and knew that he had much more to say if she could only listen. They stood there for a while as he stroked her hair and reached for her hand and squeezed it. "Mary Beth," he began. She could hear the emotion in his voice.

She could not let him finish. "I have to go now."

He continued to hold her. "Let me say just this much. I will always be your friend. Understand?"

She was afraid she knew what he meant but could not think about it one more moment. "Really, I have to go." She broke away from his arms and was afraid to look him in the eyes.

He took her hand. "Mary Beth, this thing will never be over."

"I have to go," she said once again, but she could not take her hand from his.

"Then you'll want to take this." He reached into his pocket and pulled out a small object. "I hope when you use it sometime you'll think fondly of me."

Mary Beth felt the hair on her arms raise as she looked down and saw her missing lipstick in Lt. Taylor Nelson's hand.

chapter 39

Taylor Nelson sat on the back row of the courtroom by himself as the judge read the sentence of life without parole for William McNabb. McNabb had earlier been found guilty on all counts of drug trafficking, money laundering, conspiracy to commit murder, and murder. A handful of people, including McNabb's wife, were seated together on the first two rows, but otherwise the courtroom was empty except for Nelson and a row of reporters.

McNabb's wife sat stoically until the end of the reading of the sentence, then, as if scripted, put her face in her hands and sobbed quietly. Nelson wondered how much she'd known about her husband's real business, if anything. There was never a way to punish the guilty without somewhere along the way hurting someone innocent.

A couple of reporters sat together two rows in front of Nelson. The news of the sentence would get out quickly. Nelson was pleased that Gant's testimony and the findings of his task force had been influential in putting McNabb away for good. His team had been able to show the web of murders and drug deals linking McNabb and Gant. Their evidence made Gant realize that his cooperation was the only thing between him and death row.

Nelson recalled Gant's first words as he had begun eight hours of testimony in the trial. "I always knew my day would come, but I sure as hell didn't think I would get caught like I did. I was so close to getting out of here."

The trial had taken only four days. Nelson and his task force had provided precise testimony backed by their official reports, photos of

McNabb and Gant together, and details of how events tied McNabb to the cocaine found in his car and Gant's car. Still, he could not ignore that the biggest break in the case had not been the work of his task force at all but came from an anonymous phone call to his private number that few people knew. Had it not been for the anonymous tip, he would not have been staking out the Downtown Club so early that night when Gant's car made an after-hours visit into the NAPA parts store across the street.

Nelson was ready for this assignment to be over. His team had been routinely tying up loose ends surrounding McNabb's network of enforcers, middle men, and street dealers, arresting nearly a dozen of the smaller fish who had fed off McNabb and Gant and were easily tied to the drug operation. Nelson had made sure that there were no loose ends remaining, at least none he could find. It was personal to him now.

Nelson patted his shirt pocket and smiled as he pulled out the Cohiba Cuban cigar he'd bought last time he had visited New Orleans, where the official ban on Cuban cigars hardly mattered if you knew who to ask. He held the seven inch cigar under his nose and inhaled deeply, enjoying the spicy aroma of the aged tobacco. Tonight he would indulge himself with a 1985 Fonseca Vintage Port he'd been saving because its dark ruby colors with chocolate and plums was so perfect to enjoy with his smoke in a private celebration. This trial marked the end of a chapter for him. Time to move on to another challenge. He thought of the woman who had briefly entered his life and, although she had left suddenly, her memory made him smile. He knew he would not see her again unless something went wrong. He hoped she was happy. There was a good chance no one would ever know her role in McNabb's end, and that was fine with him. At least she would be safe now. As safe as people can be. At least for a while.

Peter sat on a large blue beach towel and looked out over the calm, flat waters of Cedar Key. He sat on a small stretch of isolated beach, if this narrow strip of sandy dirt could be called a beach, facing west where he could sit alone and watch the sunset. The breeze was warm, but he knew the temperature would cool immediately after the sun was down. He enjoyed smelling the salt air, the seaweed and shellfish odors, the faint sweet charcoal of one of the town's dozens of mullet smokers nearby.

He was beginning to be at peace with the past and with himself. With the fact that Chris would not be coming back no matter how much he missed him. That bad things happen, but people can move on. Danny had once again been there for him, telling him that he couldn't take the blame for every bad turn of events. They were all adults, and they all had their reasons for choosing their actions.

As he watched the sun slowly sink into the Gulf of Mexico, he thought about his conversation with Danny the previous weekend. He had called to see how Danny was recovering after being in a coma for nearly a month and then going through six weeks of rehab to relearn to walk. Danny surprised him by how truly satisfied and happy he sounded, saying he and Juice had started an internet real estate company. They could afford to work for themselves now thanks to the three hundred thousand dollars Peter and Mary Beth had insisted they take because Danny had lost his job for being gone so long.

For days Peter had been asking himself if he would really be happy outside the advertising business. His heart was no longer there, and he knew it. Every day he felt better about a future he didn't even feel compelled to imagine yet. It didn't really matter and didn't require a plan. He needed to work, but for some reason he couldn't make the decision to buy a boat to become a licensed charter captain or even to make their move to Cedar Key permanent by buying a house. No need to rush.

He could tell that Mary Beth seemed happier, too. For one thing, they had the money to start over. His partners had agreed on a good price for

his share of the agency. John Baynes had seen to that. Mary Beth had told
Peter how concerned John had been not only for Peter's health and frame
of mind but also for their financial welfare. But Peter wasn't mentally
prepared to rush toward such a shift, so once again he found himself on
the beach, staring out at the flat, shimmering Gulf waters on a perfect
afternoon, awaiting another sunset. He thought about his motorcycle that
had been repaired. He imagined owning a bar. He daydreamed of running
a marina. Or learning to sail and taking charters to the Keys.

He and Mary Beth had talked for many hours about taking their time
and making the right decision. She'd reassured him that it was fine to go
slow. Now as he began to be at peace with himself, he and Mary Beth took
long walks together every day. They had already talked through everything
that had happened with McNabb and the drugs, and both were pleased to
look forward. They were convinced no one was tracking them. Some days
they rented a canoe and paddled out to a tiny island for a picnic. Their
relationship was like it was in the old days but even better because they had
weathered a storm. He realized what she meant to him.

Peter was glad to be far from the agency, especially now during annual
report season when CEOs and CFOs suddenly became communications
experts, which in the past had made him spend endless late nights rushing
to rewrite perfectly good copy. He knew his scowl had disappeared. That
was a good first step. Mary Beth told him it was great to see his smile again.

Although he had never been much of a sun worshiper, his tan darkened
from his shirtless afternoon runs. He was in better shape than he'd been
in fifteen years. He felt his old self returning. He was confident again and
knew that the next step he took would be the right one as long as Mary
Beth was there to take it with him.

He lit a collection of dry driftwood with his lighter and watched as the
flames curled up through the sticks. He tossed another piece he had
gathered onto the small fire and listened to the faint sound of a piece of
wood hissing.

———————

Mary Beth sat at a desk in their room in Cedar Key's only bed and breakfast, The Pelican Nest, enjoying how the light changed in the late afternoon. She was reading *The Clarion-Ledger* that had arrived that morning in the mail from Jackson and was sipping iced tea when she saw the news that McNabb's trial was over much sooner than expected. She folded the newspaper, grabbed a folder from the desk drawer, and ran the two blocks to the beach where Peter had been sitting for an hour, waiting for sunset.

She was breathing hard from the run across the sand, holding out the newspaper. "They put McNabb away for life. It's over." She brushed the hair back from her forehead and added, "Don't you think?"

Peter looked at Mary Beth with half a smile on his face but didn't answer at first. He wanted to say yes, of course, but he knew she could see in his eyes that he was hesitant to say it was over. They had already talked about how some of McNabb's network was not even in Jackson to be caught up in the sting. And Christopher's death could never be undone, the circumstances surrounding it never changing. He would always be the brother who died a criminal, using an illegal drug to cross over. That is how the world would label it. "Let's hope so."

Mary Beth sat next to Peter and wrapped her arms around her knees, watching the fire.

Peter held the newspaper toward the fire for more light. The article was a news brief. "Well-known Jackson businessman William McNabb was sentenced today to life without parole for a series of crimes, including murder, related to a cocaine drug ring. Accomplice Roy Gant, who testified against McNabb, had already been sentenced to life in a separate plea bargain. These convictions bring down what Mississippi authorities claimed was the biggest drug ring in Mississippi history."

"Now, I've got something even more important for you to see," Mary

Beth said. She opened a folder with two brochures inside and handed one of them to Peter. The brochure showed photos of twenty houses available in Cedar Key. She had circled one house with a blue ballpoint pen. Dream house. Three BR, Three bath. Sunroom. Large marble bath off master bedroom. Deck overlooking Gulf sunset. Pool. Spa. Fireplace. Boat slip.

Peter looked at her and smiled when he saw that the words 'Boat slip' were underlined. "I like that. You're really trying to attack my weakness, aren't you?"

She punched him in the shoulder. "Just being helpful. Probably shouldn't even show you what else I have in here."

She handed him the other brochure, which described a thirty-one-foot Contender with twin 250-horsepower Yamaha engines.

"Now that's a gorgeous boat. Costs more than our first house. But it's a nice ride."

"It's time to move on. Somewhere. Just make damn sure there's a seat on there for me."

Mary Beth leaned over and put her arm on Peter's shoulder. "Hey, there's more." From her bag she handed Peter a dog-eared copy of Thomas Toepfer's *American Beer Can Encyclopedia* that she'd purchased from Amazon.com, along with a cone-top can.

He looked at her for a long moment, laughing as he realized she continued to surprise him.

"Damn, Bet. That's a Red Lion from Burger Beer." Peter turned the can in his hand. "I've only seen them in pictures. Has to be one of the first cone-tops made. 1935. I can't believe you remembered me talking about it. This must have cost a fortune."

"You're worth it, Peter. I had a little extra cash sitting around," she said, grinning.

He felt his throat swelling and mumbled a soft thank you.

The two of them sat staring across the water for several minutes.

Mary Beth spoke first. "We have to begin building a new life. I want to live here, with you, really live. If not here, then somewhere else with this much sun. I want to burn our skin bronze and eat fresh crabs and track sand into our living room."

Peter turned his head and looked into her eyes. "It's not going to be that easy."

"No. It won't. But it has to be possible."

For several seconds Peter said nothing. She knew this look. She could tell he was struggling with a thought, trying to reach a conclusion. Then she saw a smile spread across his face.

He suddenly jumped up and ran toward the house, yelling over his shoulder, "Stay here. I'll be right back. I have something for you, too."

Five minutes later he returned with a large gym bag and sat next to Mary Beth with the bag in front of him. She looked at him with a question in her eyes.

"It's the last of the money." He unzipped the bag and held it for her to see inside.

"That's it?"

"This is all that's left after I paid off the repairs on my bike and the last hospital bills. It's the last thing tying us to the past."

He reached into the bag and pulled out several bundles of one hundred dollar bills. "This is for Chris." He tossed the money into the fire, leaving the bag open in front of them.

"And this is for you." He tossed another bundle into the flames.

Mary Beth just stared at the fire.

"And this is for us," he said a few moments later as he leaned over to dump the last few stacks and the empty bag into the fire.

Mary Beth spoke without looking up. "It really was just a lie wasn't it? The drugs, the money, thinking we could get even, all of it. It was a lie for McNabb and Gant, too. For everyone who touches it."

Peter didn't answer. She didn't expect him to.

After another minute, she said, "Peter."

"Yeah?"

"I take back that part about having extra cash."

They both laughed and continued to stare at the fire.

The fire gradually grew larger. The bright orange flames from the burning bills looked almost the same color as the sun slipping below the horizon and spreading its color in a thick, wavy line across the tiny ripples of the Gulf water.

Mary Beth reached into her pocket and tossed a small shiny tube into the fire.

"What was that?" Peter asked.

"Nothing. Just something I don't need any longer."

ACKNOWLEDGEMENTS

Through countless drafts my wife Virginia Shirley put up with lots of after-midnight and early morning writing, along with sacrificed vacation fun for her while I sat in front of a laptop. She has read draft after draft—including the 30,000 words that were thrown away at one point—yet somehow managed to help me maintain enthusiasm to keep working. She knows enough about the folks who inhabit these pages to tell me when I quote one of them out of character. I am grateful to live with an artist who gets it and is willing to take the risk of saying when something doesn't work. Several others along the way provided advice, counsel, information, prodding, or simply helped clear a trail. Jeanie Thompson has always been there clearing away the brush, creating a path for me and many writers, and building platforms for our work to find audiences. Without her nurturing of the literary community, I would never have found the community support to make me care about writing enough to see it through to publication. During early drafts, Ken Ritchey answered many questions about police procedure and guns, though it was so long ago he may not remember. If anything here is wrong procedurally, it's my fault for not listening well or asking the wrong questions. To *storySouth* founding editor Jason Sanford, my thanks for publishing a short story (my second accepted but first published) titled "And It Burned" that exists here in a different form, as the scene in chapter 34 when Mary Beth picks up McNabb in a bar. To my publisher Ed Garner, my deep appreciation for giving this story a home and putting his personal time into making the book much better than he found it. To my friends David Larry Baynes and Clark Powell, my thanks for challenging me in the earliest days of my writing (yes, decades ago) to keep it up and thanks for letting me steal your names for the ad agency in this book. Special thanks to cover designer James Harwell and interior book designer Felicia Kahn for their great work. Any thanks I can provide to my editor Anita Miller Garner will be inadequate to describe her guidance regarding elimination of things tedious and pedestrian, attention to detail, knowledge of what works, and grammatical knowledge. (Notice I used the serial comma in that last sentence, Anita.) Many thanks for investing time and consternation in ridding this manuscript of things that stop readers.

Of course, you, dear readers, deserve the most thanks of all for getting this far into the book. Without you, there would be no books. So, thank you most of all.

Philip Shirley

ABOUT THE AUTHOR

Since his first appearance in print—a poem in a literary journal thirty years ago—Philip Shirley has been published more than 100 times. His award-winning writing includes fiction, poetry, criticism, feature articles, speeches and business articles in a wide variety of magazines, newspapers and books. His latest publication is a novel, *The White Lie*, being released in July 2014 by Mindbridge Press.

In 2008, Jefferson Press selected his short story collection *Oh Don't You Cry For Me* as a finalist for the Jefferson Prize and subsequently published the book to critical acclaim. The next year Triumph Books published a co-authored cultural history of professional baseball titled *Sweet Spot: 125 Years of Baseball and The Louisville Slugger*.

In addition to his literary work, Philip is CEO of GodwinGroup, an ad agency headquartered in Mississippi. He is a long-time board member and former officer of the Alabama Writers' Forum, a partnership program of the Alabama State Council on the Arts. While his home is in Madison, Mississippi, much of his work is written on Dauphin Island, Alabama, or in a cabin in the foothills of the Cumberland Mountains in north Alabama a mere rifle shot from the Tennessee line. He has been married to the painter Virginia Shirley for more than 30 years.

Philip's publications also include two chapbooks of poetry, *Four Odd and Endings*. He has published poetry and criticism in numerous literary magazines and on Alabama Public Radio. His feature writing has appeared in both consumer and business magazines.

In college he was a member of the editorial staff of the *Black Warrior Review* and later was founder and editor of a literary press. He created and produced, with Steven Ford Brown, *The Poet's Corner* on Alabama Public

Radio, which received an Obelisk Award as the best radio arts program in Alabama.

He is an Alabama native and graduate of the University of Alabama (B.A., M.A.), but first attended college at Patrick Henry, now Alabama Southern Community College, in Monroeville, the official Literary Capital of Alabama.

For additional information, reviews of Philip's books, and appearance dates, visit: www.philipshirley.com

Praise for *Oh Don't You Cry For Me*

"...tightly written, closely observed...a memorable debut in the world of fiction."
– Mark Childress, author of *Georgia Bottoms and Crazy in Alabama* and 2014 Winner of the Harper Lee Award

"...consistently great stories..."
– *Pop Matters*

"...a master story teller..."
– *Portico*

"...immensely enjoyable."
– *First Draft Magazine*

"A superb collection."
– *Enter the Octopus.com*

CPSIA information can be obtained at www.ICGtesting.com
Printed in the USA
LVOW12s1106230714

395668LV00010B/119/P